I0668271

Silver Lining Summer
A Happy Montana Novel

Zanne Sweeney

Copyright © 2015 Zanne Sweeney
All rights reserved.
ISBN: 0692387811
ISBN-13: 978-0692387818

Authors note:
As a self-published author I do not have the wonderful resources that come with working with a publishing company. I love to create stories and it is important to me that what I publish is of good quality. This includes the formatting and editing of the book. If you see any errors I would greatly appreciate it if you would email me those errors, and what page they are on so I can fix them. Thank you. zannesweeney@gmail.com

DEDICATION

This book is dedicated to my girls.
You are my inspiration for creating strong female characters.
I love you! S.E.S. and S.E.S.

ACKNOWLEDGMENTS

C.N. - Editor
Nada Orlic - Cover
Thank you ladies

Chapter 1

The late May morning air invigorated Tank as he and his Sergeant-at-Arms; Grease rode towards their club's summer encampment. Tank couldn't wait to get started on the improvements he had planned for the camp. Improvements that he could now implement since his new sister-in-law, Breezy, had gifted him the deed to the one hundred acres. Tank had been leasing the long since abandoned children's camp on Happy Mountain for the last eight years, so his club's members had a place to vacation. The property came with several log cabins, a large area that served as trailer and tent campsites. A shared shower and bathhouse for the campsites and a large clearing between the cabins and campsites that was used for bon fires and group picnics. The land that housed the cabins and campsites only utilized twenty acres of the large mountain property. The rest of the property was dense forest, except for a good-sized stream that ran through the woods. The camp was remote enough that Tank's guys could get loud without any neighbors complaining. Tank loved being outdoors and the summer was his favorite time in his home state of Montana.

Tank was President of the Steel Horse Cowboys Motorcycle Club. He had been elected President ten years ago and since then he had turned the club into a legitimate business venture. The club had over one hundred patched members and every year more prospects wanted to join.

His men were from all over Broadwater County, but the Clubs main roots were in Townsend. Tank owned a service garage, a tow service, a small Harley Dealership, and an RV dealership, all located in Townsend. He employed mostly men and women from his club to work for him and because Tank initiated each business to be a profit-sharing enterprise, the club members reaped the benefits directly. The camp that Tank was headed towards was on a mountain in Happy, a small town about forty minutes north of Townsend. In the summer months, the club moved its headquarters to Happy. The men who preferred to use their vacation time during the winter months manned the Townsend businesses during the summer. It was a perfect arrangement for everyone, especially for him.

Club families would come to camp for weeks or weekends, and a few of the men like Grease, Sweets and himself, spent the entire summer there. The small town of Happy swelled in population during the summer months. There was even a bar called The Pen. His club had adopted it as their own when they first started renting the camp. It was on the edge of town across from a national park campground. At night, during the summer months, the front of the bar would be lined with Harleys, trucks, and vans.

The owner of the bar was a business mogul from New York City who needed a tax write off. There was no way the bar made any money, except during June, July, and August, when the town was full of tourists and Tank's club members were there. A new manager, Ditch had been hired late last summer. Tank didn't know much about him other than he'd been working on a ranch, thrown from a horse and landed in a 'ditch.' The accident had left him walking with a severe limp. Ditch was from upstate Montana, but now he lived in Happy over the bar. Through the winter months Ditch handled all the bar duties himself, because there was rarely anyone there. Tank was pleased when he heard that Ditch had hired a couple of guys from his club to help him during the busy summer months.

As he and Grease sped along the small paved road towards Happy, Tank thought back to when he'd first met Breezy, his brother Toby's new wife. She had come into The Pen last summer, gotten into a scuffle with his then girlfriend, Betty and proceeded to deck Betty with a great upper cut. Tank had intervened before the other females from his club sought revenge for their sister, Betty. His older brother Toby had fallen head over heels for Breezy, love at first sight, and they'd been together ever since.

Breezy was in her forties, like he was, and she had been through the ringer with her first husband. The final straw had been when she had learned that Auggie, her husband, had fathered a child and had been secretly seeing him and supporting him. Breezy had left her New Jersey home and unfaithful husband, she thought just for the summer, while her lawyer paved the way for a divorce. Breezy hadn't had a destination in mind when she'd left. Luckily, fate had brought her to Happy, Montana. A month after she arrived in Happy, her husband, and his baby momma were tragically killed in a car accident. In a crazy happen-chance turn of events, Breezy ended up adopting her late husband's son, Gus.

Breezy also had twin daughters that had just turned 21. They were going to be seniors in college next fall. Last year the girls had met two young men, Two and Bam. They were also twin's and were in Tank's club. According to Breezy, the kids were still seeing each other. Breezy was pretty without any effort. She had a great body too. Toby would pound on him if he knew that Tank even thought about his wife's figure. That thought brought a grin to Tank's face. Breezy was not only kind, funny and compassionate but she was one of the strongest persons he knew; the woman was a rock. She and Toby were so in love with each other that even an emotionally hardened man like himself felt their passion. Tank wished he could find that special someone. It wasn't likely to happen; he had resigned himself to the fact that he would never settle down. Women like Breezy were few and far between.

It wasn't that Tank was lacking for female companionship. A woman named Cara, who worked for him, had been his latest distraction. They had a mutual love of sex. It was convenient, she worked for him, knew his friends, and she enjoyed the benefits that his club offered. Tank hadn't been sampling the ladies as much anymore. When he needed the outlet there was always Cara, but his lusty appetite had dwindled and that concerned him.

He and Grease rode through the small town of Happy before turning up the small dirt road that led up the mountain towards his camp. Aspen and pine trees shaded the small road creating a tunnel like effect. It was the Wednesday before Memorial Day. Tank and Grease were riding up to open the camp for the club members who would start arriving on Friday. Toby had checked on the property throughout the rough winter months and the only major problem was a large tree had fallen across the main drive into camp. Toby was going to leave a chain saw near the downed tree because the first thing he and Grease needed to do was open up the drive.

The ride to Happy always calmed and invigorated Tank. His 2012 Harley Softail Heritage Classic (FLSTC) was his pride and joy. It was all chrome and black, and big and badass. In the winter he swapped out his Harley for his truck, but once May came he was back on his Harley.

As he rode Tank thought about the changes he was going to make in camp. The money the club saved from not having to rent the large camp was now going to be used for much needed renovations. Tank had already researched modular cabins. He had already chosen the largest one that could be hauled up the small mountain road. The lower level of the prefabricated cabin would have an industrial sized kitchen, a communal dining room, and a large open room with a bar. Upstairs, Tank wanted to put in a large office area and guest rooms. Sweets, the vice president of the club and Grease were two of his best friends. For the past three months they had been collaborating over the design and structure of the prefab cabin. The women were excited too and had added great suggestions. They were in charge of the interior, and Lolly, Sweet's wife, was already researching the best appliances to buy.

The camp was situated halfway up Happy Mountain. Toby, Breezy, and Gus lived further up the mountain, year-round. As they rode further up the mountain the canopy of trees parted, allowing a spectacular view of snowcapped Elkhorn Mountain.

They reached the driveway entrance and one hundred yards in they came across the downed tree. It was huge; five feet around and impassable. Tank and Grease dismounted and while Tank retrieved the chain saw that Toby had left them, Grease surveyed the best place to start cutting. When Tank took the saw out of its case he saw that there was a note inside taped to a large bag.

Hi Tank, can't wait to see you! I love that it's almost summer! You and whomever you brought with you please come up for supper when you're done. We have steak. Miss you!
Love, Breezy

Tank smiled at his sister-in-law's note. She was good people and Toby was a lucky son of a bitch. He then opened the paper bag and found two-dozen chocolate chip cookies, his favorite. Tank popped one in his mouth, took two out for Grease.

It took over an hour to cut through the large white pine. They cut the tree in two places; a yard in from either side of the drive. They could come back and cut more another time. Today was about giving them access to the camp. It took another two hours to saw and move the wood from the driveway. Then they neatly stacked the logs along the drive. When they finished Tank and Grease were shirtless and sweat dripped down their torsos. Grease was mopping his face with his t-shirt. His long braid was sticking in the dampness on his back. Tank had tied his blue bandana around his forehead to help keep the sweat from going into his eyes. The two men were smiling; they had loved the workout. Tank packed up the saw and put it safely behind one of the stacks of wood. Toby would have to retrieve it later. The two men mounted their bikes and headed the rest of the way into camp.

Tank was excited to see the camp. It was mind-boggling that he owned the camp. He hadn't been in Happy since Thanksgiving, that's when Breezy had presented him with the deed to the property. She had been leaving for her honeymoon and without any fanfare, in the parking lot of Happy Endings, a local restaurant where the reception had been, she handed him the envelope containing the deed. Tank had been speechless. It was easily the kindest thing anyone had ever done for him. He loved the camp and Breezy knew it. Now it was his and he was happily going to continue to share it with his Club. The two men rode through the camp stopping every so often to point out something they needed to fix, but for the most part it looked to be in good condition. They saw that raccoons were nesting in the cabin Sweets and Lolly used, and there were bats in Tank's cabin. Grease's cabin had a small tree leaning on its roof but there wasn't any damage. The other cabins were fine and just in need of a good spring-cleaning.

The camping area, where members parked their RV's and pitched their tents, had a few branches that needed to be picked up. In the large space that the children played in and the club congregated in for picnics and bonfires two small trees had fallen so they needed to be cleared. Luckily, none of the electrical poles had been toppled. Tank had already called the electric and water companies alerting them to turn the utilities back on.

Tank and Grease parked their bikes outside their respective cabins and took their leather sacks off their bikes. They wanted to take showers before heading to Toby's. Tank's cabin was the furthest away from the focal area of the camp. He loved how private it was. One of his favorite things was lying in bed at night and listening to the sounds of the forest. If he ever told the guys that he would get a good ribbing. He had a certain persona to maintain. He was Tank. the President of the Steal Horse Cowboy's Motorcycle Club. There were not too many men around that dared to mess with him or his Club, not if they wanted to stay healthy. They may not be an outlaw Club anymore, but they still garnered the respect.

Tank was big, thus his nickname. His strong arms were adorned with intricate tattoos, wide shoulders and a broad chest tapered into a defined abdomen. Athletic hips, thighs and a butt, which was often the object of female ogling, stretched his worn jeans. Tank had dark hair that he often pulled back into a short ponytail. He was ruggedly handsome; with straight, roman-like features except for his nose which had been busted one too many times. His eyes were an amazing shade of blue; like the blue of a West Point Cadet's uniform. Tank had GQ looks but a tough persona. He was self-confident and a strong leader. When he'd first been elected club President he'd often been challenged. Old timers wanting to keep the outlaw ways, young bucks hoping to raise their club status. Tank held his own, never backing down from a fight and never compromising his main objective; to take the club in a new direction.

Inside his cabin, Tank used a broom to steer the bats that were flying around his living room out the front door. They were too quick, and he was too beat so after a few minutes he gave up and just left the door open while he went to shower, hoping they would make their way out on their own. After he showered and changed he was pleased to see that the bats had left his cabin. Tank made a mental note to find and close the holes that they were using to get inside. Grease was already waiting outside to head up to Toby and Breezy's.

Chapter 2

The sun was lowering, and the air had cooled down, so Tank zipped his leather jacket up over his club's black cut. He loved his cut. It was a soft, well-worn, leather sleeveless vest with the club's insignia embroidered on the back. His vest had a President's patch sewn prominently on the front. When a man became a member of a motorcycle club he was given his cut. It was worn with pride and Tank wore his whenever possible.

Tank and Grease drove up the mountain and turned into Toby's driveway. They were met halfway down the drive by five-year-old Gus who was all smiles as he enthusiastically waved at them. When Tank reached him, he scooped Gus up and placed him on the seat in front of him. He then drove so slowly that he almost had to put his feet down to remain balanced. Tank usually had a spare helmet with him, but he hadn't brought it and there was no way he wanted Breezy on his ass for going too fast with Gus along for the ride. Grease laughed at the slow pace Tank had set and then sped ahead leaving them behind in a cloud of road dust.

When they reached the cabin, Grease was already off his bike talking to Toby. Tank pulled alongside of Grease and Toby lifted his adopted son off the bike. Toby ruffled Gus' hair affectionately before man hugging Tank.

"Good to see you bro," Tank said to his older brother, who still had that 'I'm a newlywed' look on his face.

"You too. Gus has been waiting for you since noon. Breezy told him you wouldn't get here until dinner time, but he didn't care."

Tank chuckled. "I can't believe how much he's grown."

"Yeah, and he can say his r's now."

"No more Beezy?" Tank joked, mimicking how Gus used to say Breezy's name.

"Nope, he actually has been calling her Mom now."

"That's great, and you?"

"Me what?"

"Does he call you dad?"

Toby smiled widely, "Yeah, just a few weeks ago. I fucking love it."

Tank slapped his brother on the back.

"That's great, man. You deserve it."

"Thanks. Come on in, dinner is almost ready. Breezy put the steaks on the grill when she heard your bikes."

Gus had already run inside to inform his mom that the men had arrived. Breezy had laughed at his exuberance and didn't have the heart to not act surprised, even though she had heard Toby and Grease's loud mufflers before they had even turned into their drive.

When Tank entered the kitchen, Breezy jumped into his arms.

"Hello, brother-in-law!" she said, giving him a soft kiss on his cheek.

"Hello, sister-in-law," Tank echoed her greeting.

"Okay, break it up you two. I'm still not over the fact that he met you first," Toby muttered.

Tank, Breezy and Grease laughed and as Tank released her, Toby wrapped his wife in a possessive hug and planted a claiming kiss on her pretty lips.

"Aw, come on!" Gus complained loudly. "Tank, I'm so glad you're here. They kiss all the time. I'm gunna hang with you at the camp this summer, okay?"

The adults laughed at the little boy's comment, and Breezy grinned at her adopted son.

"Is my little man wanting a kiss, too?" Breezy teased.

Gus realized what was about to happen and took off running as Breezy gave chase with her arms wide open, making kissing noises. The men could hear Gus giggling loudly from where they stood in the kitchen.

After corralling Gus and smooching him silly, Gus tapped out, something his stepsisters had taught him to do last summer. Breezy gave him one last sloppy kiss on his cheek and then headed into the kitchen. Toby had already served Tank and Grease beers and had invited them to sit at the table while he got the steaks off the grill.

Gus had placed himself between Tank and Grease and was talking non-stop. He entertained them with stories about Kindergarten as Breezy set out scalloped potatoes, salad, and green beans. Toby brought out a large, wooden cutting board piled high with sliced steak. Once again, Tank couldn't help but notice how happy his brother was with his new life as a married man.

Toby asked about the tree that they had cleared reminding Tank to ask if he could keep the chain saw for another day, so they could clear the two other trees that had fallen. While Tank talked about his plans for the camp, Breezy discreetly reached under the table and squeezed Toby's knee. Toby looked to his wife and they shared a secretive smile. They loved the excitement they heard in Tank's voice. Tank had so much going for him, yet they both felt, that for the last few months he had lost a little of his charismatic sparkle. Toby knew his brother better than anyone. Tank didn't realize he was gruffer than usual; but his family did, and Toby was pretty sure he knew why. Toby believed being single had finally lost its appeal to his younger brother; especially seeing how happy they were.

A few hours later, Tank and Grease thanked Toby and Breezy for dinner and headed out. Gus had fallen asleep curled up next to Toby. Tank would never begrudge his brother anything, much less the happiness he'd found with Breezy and their little boy, but he couldn't help the brief moment of emptiness that passed through him, as he witnessed the homey scene.

Tank and Grease drove down the mountain road passing their drive and through the quaint sleepy town of Happy before easing their large bikes into The Pen's parking lot. There were four Harleys parked in the lot that they did not recognize. It wasn't unusual for bikers to stop at The Pen, but these bikers didn't look like bikes that recreational bikers used. Grease looked at Tank uneasily as they dismounted wondering who was inside. Tank knew whomever it was inside had to have heard them pull in, so they had to go in prepared for anything.

Tank nodded at Grease conveying to him that he would go in first and Grease should wait a second before following. As Tank opened the bar's entrance door, he angled his body so his back was against the door as he stepped inside. The television over the bar was tuned to a Rockies game and four men in leather vests sat at the bar talking with Ditch. The men were patched, and it was a sign of disrespect to wear your colors in someone else's turf.

Tank stepped away from the door and Grease followed him inside. The four men stood from their stools as they approached, and Tank recognized their cuts. They were from an outlaw motorcycle club from up north called Satan's Army. Grease remained a slight step behind Tank as a sign of respect to Tank's President status, yet close enough to have his back.

"Ditch," Tank said casually, nodding at the man behind the bar.

"Tank, Grease," Ditch answered. His voice hitched slightly. Tank assumed that the four patched visitors had Ditch slightly rattled. Tank spoke to the man with the highest rank.

"Just passing through?" Tank asked.

"Yup. You got a problem with that?" the Vice President asked.

"Nope," Tank answered. All six men eyed each other warily. The air was thick with unspoken tension. Tank unknowingly rolled his shoulders; loosening them for what may come. Tank moved to an empty stool next to the VP and took a sip from the beer Ditch had placed on the bar for him.

"This isn't a highly traveled route. In fact, it's a bit out of the way for most folks," Tank said keeping his voice at an even keel. Tank knew if he and Grease were to brawl it out with the four bikers, they'd be able to inflict serious damage, but still, four to two were never good odds. Tank had actually been spoiling for a fight lately. Grease had serious bulk plus he was strong as a bull and was a hell of a fighter. The three other men stepped away from the bar to stand behind their Vice-President, who had moved away from his stool. Grease did the same and Tank put his beer down as he readied himself for the first punch. As Tank eyed the men, he noticed the distinct bulges under their leather cuts. These men were carrying. Fists versus guns were no contest.

"Well then," Tank said, "how about if I buy you guys a shot? Just to show you how friendly we are around these parts."

Grease shot tank a WTF look, but Tank continued to grin. Ditch immediately set up six shots of Jack. The tension in the room lowered considerably. The men held their glasses and Tank said, "to passing through." He and Grease downed their shots and placed the glasses back on the bar. The three bikers waited to see how their VP would react to Tank's obvious reference to them not being welcomed there.

The VP met Tanks eyes and chuckled. "I heard you were a smart son of a bitch and I know you can fight. I'd actually like to mix it up with you and your man here, but we really are just passing through and if my Pres. hadn't told us to keep a low profile we'd be having a good ole time now."

The bearded man drank his shot down and his men did the same. The VP stuck his hand out to Tank, and Tank shook it. "I'm Shooter Flynn and I know you recognize our cut."

Tank said, "I do, just as you should have recognized that you're in our town."

The air sizzled and the men on either side of their leaders readied. Tank had stood up brazenly to the outlaw VP and, had off handedly referenced them wearing their cuts on his turf.

The V.P. chuckled. "You are a bad ass and I can respect that. Perhaps another time?" he said, his meaning crystal clear to Tank. If they met again, blood would be shed.

Tank and Grease watched as the four men left the bar. It wasn't until they heard the rumble of their bikes leaving the parking lot that they relaxed.

"What did they want, Ditch?" Tank asked.

Ditch looked uncomfortable. He wasn't a member of Tank's motorcycle club, but they treated him well and he made his living off of them patronizing the bar.

"Don't know really. They asked about you, though."

"What they ask?"

"Just what kind of outfit you ran."

Grease spoke for the first time. "I don't like this Tank, something's up."

Tank was quiet for a few seconds. "Yeah, I got a hinky feeling myself."

"You have your gun?" Tank asked.

"In my saddle bag," Grease responded. Tank nodded. He hadn't brought his inside either.

Tank and Grease drank a couple beers and shot the breeze with Ditch for another hour before they headed back to camp. Tank decided he would tell Toby about the encounter, just to be on the safe side.

Motorcycle clubs were all about respect. Other clubs respected each other's turf unless they were purposely trying to stir up trouble. Most motorcycle clubs were actually legitimate clubs formed so friends could socialize and enjoy riding together.

Then there were the motorcycle clubs that were like Tank's. His club was not simply a social outlet; they were considered a family. The club owned businesses that the members worked at. They had a hierarchy and to every cut-holding member the club was their life, their number one priority. Satan's Army was an outlaw club. It had a hierarchy and to the members the club was their life too, but their club was on the wrong side of the law in every way. The Steel Horse Cowboys had at one time been an outlaw biker club. They had been involved with some seriously shady shit. Tank had been in the thick of that when he first joined up and Toby hadn't spoken to him for a year.

Luckily, the president that preceded Tank had recognized that the club was on a dangerous path. He had slowly started to pull them out of the illegal businesses. When Tank had been elected as club president he brought them all the way out. Illegal businesses paid better but the risk was too great; running guns over the boarder to Canada, or escorting trucks holding contra ban. Tank spent his first year as president detangling the club from any questionable businesses and he had still managed to keep his men working. A few years later the club was supporting everyone who chose to work, and the club was making a profit.

As Tank and Grease got to the base of Happy Mountain Road, Tank slowed to a stop and Grease pulled up next to him.

"Let's ride single file the rest of the way." Grease nodded understanding Tank's command.

"Gun?" Tank asked.

Grease patted the left side of his cut. "Right here, man."

Tank smirked and patted the same area on his cut so Grease would know that he had his gun on him now, too. "Eyes wide, friend."

"Eyes wide," Grease answered.

The men reached the camp turn off and continued to ride cautiously down the dark, dirt drive, much slower than they normally would. When they reached the cabins, Tank stopped at Grease's and they both looked around the dark campsite.

"It's quiet," Grease stated as he looked around warily.

"Yea, and I didn't see any tracks other than ours."

"What do you want to do?" Grease asked, turning back towards Tank.

"I think we're okay. Try to rig something by your door in case anyone tries to sneak in. If they ride in we'll hear their bikes."

Grease nodded and dismounted.

"Grease, if something does happen, meet me back by the swimming hole."

"Got it."

The swimming hole was a small, naturally carved out area in the stream in the woods directly behind Tank's cabin. Tank and Grease knew they could find the obscure and now overgrown path, but anyone not knowing the trail wouldn't find it.

Tank rode over to his cabin and dismounted. He vigilantly walked around his place, stopping and listening after advancing every few steps. Satisfied that no one had been near his home, he went inside. His cabin had only three rooms, a large open kitchen and living area, a bathroom, and a bedroom. It only took a few minutes to establish that he was alone. Tank was tired from the long and physically draining day he and Grease had just put in. Satan's Army showing up in Happy was not a good sign and Tank hoped they really were just passing through. He lay down on his bed but remained dressed. With his gun within reach Tank fell asleep.

Chapter 3

The next morning, Tank and Grease drove up to Toby's for coffee and breakfast. They filled Toby in on the strange visit from the four Satan's Army men and after eating Breezy's delicious blueberry pancakes, they headed back to camp to continue getting it ready for the Memorial weekend club members.

They had the two trees cleared off the children's play area by lunchtime, and in true Breezy fashion, she and Gus arrived just as they finished stacking the last pile of cut logs. Breezy unloaded a picnic basket containing fried chicken, potato salad, brownies, and iced tea. The men ate while Breezy happily filled them in on the local Happy gossip. Gus wanted to play on the old tire swing nearby, so Tank left the tree stump he was using as a seat and inspected the thick rope that was looped over a large limb. Satisfied that it was safe, he lifted Gus onto the tire and gave him a push before going back to his meal. When they finished eating, Breezy collected the garbage and told the men she expected them at dinner again that night. Tank watched her and Gus drive away, and that disturbing and unsettling wave of loneliness invaded him again.

That afternoon, Tank spent some time cleaning his cabin Grease had removed the tree from his roof and then he and Tank, together, were able to rid Sweets and Lolly's cabin of the raccoon family that had made a mess of the mattress and couch.

With those chores out of the way, he and Grease rode down to Happy, to Pete's General Store. As Tank drove the small dirt road, he made a mental list of all the things he needed for his cabin. He couldn't stop smiling when he thought how it was actually his cabin; his to do with as he pleased.

The warm afternoon air swept through Tank's dark hair as his Harley growled under him. He relished the natural beauty surrounding him. The forest buffering the road showed off slivers of sunshine that had managed to slip through the thick green awning of leaves. The air still contained a cool spring nip in it, but Tank could feel the sun's rays warm on his back. Montana was beautiful, especially in the summer, and Tank couldn't imagine living anywhere else.

When they reached Pete's General Store, Tank spent a few minutes talking with the store's owner, Pete. Tank described some of the improvements he planned to make to the old camp. Pete said he knew of a modular homebuilder that specialized in log homes and he would get Tank their information. Tank already knew exactly what he wanted, but he didn't want to offend his old friend, so he affably took the material Pete handed him.

Afterwards, Tank purchased food and hardware; including a roll of screening wire, so he could close in the places that the bats and raccoons were sneaking through. He told Pete that he would come down the next day when one of his guys arrived with a truck to tote back everything he had purchased. While he was in town he used his cell to call Sweets and tell him he and Lolly were going to need a mattress and a couch.

Satisfied with their shopping trip, Tank and Grease headed back up the mountain for dinner with Toby,

Breezy, and Gus. Tank had bought a small metal truck for Gus and a bottle of wine for dinner. He safely stored both gifts in his leather sidesaddle. Dinner that night consisted of pork chops and pasta mixed with vegetables. Toby had remained in his game warden's uniform because he had to patrol the campsite opposite The Pen after dinner. Memorial Day weekend started the migration of summer folk into the normally quiet town. The campgrounds filled up with weekend revelers and summer long campers, and Toby was kept busy safeguarding the areas national parks and the encompassing state-owned forestland.

When dinner ended, Breezy walked Toby out to his jeep while Gus entertained the two men. When Breezy returned, she was flushed, and her lips were puffy with that just 'kissed hard' look. Tank knew his sister-in-law well and he immediately stood up and hugged her.

"He'll be fine, Breezy."

"Oh my gosh, Tank!" Breezy said swatting his shoulder. "How do you do that?"

"What?" Tank asked innocently, knowing full well what she meant.

"How do you know what I'm thinking? I swear, between you and your brother..." Breezy gave Tank an endearing hug and when she pulled back, Tank held on to her shoulders gently.

"Breezy, he's good at his job, you know that."

Breezy shrugged her shoulders and sighed softly. "I know, Tank, really I do. I just keep remembering what those men did to him last summer."

"Yeah, that was rough, but look how he pulled through that."

"Yes, but they never caught them, Tank. What if they come back?"

"Honey, those men are not going to show up anywhere that Toby might see them. He can identify them remember? They won't want to risk it."

"I know you're right, Tank. I just worry."

Tank pulled her in for a quick brotherly hug and rubbed her back. "I know, me too."

After thanking Breezy for dinner, Grease and Tank headed down into Happy again to have a few beers at The Pen. The lot was empty and after they entered and sat down they had to ring the triangle bell over the well-worn wooden bar to alert Ditch that he had customers. They heard Ditch's uneven gait as he made his way down the steps from his apartment upstairs.

"Hey, Ditch," Tank greeted him as he came through the door into the open bar area.

"Tank. Grease."

"Getting ready for the onslaught?" Tank said, referring to all the club's members and their friends converging on the camp in the next few days.

Ditch gave Tank a strange look and then he simply nodded and set them up with beers and shots.

Grease shot Tank a look conveying; 'what's up?"

and Tank shrugged his shoulders not knowing why Ditch was acting strangely.

On most nights in the summer, the men and women in the club would make their way down to The Pen to let off a little steam. Tank knew when he put up the new prefab cabin that The Pen would lose business and he felt bad about it. Ditch wasn't the owner, but it was his job and he relied on his club for most of the bars business. He had been a friend to the club, but they hadn't known him for long and he wasn't patched.

Ditch wasn't in a talkative mood, another detour from his normally jovial behavior, so Grease and Tank didn't bother him. They watched the game and talked about how they planned to fix up and personalize their cabins. The bars front door opened, and Toby walked in.

"Hey, bro," Tank said. He motioned for Ditch to set Toby up.

"Hey," Toby answered, and then he thanked Ditch who had placed a beer in front of him.

"Campgrounds filling up?" Grease asked.

"Yeah, and there was already a scuffle."

"Already?" Tank asked.

"Some kids, just out of college were drinking and two guys were tussling over a girl, of course. Luckily, I was onsite. I would have been pissed if I'd been called down the mountain for a stupid drunken skirmish."

Toby took a long draw from his beer.

"Anyway, it's all good now," he said sounding weary.

Tank nodded, "Toby," Tank's voice dropped to a hush and Grease took that hint to use the restroom. "Breezy worries about you when you go out. You know that, right?"

Toby shook his head back and forth and took another sip before answering his younger brother. "She's told me, Tank, but it's my job."

"I just thought... you know, maybe she was keeping her feelings to herself again; like last summer."

"Yeah, like last summer when she confided in you before she confided in me?" Toby's voice took on an edge and Tank knew to tread lightly.

"Hey man, that woman loves you and you know it. If she had given me the slightest encouragement I would have been on her, but it was always you Toby, always. I just wanted to make sure you knew."

Toby sighed, "Yeah, I know. Sorry about being so testy. Summers are my busy time. I'm already missing her."

"You're a lucky man, Toby. What you two have... it's special, really special."

"Yeah, I know."

Grease chose that moment to walk back into the main bar area and at the same time the men heard a car pull into the gravel lot.

"Expecting company Ditch?" Tank asked.

"Never know who I'm expecting," Ditched answered quickly.

The men turned their heads to the front door as it opened, and in stepped three women dressed in short jean skirts, cropped tops and cowboy boots. The women looked at the three men and when they saw Toby in an official uniform they faltered for a second before continuing towards the bar.

All three were lookers and Grease got a huge smile on his face. Tank waited to see if the girls would retreat, seeing that it wasn't a normal bar stop for most people, but they didn't. The girls smiled sexily at the men and made their way to the opposite end of the bar.

Grease, who normally waited for women to approach him, uncharacteristically left his stool to greet the ladies, while Tank and Toby looked on. Grease was an enigma. He was the epitome of the strong, silent type. In fact, he was generally quiet around people he didn't know, but Grease was popular with the ladies. He was big and looked intimidating with his girth, bearded face, and long hair that was always held in place with a bandana. His gruff, bad boy appearance did not seem to hinder him with women though; he rarely went home alone. Rumor was that he was a gifted lover.

"Ladies," Grease said to the trio. "You just brightened this entire place with your pretty little smiles."

Toby chuckled at the charm Grease was putting out. Tank signaled for Ditch to give the ladies their first round on his tab. The ladies giggled and flirted with

Grease and then two of them looked over at Toby and Tank.

"Okay, brother," Toby said with a chuckle, "this is where I cut out."

Tank hmphed and smiled, "Yeah, you've gotten into enough trouble with Breezy in this place. Go home. Love that beautiful wife of yours."

"I plan too, baby bro. I plan too." Toby headed for the door and Tank left his stool to join Grease. Tank hadn't had a woman in a few weeks and although he could have, he just hadn't had the desire. Cara had been obvious about wanting to be with him, but he just wasn't feeling it. Maybe a good, pre-summer bang would kick start his libido. The girls were putting out serious slutty vibes and Tank and Grease planned on being very accommodating. One of them was going to have a three some and Tank didn't even care if it was him or not. For the first time in a while Tank was actually looking forward to a wild, mindless hook up. The group of five spent a good hour laughing and drinking. Tank was starting to feel a slight buzz, so he switched to water. He was surprised the little ladies were holding up well as they were. Grease was dancing with two of the women and Tank watched them grinding erotically. Grease was enjoying the attention as was apparent from the considerable bulge in the front of his jeans. Yup, his friend was having a threesome. Tank didn't mind.

The pretty brunette that was practically giving him a lap dance was all he needed for the night.

A half hour later, even though Tank had switched to water, he was still feeling a strong buzz from the alcohol. His mind was sluggish, and his vision was becoming more blurred each minute. Funny thing was; he didn't think he'd drank that much. The woman he was with was rubbing herself on his thigh and he was sloppily sucking her through her thin white tee shirt. She was moaning softly, and Tank knew she was close to coming. Grease was nowhere in sight, and neither were the other two girls. Tank's foggy mind figured Grease had probably taken them to the back hallway for some serious banging. Ditch wasn't behind the bar, and as Tank's vision doubled he knew something was very wrong.

He stood up abruptly, the brunette fell from his lap as he tried unsuccessfully to call for Grease. His hands tried to find the bar to hold him up, but he wobbled like a toddler. The girl, who he swore had been about to get off, silently sat down on a stool. He realized she did not appear to be even the least bit surprised that he had fallen. Tank's eyesight tunneled and he felt himself hit the floor hard before complete darkness engulfed him.

Chapter 4

The first thing Tank was aware of as he drifted back into consciousness was that his mouth was ridiculously dry, and his head ached painfully. Next, the sound of a motor running and men talking filtered through his hazy thoughts. Rough material covered his face and that was why he couldn't see anything, even though his eyes were open, and also why any sounds he heard were muted. His shoulders hurt and when he tried to move them he found that his hands and feet were tightly bound. He was rendered immobile, hog-tied lying on a hard, cold surface.

The bumps in the road and running engine clued Tank to the fact that he was in a vehicle on an unpaved road. He didn't want to alert whoever had taken him to the fact that he was awake yet, so he remained quiet. Waves of nausea rolled through him and he tried to thwart the bile that was threatening to come up by breathing deeply through his nose. Tank was worried that Grease was with him, but he refused want to speak because he wanted to regain his faculties before letting on that he was fully conscious.

Tank thought back to the bar and replayed the evening. The only thing that made any sense was that he had been roofied, but by who? Ditch would never do this to him. He thought about Ditch and hoped he was okay, too. The only thing Tank could come up with was that the girls had slipped him something, but why? Tank thought about the Satan's Army visit wondering if this could somehow be related.

The vehicle hit a large bump and Tank couldn't hold in the grunt after his head slapped against the hard metal floor. All talk in the vehicle ceased, Tank knew they realized he was awake. He felt someone move near him and then a vicious blow to his head sent him spinning back into darkness.

The second time Tank came to, was when he felt himself being dragged from the vehicle. He thought it must have been a utility van because he heard two creaking doors open and a whoosh of brisk air chilled his body. He was pulled from the vehicle, airborne for a second before landing hard on unyielding gravel. He grunted as his back took the brunt of the fall. He was then dragged, with his knees scraping across the ground, up a few steps, across a hard floor before he was callously pushed down a flight of steps.

Tank had no way of protecting himself as he tumbled down the steep staircase. His head was banging into everything it came in contact with, a wall, steps, and he felt something gouge into the skin on his side. When he came to rest at the bottom of the stairs he heard footsteps coming down after him. His head was swimming from the knocks it had just taken so he wasn't prepared for the kicks that began to land, first on his back and then to his ribs. No matter where Tank moved the kicks continued to land. He knew there had to be more than one person giving him this savage beating. Tank fought to remain conscious, focusing solely on the thought that whoever was dishing out the kicks, had better pray he never got free, or they were dead men.

Tank couldn't know how long the men had beaten on him for, he only knew he had passed out again, this time from a kick to the side of his head. When he came to, he vomited. Luckily the bag had been taken off his head, so he was able to spew to the side instead of all over himself. Tank's feet were tied together, and his wrists were shackled in front of him around a large pole that ran from floor to ceiling. If he wanted to stand he could, but he could barely sit up so that wasn't happening.

Tank peered around his prison and even though it was dark he could tell that he was in a stone cellar. He didn't see Grease and his concern escalated hoping that his friend was all right. Tank's head was pounding, and it hurt for him to move his neck. He could feel the dried blood on his face and when he looked down at his torso he could see that his tee shirt was soaked in blood. He also realized he didn't have his cut on. Anger coursed through him. The beating was savage, but taking his cut, well that put this attack on a whole different level. The one thing this did reveal to Tank was that this was not the work of Satan's Army. Clubs never took cuts off of patched members. You could force a man to hand his cut over by beating him and if the man succumbed, basically had had enough, he would hand his cut over. If he didn't hand it over it was still his to wear. It was the club president's prerogative to say when the man being beaten had had 'enough'. The other way a cut was taken was if a patched member had done something so horrendous that he was voted out of the club. Otherwise, cuts were sacred and considered hands off. With that piece of information tucked away, Tank struggled with not only his physical injuries, but with the fact that he had no idea who had kidnapped him or why.

Tank drifted in and out of consciousness and was thankfully not visited by anyone again. His sense of time was gone, and he had no idea how long he'd been unconscious or even if it were day or night. His mental acuity began to return, along with the horrendous pain he felt all over his body. He was cold and goose bumps rose up on his arms in the dank darkness. He knew the numerous cuts on his face and head had bled because his face felt tight with dried blood. He thought his nose might be broken but when he gingerly touched it he was reassured when he found it was not crooked. It was, however, so filled with dried blood that he couldn't breathe through it.

He knew he had a concussion and a few ribs were definitely broken. He was having trouble taking a deep breath so he was concerned one of his ribs might have punctured a lung. He couldn't see his back, but he could feel how tender it was. He was sure there were open gashes that were oozing blood; he felt his shirt sticking to him. His legs were on fire and his pants were shredded at the knees from being dragged. Both knees were skinned and caked with dirt and blood. One of his eyes was swollen completely shut and his head pounded with an unrelenting beat making him nauseous. He ran his tongue across the front of his teeth and was relieved he didn't feel any gaps.

Tank needed to take a piss, so he maneuver himself upwards, using the pole to steady himself as he stood. He couldn't stand up right he was in too much pain. He pressed his pelvis to one side the pole and carefully lowered his hands to undo his fly, but his fingers wouldn't stretch around the bar. He was dreading the fact he would have to pee in his pants. He managed to partially unzip his fly, but he just couldn't unsnap his button.

He heard a noise coming from near the bottom of the stairs. It was too dark to make out who or what it was. Tank was tough, but he knew there was only so much he could physically endure before his body gave out. He was badly beaten and in more pain than he'd ever felt of pain. Tank knew with his current injuries he would live, but Ii he had to endure any more, he might not survive. Maybe that was the idea, he thought grimly, dreading what was about to happen. Tank heard light footsteps padding towards him, too light to be one of his former abusers. When he was finally able to see whom it was, he audibly gasped. He thought it was a woman, but her clothes were so baggy he couldn't tell for sure. She was filthy. Her ill-fitting clothes hung off her skeleton like frame. Greasy, stringy, long dark hair hung in front of her face totally obscuring it. Her feet were bare and black from dirt. As she slowly approached him, Tank tensed. Her movements were tense and skittish. The woman produced a small plastic sandwich bag filled with water. She opened the top of the bag and tilted it towards Tank's mouth. Tank didn't hesitate, he drank the entire bag of water and then realized he was definitely going to pee himself now, but the water tasted great and he had really needed it.

"Who are you?" Tank asked quietly.

She put her finger to her mouth and Tank understood they needed to stay quiet.

He nodded then he whispered, "can you get me out of here?"

She shook her head back and forth. No.

Tank didn't know if she was mute or just too afraid to speak.

The unkempt woman then pointed at his unzipped pants.

Tank looked to where she pointed.

"Yeah, I have to piss," he whispered uncharacteristically embarrassed.

The woman hesitated for a few seconds before she quickly unsnapped his jeans and reached her dirty fingers into his boxers to pull out his dick. She positioned it in the plastic bag then shyly looked away. Tank was taken back, but he realized she was trying to help him, so he quickly got past the fact that some unknown, scraggily woman was holding his dick into a plastic bag and he quickly emptied his bladder. He had to stifle a moan at how good it felt to relieve himself. When he had finished, she tucked him back in, zipped him up, and refastened his button. Tank could tell that she was as uncomfortable as he was.

"Thanks," Tank whispered feeling awkward.

Tank watched her go to a dark corner of the room where he heard her dump his pee out. She then walked back into his line of sight and he watched her as she took the empty bag and stuffed it into a crevice in the wall, away from wherever she had dumped its contents. She was smart. A sliver of hope shot through Tank. Maybe, just maybe, he could persuade her to help him.

The girl nervously walked out from the shadows of the room, and timidly pushed her greasy hair behind one ear exposing part of her face. This allowed Tank to see her features for the first time. Her face was gaunt, and she appeared to be a young woman. Her clothes hid her shape, but the way they hung on her he knew she was seriously under nourished. He studied her dirt-smudged face trying to look past the grime. She had full lips that were dry and cracked. Her high cheekbones were pronounced more likely from being so thin. Two bruises showed through the filth covering her face; one on her chin and one under her eye. She had been averting looking directly at him but when her eyes timidly found his Tank sucked in an uneasy breath. Her eyes were captivating. Even in the darkness of his underground prison, Tank saw that they were a vibrant shade of blue. His first thought was that they were the color of the Montana sky or a cloudless day. If Tank didn't know better he'd swear she wore contacts. Underneath her pretty eyes were dark circles, and her body odor indicated that she hadn't bathed in a while. In fact, she smelled horrible.

She'd been quietly staring at him the entire time he had been studying her. Then, without warning she leaned towards him and ever so quietly whispered, "try to live. I'll be back."

With that, she soundlessly hurried up the wooden stairs.

Chapter 5

Time was non-existent for Tank. The men descended on him daily. They enjoyed taunting him, accentuated with kicks and punches. The strange woman would always come to him before his beat downs and blindfold him, so Tank never saw his attackers. He figured that they were purposely keeping him weak, but for some reason they had not killed him. He still had no clue as to why he had been kidnapped. Tank was taken to the bathroom twice a day. After the men had their sick fun with him and then later in the day. He was always kept cuffed and blind folded, so any thoughts of escaping were discarded. Twice a day the woman would come down to the cellar and feed him. The first two days he could only stomach broth. Tank had a feeling that she was only supposed to be feeding him the soup, but when she came the second time each day, she fed him scraps of meat and pieces of bread. Tank was weakening and losing hope.

"How long have I been here?" Tank asked the woman as she was feeding him soup that was no longer warm. He had taken a few serious punches to his ribs a few hours earlier and it was hard for him to breath.

The woman paused mid spoon. "Four days," she whispered uneasily.

Tank couldn't believe she answered him.

"Where are we?"

"I don't know," she paused. "I'm not supposed to talk to you. If they catch me they'll do something bad to me. They're asleep and don't know I'm down here now."

Tank nodded. He didn't want to get her in trouble, but he had to know. "Just tell me your name."

"Tess," she whispered. "Now shush and eat."

Tank relented and had soon finished the soup.

The next day, Tess came down the steps with a man. She didn't secure the sack over his face like she did before the men visited him. The fact that the man was letting him see his face was not a good sign. The man was large, though not as large as Tank. He had long hair that was tied back with a piece of leather. He looked to be in his thirties. His teeth were yellow with tobacco stains and he had a scar on his neck.

"You've been talking to her," the man said holding Tess firmly on her bicep.

Tank kept his mouth shut. Tess was not looking at him and she was visibly shaking.

"I heard ya," the burly, redneck hissed.

Tank picked up on the man's accent and knew it was from upper Montana.

Tank still didn't answer him.

"I told her not to talk to ya," he yelled at Tank, spraying saliva. He shook Tess violently.

He turned to Tess, "Din I tell ya not to talk to him?" He then slapped her so hard across the face that she was lifted off her feet.

Tank was outraged. "Leave her alone," he yelled, only his voice came out in a raspy wheeze. His body was shutting down, and Tank could feel how weak he had become.

Knowing Tank was no threat to him he remained focused on Tess, who lay on the floor.

"I've saved your sorry ass more than once. You repay me by talking to this trash?" he asked, pointing at Tank.

Tank could see that Tess was crying softly. Her hand was holding her cheek as she remained cowering on the floor.

The man was seething, pointing his finger at Tess. "He's gunna to be gone soon. Don't forget who owns you, woman."

He then grabbed Tess by her hair and hauled her upright before forcing her up the steps in front of him.

The next day, Tess only came down to feed him once. She leaned into him. Tank couldn't believe she was going to risk talking to him again.

"They're waiting to hear from someone about what to do with you. I think they want to kill you but don't know how to do it. It needs to look like an accident. If I can help you I will, but if they catch me they'll kill me too, or worse." Tank didn't understand what could be worse, but he didn't risk asking her.

Hours later two men came down the stairs. They uncuffed Tank from the pole and dragged him upstairs. He was so weak he could barely support his own weight. Tank saw looked out of the windows and saw nothing but trees. The home looked rustic and Tank realized it was probably a hunting or summer cabin.

Tank was hauled into a small room off of the main room. He was stripped of his clothes; his boots and socks had been taken from him on the first night he was there. He was forced onto a twin-sized bed and the chain around his wrists was replaced with a rope. He was secured to the metal bed frame face up, spread eagle and completely naked. If they were going to torture him more Tank knew the end was near. He wanted to taunt the men. He figured they would lose control and kill him quicker. How bad was it that he was only hoping for a quick death? Sadness blanketed him as he thought about his family and his club. The only positive thought was that Toby, Sweets and Grease, if Grease was alive, would not rest until these fuckers were found.

He heard muffled cries coming from the doorway and saw that Tess was being carried in just as naked as he was. She had a gag in her mouth and was fighting them with everything she had. The men laughed at her weak attempts to free herself. Tank noticed that the man that had hit her wasn't with them. They tied Tess so that she was spread eagle on top of him, so they were face to face. Tess was still trying wiggle free and every move exacerbated his own injuries. He knew she was scared out of her mind and he wished he could comfort her. He remained quiet not want the men to know he was fully cognizant. He'd been pretending to be out of it since his last beating.

When Tess was finally secured the two men joked about their sick rendering of human artwork. Tess's hair was covering his face making it hard to see but Tank heard liquid being sloshed around their tiny room. Tank knew from the noxious smell that it was gasoline. Tess's eyes were crazed with fear as saw what the men were doing. Tank knew what was coming next and he quickly scanned the room praying for anything that might save them.

"Any last words tough guy?" One of the men asked him crudely.

Tank didn't say a word hoping he looked bewildered. He was however, memorizing their faces.

They heard the men leave the cabin and a car start up. A few moments later a loud whoosh shot through the wooden cabin. Tess was screaming into her gag.

"Tess...Tess..." Tank was trying to get her attention, but she was completely panicking and pulling on her ropes.

"Tess..." Tank knocked his head sharply against hers to get her attention.

Tess looked down at him and stopped struggling. Tank used his mouth to pull the gag from her mouth.

"Our hands are near each other. Let me try to untie you. You have to stop moving, you're making the knot tighter."

Tess stilled and Tank went to work loosening her knot. Tess focused her attention on their other wrists, and she worked her fingers to try to undo the knot binding them together to the bed frame. They could hear the fire eating away at the wooden house they were trapped in. The heat was making their bodies slick with sweat, and it actually helped Tank to work the rope. Smoke was becoming a factor and Tank tried not to cough because his ribs were killing him. Finally, Tank was able to loosen one of the ropes just enough that Tess could slip her thin wrist through the small loop. She quickly untied Tanks wrist from the frame and then freed their other wrists. When Tank's hands were liberated, he pushed Tess into a sitting position between his feet so he could untie their feet. Bending over was painful and Tank fought the waves of darkness that threatened to engulf him.

The flames were only a few feet from the bed and Tess was coughing miserably. Tank told Tess to scream bloody murder. She looked at him like he'd lost his mind for a half a second before she shrieked out a long and loud wail. Tank let out a bellow of his own. Tank finally managed to get them completely untied. The flames was so close to them that it had ignited the mattress beneath them. They leapt off the bed and Tank grabbed his clothes that had been thrown on the floor nearby. He slapped the flames off his jeans and grabbed Tess's hand urging her to follow him.

They crawled out the bedroom door towards the back of the cabin. Flames crawled up the log walls around them and embers swirled ominously around them. Tank stopped under a window and cautiously peered over the window ledge. Not seeing anyone he quickly lifted it. He motioned for Tess to go out the window and when she scampered through he followed her. His body was so battered and weak that he tumbled to the ground, grunting from the impact, but managed to get to his feet with Tess's help.

They ran towards the cover of the nearby trees. After running a few hundred yards into the thickly wooded area they stopped to rest. Tank was in agony and black spots were fading in and out in front of his eyes. He was gasping for breath. Tess was winded too and leaned back against a tree. It was then that she remembered she was naked. She slid her thin body to the other side of the tree, out of Tank's eyesight. Tank threw his shirt towards her and then he painstakingly pulled his pants on.

"Tess, we have to keep going," Tank panted. She was still behind the tree.

"They're going to make sure our bodies are in there before they leave, unless someone spots the smoke and they run. I guarantee they are sitting down the drive waiting for the fire to burn off. We have to get out of here."

"That's why you had me scream?"

Tank nodded.

Tess came out from behind the tree wearing his blood caked, olive colored shirt. It fell to just above her knees and the sleeves sat near her elbows. She had her arms crossed in front of her body and she kept her face to the ground.

"Can you keep going?" she asked so quietly that he almost didn't hear what she had said.

It was the first time she acknowledged his injuries.

"I have to," Tank said seriously.

They kept walking in the opposite direction from the smoke. Their ears were listening for any sounds of the men tracking them. Their progress was slow because neither of them had shoes on. Spikey pinecones and hidden tree roots littered the forests ground and cut into their bared flesh.

As the sun started to set, the woods grew darker and the air around them moistened with the chilly onset of nightfall. Tank stopped walking and Tess must have been looking down because she plowed into his back.

They both groaned at the impact.

"It's getting dark. We need to find a place to sleep."

Tess eyed him nervously. She walked over to a nearby tree and sat down tiredly. Tank watched her then limped to a tree adjacent hers and eased himself down. Cutting pain sliced through his chest, and he knew his breathing was becoming more labored. His knees were raised. He propped his arms across them, leaned his forehead against his bare fore arms, and shut his eyes. The position hindered his breathing, so he uncrossed his arms and straightened his legs leaning back against the tree. He knew it was going to be a long and uncomfortable night.

Neither spoke as the woods came alive with animal noises. Normally Tank would have loved listening to those sounds, but he silently prayed that tonight wasn't his last time hearing them. They remained quiet and Tank thought Tess had actually fallen asleep, but then she turned towards him and he was able to see that her eyes were open.

"Can't sleep?" he asked.

"Uh-uh."

Tank noticed that she had pulled her arms inside the shirt and had tucked her legs in also.

"Are you cold?"

"A little. You must be, too. You don't even have a shirt on."

"Yeah, I'm a little cold," Tank lied. He wasn't cold because he knew he was running a fever.

They grew silent again.

"Tess, tell me about yourself. Why did they have you with them? Do you even know who they are?"

Tess sighed deeply. "I don't even know your name," she answered him sullenly.

"It's Tank."

"Like the army truck, Tank?"

"Yeah," he chuckled then grimaced with the pain that had brought forth.

"Do you have another name? I don't really want to call you Tank. A tank is destructive."

"My given name is Terry, but I've been called Tank ever since I was little."

"Because of your size?"

"Yeah."

"Can I call you Terry instead? I really like that better."

"Sure, why not."

"Okay, Terry," she said softly. "Have you ever heard the saying; if I tell you I'd have to kill you?"

"Yeah?" Tank answered warily.

"Well, if I tell you who I am ..."

"You'd have to kill me," Tank finished dryly.

Tess sighed deeply, "first, I'd never kill you, or anyone for that matter, on purpose that is..." Tess's voice trailed off as if she was deep in thought.

"I'm not trying to pry, Tess. I just want to know more about the woman who saved my life." Tank's voice was gentle, and it helped to put Tess at ease.

"What state is this?" she asked. "Do you know?"

"I think we're in Montana."

"It's pretty. I liked looking out the windows."

"So, tell me your story, Tess. I may be dead by morning so you wouldn't have to kill me." Tank tried to jest.

"Don't say that," she admonished.

Tess snuggled deeper into his shirt. "For starters, my name is Tess Green. I was taken against my will by those men and I don't know how long I've been with them, but I was taken on April 21st."

"Geesh, Tess, that's a long time."

"Why? What's the date?"

"I'm not sure exactly, but I was taken right before the Memorial weekend."

"A month and a half," she murmured.

"Yeah, a month and a half," Tank repeated softly, looking at the slip of a thing that had been held captive for so long.

"So, here's where the 'I'd have to kill you' part comes in," Tess said nervously, as she fiddled with the hem of the shirt. "I had a boyfriend, well he said he was my fiancé, but he never gave me a ring or anything. He said it was our little secret. Anyway, we met in New York City. I was waitressing at a bar, and we just connected."

Tank nodded his head as a form of encouragement. He could tell she was nervous.

"We fell in love. Well, I thought we did anyway. I don't have money and I don't have any family." Tess chuckled gently, "I'm on the ten-year plan for college, so when this handsome, nice, wealthy man said he loved me; well, stupid me actually thought he did."

"Ten-year plan?" Tank interrupted.

"I could only afford a few credits a year while I worked." She shrugged like it was no big deal, but Tank thought it was admiral.

He took one of her hands in; he knew her story did not have a good ending.

"So about nine months into our little romance he loses everything in a Ponzi scheme. I told him we would start again, build up his financial assets, as long as we were together we'd be okay. I was such an idiot. He looked at me and started laughing. I was shocked. I thought maybe he had lost it, you know, gone bonkers. He was laughing so hard that he could barely stand up straight. That's when he told me he was married and if his wife found out that he had invested her money in a shady investment that she'd divorce him."

"Wow, that stinks."

"Yeah, but there's more. I kind of lost it and I was ranting and raving telling him that I was going to tell his wife, you know the whole scorned woman thing, and that's when he got scary. He stopped laughing and told me he'd never let that happen and then he left."

"So, how'd you end up with those men?"

"I was on my way home from work the next week. I worked the night shift at a bar. I was snatched out of a parking lot and shoved into a van. They forced some drink down my throat and I was out. When I came to I was tied up. I couldn't escape and believe me I tried. Then the one man, Lester, he was sort of in charge of me."

"The one that slapped you?"

"Yes. He told me that my ex-boyfriend, Dan Randal had filed charges against me in New York. He said Dan had proof that I had stolen all the money he lost. On top of that bull crud, Dan's wife was found dead and Lester told me there was a warrant out for my arrest for her murder."

"Holy smokes, Tess, that's bad, really bad."

"Yeah, believe me I know. I don't know if Lester was lying, but it wouldn't surprise me one bit if Dan killed his wife and framed me."

"Shit."

"Lester said that if I did everything he asked, he'd keep me hidden from the law and safe from the other men."

"So, you think your boyfriend had you kidnapped and framed?"

"It's the only thing that makes sense. I sure as heck didn't steal any money or kill anyone."

"Did he? Did they...?" Tank couldn't say the word.

"They tried," Tess said, realizing what Tank was trying to ask. "But I fought like mad. Then Lester stepped in and stopped them. I know he's a bad man, but he did save me from that. I tried to escape, I really did, but I didn't get far. They took my clothes after I tried to escape for the second time. Then a few weeks ago they gave me the ones you saw on me."

"Did they feed you?"

"A little. I was afraid to eat too much because I didn't want to be drugged again."

"And no bath I suppose?"

"I tried to wash myself, but we were never at a place with running water. I must smell awful?" she said awkwardly. "At that last cabin, the electricity and water turned on the day after they brought you there. I don't think the cabin belonged to them, and I think that's why they were getting nervous. I think they thought the cabin's owners were coming soon."

"Do you know why they took me?"

"No, sorry. Lester told me not to talk to you because you were really bad and mean. He said that if I got too close to you, you'd try to hurt me."

"Why didn't they just kill me at the beginning? Why did they keep me around?"

"I heard them say they needed it to look like an accident. If it looked like murder your brother would get involved and he wouldn't let it go."

"Yeah, he would, too," Tank chuckled.

"Lester said you liked woman, a lot, so they were going to make it look like you took off with some lady from the bar you were at. Then, as you saw, they wanted to make it look like an accident, like you and her died in bed, together. The woman they were going to use never showed tonight. She was a hooker they would use sometimes, Riyanna. I think Riyanna knew something wasn't right, so she didn't show up. That's when they decided to use me. Lester fought them but they knocked him out. They said our rope ties would burn off and it would simply look like two lovers were caught in a fire and died in bed."

"That's pretty diabolical. There is no way they could have masterminded that."

"No, I don't think so either. I thought maybe Dan was behind my kidnapping, but yours? He doesn't even know you."

"Yeah, it's strange."

"Didn't that woman try to help you?"

"She never knew I was there," Tess answered, suddenly tired. She yawned relinquishing Tank's hand.

Tank watched as she curled into a small ball and snuggled into the uncomfortable ground.

"You're not that mean Terry." He heard her say drowsily as she drifted off to sleep.

Chapter 6

Tank closed his eyes and was able to doze off a few times during the night. When the first rays of sun filtered through the thick cover of trees overhead, Tank awoke to find Tess curled up on his lap. He didn't want to wake her, but he wasn't feeling well. He was uncomfortably warm, and he should have been freezing.

"Tess," he said gently, "Tess, it's time to go."

Tess awoke and when she realized she was wrapped around Tank's lower region she flew off of him and smacked into the tree behind her. She turned an adorable shade of pink and stared at the ground as she mumbled, "I'm sorry," as she rubbed the back of her head where it had banged against the tree.

"Tess, it's okay. Your body just sought out a heat source. Are you okay?"

Tess still couldn't look at him, but she nodded that she wasn't hurt.

"We have to get going," Tank said changing the subject and hoping to get her past acting so skittish around him.

He tried to stand up and wobbled, almost falling face first. Tess quickly jumped to her feet and pushed her bony shoulder under him for support.

"Thanks," Tank mumbled, hating the fact that he was so frail.

"You're really hot, Terry," he heard the concern in her quiet voice.

Tank felt like crap, but he couldn't resist teasing her.

57

"Why, thank you, my dear," he jested using a British accent.

"I..., you know that's not what I meant." She reddened with embarrassment. "I mean you are... well you..." Tank started to chuckle but stopped and clutched his side hoping to diminish the sharp pain that was slicing into him.

"I know what you meant, I just wanted to see you blush again."

"Terry, stop. I know you're hurting."

"Yeah, I don't feel great that's for sure. We have to get out of these woods, and I have to get in touch with my brother. He's the only one we can trust right now."

"We?"

"Yeah, you and me."

"Uh-uh, once I get you someplace safe, I have to leave. I can't risk being caught. I don't want to go to jail and I know I'll end up there. I can't afford a lawyer. No, I'm going to get lost somewhere."

"Tess, you're not going anywhere. My brother will help you. Please trust me. I'll take care of you."

" I can't risk it. Please don't ask me to."

"I can't argue with you now. We have to get out of here. I don't think either of us would last another night in the woods. Let's talk about this when we're someplace safe."

"You're pretty confident we're going to survive this," she mumbled under her breath.

"I heard that, Tess, and we will survive this," he said with more confidence than he was feeling.

"Okay, but I'm not changing my mind."

"Yeah, I hear you. Come on, we need to head east."

Tess nodded and they set off once again, moving slowly through the cool morning air of the awakening forest. Tank was breathing erratically and if Tess hadn't remained glued to his side, he would have fallen a couple of times. They broke for a rest and Tank leaned against a large boulder while Tess collapsed to the ground burying her head in her arms.

Tess looked up at Tank. His eyes were closed, and she watched his uneven breathing.

The man was a paradox. He was big and strong, well he had been, before he'd been kidnapped. He was tough enough to survive the beatings the men had administered to him every day, yet he had a gentle side to him. The sheer fact that he had empathized with her after she had told him her story sent a small jolt of hope into her pessimistic future.

It was almost sinful how good looking the man was. He had dark hair that fell below his jaw line, high cheekbones, and perfect sized lips for a guy. He now had a five-day growth on his face, but she'd seen him when he'd first been dragged into the cabin, before his beating. She'd noticed how attractive he was. She couldn't guess his age, but he had little crinkles in the corner of his eyes that belayed he might be older than he appeared. He had the biggest biceps she'd ever seen, accentuated with tattoos that she normally would have shied away from, but on him they were sexy. His arms connected with strong wide shoulders. His neck was thick, and his chest was large. She didn't see any fat on him, especially now that he'd been purposely under fed. His eyes fascinated her. Holy Toledo, they were lethal; a blue gray color with long dark lashes.

Tess colored when she realized she'd been staring at the man, but then she saw that his eyes were closed, and he'd never even noticed. She didn't like how pale he was, and it worried her. Sweat was dotting his battered chest, and Tess knew he was much worse than she'd originally feared.

"Terry can you sit?" she asked, as she stood and walked towards him.

"I'm afraid if I do I won't get up again," he said honestly.

"Yeah, that's what I figured. Come on, I'll help you." Tess helped ease Tank to a sitting position and then she knelt down next to him.

"Listen, I'm going to go for help, and you need to stay here. I can go faster alone."

Tank looked at her and then used his fingers to tuck a piece of stray, dirty hair behind her ear.

"I know you're right, but I don't want you to get hurt or lost. Maybe we should camp here and try again tomorrow?"

"I know you're being the tough guy, but you need help, we need water, and I'm cold. I don't want to sleep out here again." Tank saw the resolve in her grimy face and couldn't help but to admire her.

"But what if you get lost?"

"I have a great sense of direction. I'll leave markers so I can find you again. I'm more worried about you."

"Yeah, I'm a little worried myself," Tank said grimly. "Okay, don't try to move too much. I'll be back as soon as I find some help. "

"Tess, you have to get in touch with my brother. He's the game warden in Townsend County. His name is Toby O'Brian. You'll first have to call the Sheriff's office in Happy. Ask for Sheriff Liam Ross, he's a friend. He and Toby share a radio channel."

"Terry…" Tess tried to interrupt him.

"No, listen, Tess. I know you're afraid, but who ever took us is still out there and we can't trust anyone else. I promise you'll be safe. Please, get Toby."

Tess put her small hand on Tank's shoulder. "Okay. Are you going to be okay alone?"

"Yeah, just leave me with that big stick over there," Tank said, pointing a large limb laying a few feet away.

Tess handed him the large stick. She knew he wanted it in case an animal came near him and that sent a shiver of fear through her.

"I'll go fast, Terry. I promise. Please stay safe until I get back."

Tank grabbed her hand as she was standing, forcing her to bend down even with him again.

"You stay safe, Tess. Please be careful about who you approach for help. I know you're worried, but I promise if we get out of this, I'll help you clear your name."

"Terry…"

"No, I will. I know you didn't kill that woman. I will help you."

Tess nodded and tried to give him a confident smile. "Okay, I'll be safe. Now let me get going so we can get out of here."

Tess stood up and headed east. She looked back a couple of times just making sure he was still upright; she really was worried about him. He had said that she had saved his life, but she knew darn well that she would have perished in that fire if he hadn't been so calm.

Every hundred yards Tess stopped to arrange a small pile of rocks or break off a branch to mark her path. Ominous thoughts pushed to the front of her brain, like what if she got back and he was dead? Would she be blamed for his death too? Tess brushed the negative thoughts away. He was tough she just had to find help. She wasn't sure how long she had walked for but all of a sudden she came to a dirt road. She knew she needed to follow the road, but which way?

Tess arranged a large tower of rocks where she came out of the woods and then bent down all the limbs she could reach on the nearby trees. When she was satisfied that she'd be able to find the entrance again she turned right and walked down the road. Her feet were bleeding because she had pushed herself hard hoping to bring help back to Tank quicker. She mentally sent up a prayer that he was still okay. Tess quickened her pace, keeping to the roads edge. She wasn't going to flag down a car. In fact, if she heard one coming she planned to hide. What she wanted to find was a house, and hopefully one with a woman in it. Right now, her trust level in the male species was at zero.

A mile down the road Tess heard a loud rumbling behind her. She quickly jumped into the adjacent roadside ditch for cover and watched as a school bus passed by her. She watched as the buses flashing lights came on, first yellow and then red as the bus stopped. A boy hopped out from the hinged doors. When the bus pulled away Tess left the ditch and walked towards what she prayed was a way to save Terry.

When Tess reached the driveway, she saw a ranch style home with an exterior garage structure. The house say about thirty yards off the road. Tess skirted the drive, keeping near the edge of the large wooded lot. She watched as a woman dressed in jeans and tee shirts walked along side of the boy that she had seen get off the bus. They both disappeared inside the home's front door.

Tess picked her way through the forests edge so that she was even with the home, yet still hidden by the trees. She debated what to do next. With her appearance, she knew she would most likely frighten anyone that saw her. She also didn't want to get shot for trespassing. Tess was still debating how to approach the house when she heard a young voice.

"Momma, look."

Tess looked to her right and saw the young boy pointing at her. The woman who was standing near a clothesline dropped the laundry basket she was holding and ran to her son pushing him protectively behind her. Tess froze she hadn't heard them come outside. They had to have exited from a back door. Tess took a step out of the woods and onto their lawn then stood still. She held her hands up to show them she was not carrying any kind of a weapon.

"I'm sorry, I didn't men to scare you. I'm alone and I need help."

The woman said something to the little boy, and he scampered into the house. She never took her eyes off of Tess.

"What do you want?"

"I need help. I need a phone. I won't come any closer, I promise."

"Who are you?"

"Please, can I use your phone? I need to call the Sheriff in Happy, Montana."

Tess thought that saying that she wanted to call a Sheriff may help facilitate a little trust.

"Don't come any closer, okay?"

"I won't," Tess said as she sat down tiredly on the plush grass lawn.

The little boy came out with a phone and handed it to his mother before running back inside.

The woman was talking to someone on the phone and Tess anxiously waited. If they arrested her without helping Terry first, he'd die in the woods. He might be dead now for all she knew. He had looked terrible when she'd left. Tess's heart did a slight bump against her chest at the thought that Terry could be dead. She had to help him.

"Please call Sheriff Liam Ross in Happy. Tell him it's about Tank O'Brian. I'll stay right here. Please call him. My friend is hurt in the woods and he is really, really sick."

The woman said something into the phone and then held it to her chest.

"I was just talking to my sheriff. He's going to call the sheriff you mentioned."

"Thank you," Tess said. The woman continued to stare at Tess and Tess could see the little boy pressing his little face on a windowpane, staring at her, through the safety of his home.

Tess heard the phone ring and watched with trepidation as the woman answered it. Tess saw her nodding and then she motioned to Tess to come closer. Tess stood up and approached the woman slowly. She could see her taking in her appearance and Tess suddenly became self-conscious about how awful she must look. Tess stopped about ten feet from the lady.

"I probably smell awful," Tess said, explaining why she stopped so far from her.

The woman tossed Tess the phone. "That Sheriff's on the phone."

Tess caught the black wireless handheld and put it to her ear.

"Hello?"

"This is Sheriff Ross in Happy. Who is this?"

"I'm a friend of Terry's... of Tank's, he needs help."

"Who is this?" he persisted.

"Please, he really needs help. Can you get his brother on the phone for me? He wants his brother. Please." Tess knew her voice was bordering on panic as tears welled in her eyes. "Please."

"Okay, okay, according to the sheriff that called me you're about two hours north of Happy. Stay where you are, and we'll be there as soon as possible."

"Please hurry, he's really hurt."

The Sheriff disconnected so she tossed the phone back to the lady. She wiped the tears away and once again said a silent prayer for Terry's safety.

Tess looked to the ground and then turned back towards the woods.

"Where are you going? The sheriff said to stay here," the woman said nervously.

"I don't want you to be afraid. I'm just going to sit back down by the woods."

The woman nodded. When Tess was once again sitting the woman motioned for the boy again and when he came out she said something to him and then he went back inside. A few minutes later he reappeared with a blanket and a large plastic solo cup. The woman took both things from him and started walking towards her. About halfway between them the woman put the cup on the ground and backed away.

"That's water."

Tess stood up and quickly made her way to the unexpected handouts. She picked up the cup and gulped down the entire contents, choking violently when it went down the wrong pipe.

"You need more?" the woman asked.

Tess nodded her head yes.

The woman approached her, and Tess stood still. She took the cup from Tess and the little boy reappeared to take them. This time when he returned he had two cups.

Tess drank another cup quickly. She'd been so thirsty, and she wished she could magically send some to Tank.

"You were kidnapped?" the woman asked.

"Yes, and my friend."

The woman seemed to trust her more and Tess didn't want to do anything to make her shy away.

Tess and the woman heard gravel churning and Tess saw a truck fly quickly into the driveway. A man in jeans and a flannel shirt jumped out of the truck and ran to where they were. He moved immediately to the lady and tucked her under his arm, keeping his eyes on Tess the entire time.

"Who are you?"

"She's been kidnapped, Ed," the woman said, hoping to calm her husband down.

"Who are you?" he asked again. This time his voice was hard.

"My name is Tess, and my friend Terry O'Brian is hurt in the woods. I had to leave him to get help. I swear I just need help for my friend."

Ed was taking in her scraggily appearance when another car rumbled into the driveway. Tess saw it was a sheriff's car.

The man in uniform stepped out of the car and jogged to where the three of them stood.

"Everyone okay here?" he asked the young couple.

"Reg, she says she's been kidnapped," Ed told the sheriff, who was studying her appearance.

"Yeah and she could be telling the truth. The sheriff in Happy says his friend Tank has been missing. His brother is the game warden and they've been going crazy looking for him."

"When will his brother get here?" Tess broke in, her voice scratch with fear.

"The ride usually takes about two hours, but I bet they'll get here sooner. Ed, I gave them your address."

Ed nodded.

"If you're telling the truth, and my gut says you are, plus I've known Sheriff Ross for years and he's a straight shooter, we better get your friend out of the woods."

"Please," Tess said softly, "I'm so worried about him."

"Ed, your ATV got gas in it?"

"Yeah, just filled it."

"Lisa, can you get this lady something to wear and pack us a blanket or two?"

Lisa hurried into the house, and Ed went to get the ATV.

"Can you find your way back to him?" the Sheriff asked.

"Yes, I left markers. Can we bring him some water please? He had a fever when I left him."

The Sheriff nodded. Tess heard a small engine start up and a green ATV pulled out of the garage moving towards them. It had two front seats and a bucket back seat.

Lisa came out of the house and handed Tess a pair of sweatpants, flip-flops, and a tee shirt.

Tess took the clothes but didn't know what to do about changing into them.

"Go change in the garage," the Sheriff said, realizing her dilemma.

Tess nodded then she turned back. "Can you put this shirt in a bag or something, in case there is DNA or something on it?"

The Sheriff smiled for the first time.

"Smart girl. Yeah, bring it back out when you come. I'll get a bag."

When Tess came back out she was wearing gray sweatpants that she had rolled the cuffs up on. The flip-flops fit her pretty well but the cuts on her feet were rubbing on the black rubber and Tess didn't want blood ruining them, so she took them off. The tee shirt was the woman's and fit her better than Tank's. She was self-conscious of not having a bra on, so she intentionally crossed her arms to hide her chest after she handed the sheriff Tank's dirty shirt. The sheriff placed it in a brown bag and sealed it. Then he saw she wasn't wearing the flip-flops.

"Don't they fit?"

"They do but my feet are cut, and I don't want to ruin her shoes."

"Let me see your feet," the sheriff said.

"Can we just go? Please, I'm afraid for Terry."

The sheriff knew the man she wanted to get to must have been bad off because he heard the concern in her voice, so he nodded and motioned for her to get into the back of the ATV.

"While we're driving, you bandage those feet, little lady, deal?"

"Deal."

Lisa returned as they were all getting settled into the ATV and handed her husband a bag, a thermos of water, and a couple of blankets.

Ed kissed Lisa on the forehead and told her to stay inside the house while he was gone and to only come out if the other sheriff arrived. Tess watched the obvious love the husband and wife had for each other and an undulation of loneliness swept through her.

They took off down the road under Tess's directions. She bandaged her feet using antibiotic ointment and Band-Aid's that she found in the large canvas medical bag that the sheriff had brought from his car.

Tess pointed out the opening into the woods and the sheriff complimented her on how well she marked her trail. The ATV slowly traversed the forest, and Tess became nervous about what they would find when they finally reached Tank. It took about forty minutes before Tess yelled stop and jumped out of the vehicle. The sheriff told her to wait but she ignored him.

Tess ran to where Tank lay motionless on his side. He looked dead. She knew his side was hurt so this was not a position he would have chosen to rest in. "Terry... Terry please...I'm back."

Tess was shaking his shoulder and tears ran down her grimy face leaving trails on her cheeks.

The sheriff and Ed joined her, and the sheriff felt for Tank's pulse.

"He's alive but his pulse is weak. Shit, he's been beaten pretty badly."

Tess only nodded, refusing to move away from him. They heard Tank moan and Tess got down even with his face. "Terry, I'm back. Please wake up."

Tank's eyelids fluttered and she saw that he was trying to focus.

"Tess..." he said weakly.

"I'm back. I talked to your sheriff. They're coming Terry. They're on their way."

Tank realized Tess wasn't alone and tried to sit up, but he was too weak.

The sheriff saw him struggling and helped him to sit up.

"Hey, my name's Reg Porter. I'm the sheriff here. I talked to Liam. He and your brother are on their way."

Tank nodded, still not completely alert.

"We have to get you out of here, Mr. O'Brian. We're going to get you up and into that ATV, okay?" The sheriff was pointing at the green four-wheeler.

Tank nodded and the two men helped him up. Tess watched his face contort in a painful expression. They got Tank into the back seat, and Tess followed him in, immediately covering him with a blanket.

"Tess, get some water into him and see if you can get him to swallow the Advil."

"He hasn't eaten. He won't be able to hold it down." Ed handed her the thermos and the bag.

"Give him something to eat."

As the ATV made its way out of the forest, Tank moaned as it bumped its way over the thickly rooted uneven terrain. Tess gave Tank water from the bottle and made him drink it slowly so he wouldn't choke like she had. She knew that would really hurt his ribs if he had to cough. Then she unwrapped a peanut butter sandwich from foil and broke off small pieces, coaxing him to eat. When she was satisfied he'd had enough, she fed him two Advil and held a cup of water to his lips so he could wash it down.

When she thought he'd had his fill of water, she tucked the blanket around the two of them and held him gently against her small frame, hoping to buffer him from the bumpy ride.

The sheriff kept looking back at them while Ed maneuvered the ATV as fast as he could while steering the ATV away from any large roots or stones.

Finally, they reached the road and Ed flew towards his house. When they got close, Tess saw another sheriff's car in the drive. Two men were standing next to it and as they approached, the one man that looked like a slightly smaller version of Tank practically jumped into the ATV before it stopped. "Tank. I'm here, man. Oh my God, who did this to you?" Tess saw that he knew his brother had been beaten severely.

"Toby?" Tank said in a hushed breath.

"I'm here man. Just hold on. We're taking you to the nearest hospital."

"Tess?"

Toby looked at the small woman who was holding Tank against her.

"I'm here, Terry," she said.

Tank opened his eyes and gave her a feeble smile. "You found him."

"I told you I would," she said softly.

The men helped Tank from the ATV and into the back of the sheriff's car. Tess stood outside the car, unsure of what to do.

Toby got Tank as comfortable as possible using blankets to wrap around him. He stood to shut the car door as Tank grabbed his hand.

"Tess. Bring Tess."

Toby looked at the sheriff and he saw Liam look at Reg and Reg nodded.

Toby motioned for Tess to get in the back, so she got in and placed Tank's head on her lap. The back seat was not ideal for Tank's big frame, but with his knees bent he fit.

The two sheriffs spoke quietly for a second before Sheriff Ross got in the car. Sheriff Reg knocked on the window near Tess to get her attention, but because it was an official vehicle she couldn't roll it down. He moved to Liam's window and spoke to her through that.

"Whatever happened to you happened in my jurisdiction. We still need to talk so don't go anywhere with letting Sheriff Ross know, okay?" Tess nodded and fear gripped her. She was so concerned about getting help for Tank that she had forgotten about her own predicament. The sheriff's car took off with its lights flashing.

Tess smoothed back Tank's hair with her left hand. Her other hand rested lightly on his chest. Tank was covering her hand with his and that's what Toby saw when he turned around to check on them. Tess was gazing down at his brother with a concerned look and Tank was holding her hand almost reverently. It made Toby really look at Tess for the first time.

He had noticed that she was pretty raggedy looking at first glance, and he and Liam had both noticed how she and Tank did not smell great. Body odor, old blood, and smoke were the mixture of smells that permeated the air around them.

Toby saw that Tank's eyes were now open and looking up at Tess. Toby saw Tess smile gently at his little brother and it reminded him of how Breezy looked at him.

"Toby." Tank saying his name jolted him back from thoughts of his beautiful wife.

"You okay?" Toby asked nervously

"Been better. Is Grease?" He couldn't even say what he was thinking.

"Grease is fine. He was drugged and when he came to you were gone. He's been a mess."

"Thank God," Tank said visibly relieved. "Take me home Toby."

"Tank, we're heading to a nearby hospital. We're in Teton County."

"No, Toby." Tank was struggling to talk. "Happy."

Toby looked at Tess.

"He doesn't know who kidnapped him or why. He doesn't trust anyone."

Toby nodded and told Liam to head home. Liam handed the satellite phone he had to Toby and Toby radioed someone in Happy. Tess presumed it was someone in a medical facility, because she heard him tell the person on the other end that they needed, x-rays, an IV set up, and the doctor needed to be there.

Chapter 7

Tank drifted in and out of sleep, and Tess was having trouble keeping her own eyes open. She felt the car slow and saw they had pulled into a small lot with a sign saying Urgent Care 24/7. Toby jumped out when the car stopped and assisted Tess from the backseat before he and Liam helped Tank to sit up and get out of the car. Tank leaned heavily on the two men as they helped him to walk inside. Again, Tess felt like an intruder, so she simply followed along behind them. Tank was taken into a room and the doctor shut the door leaving, her in the hallway. Tears welled in her eyes. She felt so alone at that moment, yet she was relieved that Terry was going to get the care he needed.

Tess turned back to the receptionist area and walked out the front door. She knew she was supposed to stay where the sheriff could reach her, but all she could think about was that she was probably going to be thrown in jail. She knew she'd never get out if Dan had his way. So, Tess walked quickly through the lot debating on where she should go. It sucked not having any money.

"Tess!" She heard her name being called turning around. She expected to see the sheriff coming towards her with handcuffs. Instead, she saw that it was Toby and he was jogging towards her.

"Where are you going?"

Tess just shrugged her shoulders.

"Tank is asking for you. Please come back inside. You need to be looked at, too."

Tears rolled down her gaunt cheeks, partly relieved that she wasn't being arrested and partly because Tank was asking for her. Toby took her hand and led her back inside.

He took her to the door that had previously been closed to her and brought her inside. The doctor stood over Tank and the sheriff stood quietly in the corner. An IV hung off a pole pushing fluids into Tank's arm. When he saw Tess, he reached his hand out to her and pulled her in close.

She bent towards him so he could whisper in her ear.

"Don't you dare leave, woman," he said softly.

"I'm scared, Terry," she whispered back.

"I know, baby. Don't be. I promise I'll take care of you." Tess straightened a little and smiled down at the large man smiling up at her. She wiped some dirt from his chin and nodded. When he called her baby, her heart did an unexpected pitty patter dance, which caught her completely by surprise and sent a warm feeling through her body.

"Doc, you gotta look at Tess, too," he said weakly.

"I will, Tank, just let me get you comfortable first." Tank nodded, never taking his eyes off Tess.

A couple hours later, Tank was resting comfortably. He had cracked ribs and bruised lungs and kidneys. The gashes on his head and torso had been sutured and he was being given more fluids and antibiotics.

Tess was in another room, also with an IV drip. She didn't have the injuries Tank had, but the doctor told her she was severely malnourished and dehydrated. They were both to remain overnight in the clinic, and the doctor assured Toby that he would sleep in the office so he could check on them regularly.

The doctor must have administered her a sedative along with the antibiotics she was given through her IV, because Tess fell asleep and did not wake up until the next morning. She knew it was daytime because soft rays of light sifted through the blinds in her room. The doctor came in, took her off the IV, and Tess used the toilet. She tried to scrub off some of the dirt on her face and she scrubbed her hands. Her fingernails were disgusting, and her hair was stringy and oily. How could Tank even look at her without vomiting?

Tess knocked on Tank's door and opened it slowly. When she saw him, she couldn't believe how much better he looked.

"Hey," he said.

"Hey," she said, smiling at him.

"You okay?" he asked.

"Yes. How are you feeling?"

"So much better. Doc says we can leave today."

"Terry..."

"Don't say it, Tess. You're going with me. I haven't told anyone your story. Right now, to them, you're the girl that saved my life."

Tess nodded. "You saved me Terry. I would have died in that fire."

"Well, then we saved each other."

Just then the room's door flew open and an attractive blond woman ran through it and right into Tank's arms.

She was crying and her face was tucked into his neck.

"Tank, we were so scared."

An uncomfortable feeling pummeled Tess as she watched the pretty female hugging Tank. Tess nervously stepped back from his bedside. Toby walked into the room and placed his hand tenderly on the woman's back.

"Breezy," he consoled her gently. "I told you he was going to be fine."

The woman he called Breezy stood up and wiped tears from her face. Tess watched as the woman began to relax.

"Tank. How you doing?" Toby asked. Breezy's hand remained on Tank's arm and Tank was smiling up at her fondly.

"Breezy, I'm okay."

"What happened?" she asked.

Toby interrupted, "Liam's coming by later today. He will tell us all at the same time, after we get him home. Okay?"

Breezy nodded.

"Breezy, this is Tess," Tank said, motioning to her. Tess didn't know how she was going to be received, so she hung back.

"She saved my life."

Breezy stepped around the bed and hugged her. Tess was completely caught off guard.

"Thank you Tess."

Tess smiled uneasily. Looking over Breezy's shoulder she saw Tank smiling at them. She didn't know why, but that somehow made her feel better.

The doctor walked in and checked Tank's vitals before unhooking the IV.

"Okay, you can go home but you are to take it easy for at least a week. You're going to Toby's tonight right?"

"Yes," Breezy answered for him.

The doctor turned towards Tess.

"And you?"

"She's coming too," Tank answered for her.

Tess saw Breezy nodding to confirm that she was indeed going home with them, too.

Toby helped Tank get into the front of a brand-new Jeep Cherokee, and he then motioned for Tess, who was still apprehensive, to get into the car. Breezy got in the back with her and Toby took the wheel. Breezy filled Tank in on what had been happening since he'd been gone. Toby interjected pieces of information every so often. Tess was able to garner that Tank's friends were currently residing somewhere in Happy. They had been really worried about him. It occurred to her that Tank had asked about her, but she hadn't asked him anything about himself.

The jeep was making its way up a beautiful mountain dirt road, and Tess was marveling at how gorgeous it was. Every so often the trees that loomed on both sides of the road would open up and she was treated to a glorious view of snow-capped mountains.

"That's the Elkhorn Mountain Range," Tank said, noticing what she was staring at.

After climbing the steep mountain road for twenty minutes, they passed a small road on the right and Toby looked to Tank.

"I'm not ready, Toby. I don't want anyone to see me looking weak and I still don't know who's behind my kidnapping."

Toby understood and kept driving.

Tank turned his head back towards Tess. "That drive back there is to a summer camp that I own. I'm the president of a motorcycle club, Tess, Steel Horse Cowboys." He waited to see how she'd handle that. When she didn't react, he continued. "We're completely legal in all our business dealings." Tess remained quiet. She had known he was part of a motorcycle club because one of the guys, Bo, had taken the leather cut from Tank after they had beaten him unconscious that first day.

"Breezy gave me the camp last Thanksgiving," he said nodding at Breezy. "I spend my summers at the camp with members of my club. I can't wait for you to see it," he said with a smile.

Tess liked that he wanted to show her his camp. It made her feel special and that wonderful warm feeling pushed through her again.

"Tess?"

"It's beautiful here," Tess said.

"I know. That's one of the reasons I summer here. Did you hear what I said, though?"

"Yes. I figured you were part of a motorcycle club, Terry. I was upstairs when Bo came up with your leather vest."

"That's when I knew this wasn't some club crap," Tank said to Toby. "No motorcycle clubs patched member would ever take a cut. It's just not done. It's law."

"That's the first night I snuck down to you. They all got drunk and Lester thought he locked the closet...

"Closet?" Breezy said horrified.

Tess colored and looked out the window embarrassed. "Breezy, Tess was kidnapped in April. It's a long story and we aren't going into it now." Tess continued to look out the window and Tank watched her from his side mirror thoughtfully. She was so sweet and timid, yet she was also strong and smart. Toby turned into his drive and Breezy asked Tess and Tank if they'd like to shower before or after they ate. They both answered before at the same time and everyone in the car laughed.

"Good man," Toby said teasingly, "cause, bro, you stink."

Chapter 8

When Breezy left Tess in her master bathroom, her lasts words to her were 'take your time.' Tess smiled because she was going to do exactly that. She washed her hair three times and then conditioned it twice. She shaved and washed her body until her skin was pink from all her scrubbing. She trimmed her nails and scrubbed herself all over again with wonderful smelling soap. Lastly, she brushed her teeth with a toothbrush Breezy had given her, not sparing the Crest.

When she got out of the shower she used lotion and then she dried her hair. She felt ten pounds lighter with all the filth finally off of her. She walked back into the bedroom relishing the clean feeling she had missed so much, but she was dreading putting back on the clothes Lisa had given her, knowing her previous stench probably still clung to them. To her surprise, there was a pair of underwear and a little halter-top sundress lying on the bed where her loaner clothes had been. Tess put them on and looked at herself in the mirror.

She didn't even look like the same person who had entered the shower. Her honey colored hair was shining, and her face was luminescent. She had dropped a considerable amount of weight and the dress was a little big on her, but it wasn't a bad fit and it flattered her tiny waist and slim hips. Her shoulders were a little bony, but she was alive and free.

Satisfied with her appearance but nervous as to what Terry would think, Tess made her way out to the kitchen somewhat hesitantly. When she appeared in the doorway, all conversation stopped. Breezy said, "Wow!"

Toby looked stunned and kept looking between her, Tank.

However, it was Tank's response that she was focused on. He was motionless. The spoon that he'd been lifting towards his mouth was stopped mid-way between his bowl and mouth, and his eyes were fixated on her.

"You're a blonde," he said softly.

Tess nodded.

Tank put his spoon down and slowly stood up. He pulled a chair out next to him and motioned for her to sit down. Tess was charmed by his manners.

"Thank you," she said, as she sat down.

"Tess, I knew the inside of you was beautiful, but let me tell you, Honey..." He was having trouble finding adequate words to describe the gorgeous creature in front of him. "Tess, your outsides match your insides."

Toby started laughing and Breezy slapped him. "I'm not laughing because that was corny," Toby said. "I'm laughing because I never thought I'd hear Tank say anything so philosophical."

Tess smiled shyly.

"Thank you, Terry," she said in a quiet voice.

"Tess, please eat. It's my homemade chicken noodle soup." Tess nodded and picked up her spoon. Before she dipped into the steaming bowl, Tank grabbed her hand.

"You're so pretty, Tess." he said seriously.

Tess blushed and her heart gave an unexpected lurch at his compliment. She then concentrated on eating her soup. Two bowls and several crackers later, Tess excused herself to brush her teeth again. She loved how clean she felt, and she wanted to keep that feeling. When she returned, Breezy was washing dishes and she told Tess to join the men in the living room.

Toby was sitting in an easy chair and Tank was on the couch. When she entered the room, the men stopped talking and Tank motioned for her to come sit by him. Tess was still battling the effects of being isolated with unscrupulous men for two months, so when Tess sat down next to Tank, she unconsciously tucked her small body into his protective large frame. Tank looked down at her and when she realized what she'd done, she started to pull away, but Tank held her to him with his strong arm. He bent his head towards her. "No stay. I like it when you're close," he whispered.

Tess looked up at him and her eyes must have conveyed her trepidation because Tank leaned in again. "Really."

Tess relaxed and all but disappeared into Tank's side. Tess listened as Toby was telling Tank how they had searched for him. Her eyelids grew heavy from a full belly, and before Tess knew it she was fast asleep. She awoke to Tank shaking her shoulders gently.

"Tess, the sheriff is here."

Dread gripped Tess and she looked around wild-eyed. Tank felt her tense up. "Tess, he just wants to hear our story."

Tess met his eyes and Tank saw that they were rimmed with tears.

"Baby, he's not going to take you away." He had read her correctly and she wiped her eyes, burrowing into Tank's side even further, if that was possible. He made her feel safe and she couldn't remember the last time she'd felt that way.

Breezy brought everyone iced tea and sat down on the ottoman near Toby's chair.

Liam began the inquisition. "Tank, I promised Reg I'd tell him what happened, and quite frankly, I need to know, too. Kidnapping is a federal offense."

"Okay, I'll tell you what I know, but we aren't ready to discuss anything about Tess yet. You understand?"

The sheriff looked shocked. "No. You need to tell me everything. She's not a criminal is she?"

Tank hesitated for a second and Tess cringed. She heard Toby mutter, 'shit' under his breath.

"Terry, I don't want you to get in trouble," Tess
whispered.

Tank put his hand on her knee to reassure her.
"If she tells you her story, you may be forced to do
something in accordance with the law and then
you'd have trouble with me. I'm telling you now,
leave it alone." His voice was hard, and Toby and
Liam exchanged a knowing look.

"Okay, Tank, I'll leave it alone for now. Tell me what
happened to you."

Tank explained how he and Grease had gone to The
Pen, and that Toby had stopped in and left when
the three women came in.

"Smart man," Breezy said sarcastically. Toby
reached over and grabbed his wife's hand.

Tank continued, "we were drinking but nothing
crazy. Grease disappeared with two of the girls,
Ditch was nowhere to be seen and I was with the
other girl." Tank felt Tess stiffen next to him and she
tried to pull away a little, but he held her fast. Two
things became evident to Tank; one he did not like
Tess hearing about his past with other women and
two, Tess didn't like hearing about him with other
women. The male in him actually liked the second
detail because that meant she cared, and he
realized he wanted her to care.

"I think she was in on it because when I started
staggering and seeing double she just stayed by the
bar and watched. I remember thinking that I hadn't

drank that much and then my vision blurred and the last thing I remember was going down."

Tess watched Breezy's face crumble and Toby must have sensed she was having trouble hearing about her brother in laws ordeal, so he pulled her on to his lap.

"When I woke I was hog tied with a bag over my head. When we got to the cabin I was dragged inside and beaten pretty badly. I was handcuffed to a pole and every day I was beaten again. I think they were just trying to keep me weak."

"They were." Tess affirmed, surprising herself that she had spoken out loud. When she saw they were looking at her she shrank back into Tank's side.

"Tess?" Tank encouraged her softly.

"I heard them say they were afraid of you regaining your strength. They were waiting for someone to call them to tell them what to do with you. I don't know who," she interjected quickly.

"Tess would sneak downstairs at night to where I was being held to give me extra water and food. I wouldn't have survived if she hadn't. Every night they'd lock her in a closet, but she managed to unlock it and sneak down to me." Tank looked at Tess who was looking down at her lap, uncomfortable with the attention.

"Then two days ago they came down and got me. I had no idea what was happening, but I knew it couldn't be good because I saw they let me see their faces. They tied me to a bed upstairs and then brought Tess in and tied her up with me."

Tess was so relieved he didn't tell them they had been naked.

"They set fire to the cabin hoping that when our bodies were found it would look as if we were lovers who died in bed. Tess told me later that they were told to make it appear as if I had snuck off with the woman from the bar and that I'd been shacking up with her."

"They were going to use a prostitute, Riyanna but she didn't show up, so they decided to use me instead." Tess filled in quietly. Tank nodded squeezing Tess's hand gently.

"We were lucky to escape the fire and the cabin without them knowing. We spent the night in the woods, but I was too weak to go on. Tess went on to get help. You know the rest."

Breezy was sobbing softly into Toby's shirt and Tess wrung her hands unsure of what would happen next.

"Tess do you have any idea who these guys are?" The Sheriff asked.

"I don't."

"Why were you with them?" He asked.

"Liam, come on." Tank said exasperated at his friends attempt to forage for information.

"Okay then I'm going to call Reg and fill him in. I'm sure he's aware of the fire by now so I'll ask him to check it out."

"It's a summer cabin Liam, no insulation. I was kept in a stone cellar. The water and electricity came on when I arrived."

"That's good info, Tank, thanks." Liam stood up, and Breezy and Toby followed him to the door.

Tess turned to Tank, her nervously fingers fiddling with the front of his shirt. "Tank, I really think I should just go."

"Tess, if you leave I can't help you. You need to stay so we can figure this out together."

"I feel like I'm intruding...I"

Tank clamped his hand over Tess's hand that was on his chest. "Tess, get this through that sweet head of yours. I. Want. You. Here."

Tess wiggled fretfully.

"Tess, look at me." Tess looked up and met his concerned blue eyes. "Do you want to leave here because you're uncomfortable around me? Are you trying to get to someone?"

Tess stopped fidgeting and looked up at him. She could sense that he was worried.

"No, Terry. I'm not trying to get to someone. I honestly don't want you to get into trouble." Tess lowered her voice to barely a whisper. "I'm a fugitive, remember?"

"One thing at a time, Tess," Tank said, relieved. "First, we get healthy. Second, we find these bastards. Then with what they hopefully tell us, we deal with your jerk wad ex-boyfriend."

Tess laughed out loud when she heard Tank refer to her ex as a jerk wad, and Tank looked at her, completely enamored. "I love hearing you laugh, Tess." Tess tucked her head into his side, embarrassed.

After Liam left, Breezy, and Toby told them they had to go out and they'd be back in an hour. Tank declared that he was tired and stood up. He held his hand out for Tess to take.

"Come nap with me, Tess." Tess looked at him skeptically.

"We are in the twin's room, with twin beds, so you're safe, Sweetheart; for now." He then gave her a sexy wink.

Tess's heart boomed inside her chest seeing his wink. She needed to be careful around him, she thought regrettably. She followed Tank into the bedroom and saw that there really were two beds. Not that she doubted him, but she had heard he was notorious with the ladies and she had no desire to fall prey to his obvious charisma. Tess sat down wearily on the one bed and watched Tank nervously as he went to the other.

"Really, Tess, we both need to sleep. Lay down. I want to take you to my camp tomorrow. Toby said my friends have been really worried and want to see me in person. He's going there now to tell them that I'll be down tomorrow. They all wanted to come up here tonight."

"They must really love you."

"We're family. It's hard to explain."

"You have two families," she quietly mused.

"Yeah, it's nice." His face had a tiny smile on it and Tess couldn't help but notice how handsome he looked at that moment, bruises, and all.

Tess was quiet and he knew what she was thinking about.

"You're with me now, Tess and, that means my family is your family."

"Terry, you hardly know me." Her voice was solemn, and Tank hated hearing her sound so despondent. He hated that she felt so alone.

It was true he had barely known her for a week, but there was something unique about her. His protective instincts flared to life when she was near.

"I know the important things about you and that's enough for now. Now get some sleep, angel."

Tess smiled at his endearment and slid under the sheets. She wished she could take her pretty dress off, but she didn't want to impose any further than she already had by asking for pajamas. Tess was exhausted and within minutes she was fast asleep.

Tank lay quietly in the bed next to hers thinking about the mysterious woman who had saved his life. When she'd helped him pee he had been so uncomfortable that he hadn't thought about how difficult that must have been for her. He remembered how her stringy hair had hung in front of her face, hiding her features, and how filthy she had been. Every night she had risked sneaking downstairs to him, trying to ease his discomfort. Not only had she given him water and food, but also she had wanted to clean his wounds. Tank had stopped her, telling her that the men would notice. She had known they would, too, but she had whispered to him that she hated how angry his wounds looked and she was worried about infection setting in. She had tried so hard to make him comfortable even though she wasn't much better off than he was. Tank knew she was kind and gentle. It was when Lester had hit her that he knew she was also brave and tough. He admired her courage and even when she looked haggardly, he had felt a connection to her.

When she had appeared in the kitchen doorway after her shower, he had been blown away. She was so pretty that she had literally taken his breath away. He was a bruised and battered man physically, but his one body part had no trouble responding to her attractiveness. He knew he needed to tread lightly with her, though. She was resilient, but timid. She'd been through the wringer and she had completely justifiable, very major, trust issues with men. If he were able to clear her name it would go a long way towards proving how much he actually liked her. And yes, he liked her. His heart thudded when he was around her. She made him want to be a better person, to equal how good she was. What she had him thinking about now were things he had previously thought were not in the cards for him. He didn't want just that one pleasurable night with her; well he did, but he wanted other things too, boyfriend things. He wanted to really get to know her. He envisioned her sitting behind him on his Harley, going to dinner together, sitting with her around the bon fire at camp. It was unnerving how close he felt to her. They really didn't know each other, but one thing he did know, without a shadow of a doubt; he would get to know her, intimately. It was to those thoughts that Tank drifted off to sleep.

Chapter 9

The bedroom was flooded with sunlight when Tess woke up, and she realized she must have slept through the night. Tank was still sleeping so she tiptoed out of the room, closing the door behind her, and went to use the toilet. After hand combing her hair and splashing water on her face, she made her way to the kitchen where she found Toby eating pancakes, and Breezy leaning on the counter and sipping coffee.

"Good Morning," Breezy said cheerily. "Would you like some coffee?"

"Oh my, yes. I haven't had coffee in so long. Thank you."

Breezy handed Tess her cup and pointed out the cream and sugar. While Tess doctored her coffee, Breezy asked how she had slept.

"I don't think I moved the entire night. Terry's still out."

"If I had known you were going to sleep for the night, I would have given you pajamas. I feel terrible that I didn't give you any."

"Breezy, you've already done so much."

Tess felt his presence before she saw him. Her heart rate sped up and she slowly turned to the doorway to see Tank standing shirtless, with his sculpted tattooed arms reaching above him, his hands gripping the top of the doorframe. He was magnificent to look at. He had shaved the growth from his face, and his mesmerizing eyes twinkled as he smiled. His jeans hugged his athletic hips, and a dusting of hair trailed from his abs down to hide under his jeans. Tess's eyes traveled his body noticing how bruised his torso was. Her mouth strangely became dry, so she quickly took a sip of coffee and sat down.

Tank's eyes were shining, and she knew he had noticed her ogling him.

"For gosh sakes, Tank, put a shirt on," Breezy chastised him.

Toby continued to sit at the table, but now he had a lopsided, smirky smile on his face. He knew exactly what his baby brother was doing with his shirt off.

"Morning everyone," Tank greeted them with a gravelly morning voice that only added to his sexiness. "Tess how did you sleep?" His eyes hadn't left her face.

"Good, thank you, and you?" She hoped her voice wasn't quivering. She'd been thinking it was ridiculous that any one man should look so damn good, and in the morning no less.

"Pretty good, considering my feet were hanging off the end of the bed."

Breezy laughed, "I'm sorry Tank. I knew it would be a bit short for you, but I wanted you to be in a bed and not on the couch."

"No problem. I appreciate you letting me stay here last night."

"You staying here tonight?" Toby asked.

It was now Tank's turn to laugh. "No, big bro, I'm heading to camp in a bit. I don't want to stifle your empty nesting."

Breezy's twin daughters weren't due back from college for a week and Gus was away camping on a Cub Scouts trip that had started yesterday. Toby and Breezy were going to be able to enjoy two more nights of coveted alone time. He knew that becoming a father to a rambunctious 5-year-old had probably put serious kinks into his brother's romantic endeavors.

Breezy handed Tank a cup of coffee then left the kitchen. Tank joined Tess and Toby at the table. Tess was having trouble looking up from her coffee. Tank's bare chest was at her eye level, and she was having trouble focusing on anything other than that. Breezy walked back into the kitchen and like a mother helping a toddler, placed Tank's head through the neck opening of a black tee. Toby laughed outright but Tank simply grinned and allowed Breezy to continue pushing the shirt over his head. She held out the arm opening and Tank, after putting his coffee down, pushed his hands into the armholes and then pulled the tee shirt down his torso.

"There! That's better," Breezy said sitting down on a chair next to her husband.

"Having trouble concentrating, wife?" Toby asked with a smirk.

"No red-blooded female wouldn't," she answered quickly with a giggle.

"Phew, I'm glad I wasn't the only one..." Tess said and then she clamped her hand over her mouth, horrified that she'd said that aloud. Her cheeks turned a bright red and her face heated. Toby laughed and Tank grinned roguishly.

"That was his plan, Tess. I swear the O'Brian men are not above playing dirty when it comes to wooing women."

"Hey!" Toby objected.

"Oh, he's not... I mean...we're... he's not wooing me, Breezy," Tess stuttered, her face still crimson.

Tess was so flustered that she quickly stood from the table. She composed herself by walking to the sink and placing her mug in it.

"Can I use the shower again?" she asked when she got her voice under control.

"Sure, but how about eating some pancakes first? I made them especially for you two."

Toby looked up from his plate, and Breezy, who had stood up, leaned down and planted a kiss on the top of his head. "And for you too, my sweet husband." Toby smiled and went back to eating.

The four of them finished off all the blueberry pancakes Breezy had made. Tess was so full she thought she'd never be able to move from the chair. The men began to rehash the mystery of Tank's kidnapping. Toby explained to Tank how he had personally questioned Ditch the next morning, but he had been no help. Toby quoted to Tank what Ditch had said. "The men were getting 'nasty' with the women, so I went upstairs. When I came back down later that night, they were gone."

Breezy saw how uncomfortable Tess was with the conversation.

"Tess, let's get you some other clothes so you can shower okay?"

Tess welcomed the interruption and practically leapt out of her chair. With both women were out of the room, Tank shot Toby a serious look.

"Can you cool it on the stuff about me and that woman at the bar?"

"What do you mean?" Toby was enjoying this. He knew exactly what Tank had meant.

"I don't want Tess thinking I'm some man whore."

"You are a man whore," Toby smirked.

"Toby!' Tank said, exasperated.

"You like Tess?" Toby asked earnestly.

"Yeah."

"You've known her a week. You sure it's not just that you went through some bad shit together? It could be an adrenaline bond."

"I thought about that, but no. It's different, hard to describe."

"Think about her all the time?"

"Yeah."

"Feel calmer yet strangely unsettled when she's around you?"

"Yeah, weird huh?"

"Tank, man, I think you actually might like her." Toby gently slapped his brother on the shoulder. "So, stop bringing up the other women, okay?"

"Okay, bro."

Breezy walked back into the kitchen.

"Toby, stop making Tank out to be such a whore. It bothers Tess."

The men laughed. "We were just talking about that," Toby told her as he pulled her down on his lap, softly nuzzling her neck.

"It bothers her?" Tank asked quietly.

"Yes, Tank, I think it bothers her."

"Did she say that it did?" Tank asked hopefully.

"No, but I can tell it does." Breezy paused for second, weighing her words. "Tank, don't play with this one," she said, referring to Tess. "She's not your normal conquest. You could really hurt her."

Breezy left Toby's lap and started clearing the table

"I know she's different, Breezy," he acknowledged softly. "Breezy, I have a favor to ask,"

Breezy wiped her hands on a towel and turned back to the table.

"Would you go to Townsend and buy Tess clothes and stuff she might need? I'll give you my card."

"Oh, Tank, that's so sweet."

"Thoughtful, bro," Toby added.

"Want me to take her with me?"

"No, it's best she stays out of sight right now."

"Is it bad, Tank? What she's involved in?" Breezy asked concerned.

"Yeah, pretty bad, but she's innocent."

"You know this for a fact?" Toby countered.

"I wasn't there, but yeah, I know. I swear. I know."

Toby and Breezy exchanged a look as Tank stood from the table.

"Well, I'd be happy to go get her some clothes and female essentials. How much do you want me to spend?"

Toby laughed, "better give her a hard limit, Tank."

Breezy swatted her husband.

"No limit. Just get her clothes and whatever else you females need."

"Oh, this is a fun assignment!" Breezy laughed gaily. Twenty minutes later, Toby had left for work and Breezy, Tank, and Tess were in Breezy's jeep heading down the mountain towards Tank's camp. When they turned down the dirt drive, Tess saw that Tank had an enormous smile on his face. Even though she was nervous, just seeing how happy he was made her smile too. When the car cleared the forest, she saw rustic log cabins to her right and to her left she saw trailers tucked into the woods. A huge fire pit was rimmed with large rocks and a barbeque pit stood in another open area.

Everywhere she looked were people, young and old. When they saw Breezy's car they came jogging towards it. Breezy stopped at the cabin furthest away and Tank opened his door and stepped into the large group of people that swallowed him up. Tess saw men gently slapping his back and woman hugging him. She remained in the back seat, totally unnerved. She watched as a long-legged brunette approached Tank and the small crowd parted for her, giving her unfettered access to him. She wrapped her arms around him and buried her pretty face in his chest. Tess could see she was crying. Tank was comforting her by rubbing her back.

A powerful wave of loneliness ripped through Tess as she watched Tank with the woman. She'd been a fool to think Tank didn't have girlfriends.

Breezy opened the back door, forcing Tess to look away from Tank and the woman he held in his arms. "Come on, Tess, I want to introduce you to Lolly. She's married to one of Tank's best friends, Sweet. She's awesome."

Tess got out of the car and meekly followed behind Breezy. Breezy stopped walking and waited for her to catch up, and then she linked arms with her and continued walking.

Tess could see that Tank wasn't entangled with the woman anymore, but she was still near him. She couldn't help noticing how the woman kept reaching out to touch him. Breezy saw what Tess was looking at.

"He has lots of friends, Tess."

"I know."

Tess had thought there was something special growing between them but her track record with men and relationships was terrible. Staying at Tank's camp was probably not going to be a good option for her.

They rounded the jeep and a pretty woman, who looked to be in her forties with a long braid hanging down her denim vest, stepped towards them.

"Hey, Breezy."

"Lolly, this is Tess, a friend of Tank. She saved Tank's life."

"We heard some woman had helped him. Welcome, Tess." Lolly gave her a hug.

"Lolly, I'm running into Townsend, can you show Tess around? Tank's a little busy."

Lolly laughed, "sure thing. Come on kid."

"Breezy..." Tess wasn't sure she wanted to be left at the camp.

"Can I come with you?"

"Tess, Townsend's a pretty big town. Won't you be safer here?"

Tess got her message. "Yeah, I guess."

"Come on, Tess, let me show you the camp," Lolly said, seeing that Tess was anxious about being left alone.

Tess nodded and Breezy gave her arm a reassuring squeeze.

"I'll come back in a couple hours. If you want to leave then, you can come back home with me, okay?"

Tess nodded. She didn't want to impose on Breezy, but she didn't know if staying at Tank's camp was smart either. Tank had worked his way into her very guarded heart and it scared her.

Lolly hooked arms with Tess, and the two women said good-bye to Breezy. Lolly turned them so they were headed towards the trailer area of the camp when Tess heard Tank calling her name. They stopped walking. Lolly turned around but Tess didn't.

"Tank, I'm glad you're home safe and sound. You got banged up good, didn't ya?" Tank acknowledged Lolly with a peck to her cheek.

"Tess?" Tank could see something was off.

Tank moved so he was now in front of her. "Lolly, give me a minute please."

Lolly walked down the path a ways. Tess saw that a man joined her giving her a gentle kiss on her lips as a greeting.

"Tess, I'm sorry. They were just so worried and..."

"Tank, don't worry about it." Tess plastered a smile on her face trying to appear unfazed.

"Tank?" he echoed. Now he knew he was in trouble. His voice was soft, and Tess felt guilty for acting like a child.

"Lolly's giving me a tour of your camp."

"I wanted to do that," Tank said sheepishly.

"You really should be taking it easy," Tess replied carefully. She couldn't do this. Her mind was racing, her chest ached, and she didn't like it. They'd been together for a week and somehow he had managed to stoke a desire in her that she didn't think she'd ever have again.

"Are you mad at me?"

"No," she sighed, "I'm mad at me."

"Baby..."

"Don't! Don't you dare call me baby." Her eyes had darkened, and Tank cocked his head, unsure of how to proceed.

"I don't understand?"

Tess's eyes welled and she looked like she was getting ready to cry. Tank tried to pull her into his chest, but she stepped backwards, out of his reach.

There was no way she was putting her face right where the other woman had. Tess dissolved into tears, sobbing into her hands.

"Honey, what's the matter? Jesus, Tess, please tell me what's going on?"

Tank stepped up to her and this time when he reached for her to pull her close, she let him. Tank rubbed her back affectionately, letting her get her emotions under control. When she pulled back, she tried to move away from him, but he wouldn't allow it.

"Oh, no you don't, Angel. I know it's been awful for you and the last week has been a nightmare, but if you're upset you need to tell me why. Otherwise I can't fix it."

Tess stared up at the handsome man who was showing her so much kindness that it almost set off more tears.

Tank wiped an errant tear that was trickling down her cheek. "Talk to me, Tess."

It took her a few moments to compose herself, but she finally managed to speak.

"I'm sorry. I don't know what's going on or why I'm acting like this. I am so grateful that you found me a place to sleep last night, but I don't think I can stay here tonight. You have a life filled with two families that need you. I can't impose on you any longer. I know we went through something that was pretty devastating, but once your life returns to normal you're not going to want me hanging around, reminding you of what you went through."

"Tess, we've been through this."

"Tank…"

"Terry. I'm Terry to you," he said quietly.

She sighed. She hated how she was feeling. "Terry, your girlfriend is not going to be happy I'm here, friends or not. I just…"

"I don't have a girlfriend," he interjected quickly.

Tess eyed him suspiciously. She was not good at fettering out lies so she just looked at him.

"What? I don't."

Now it was Tess's turn to cock her head, sending him a frustrated look.

"I'm no saint, Tess, but I swear to you, I don't have a girlfriend."

"It sure looks to me like you have a girlfriend."

Tank finally realized what Tess what referring to. "I know…" he interrupted, "I know what you saw. That was Cara. We've been together, yes, but she knows it was just sex."

Tess physically cringed.

"Oh, God, I'm screwing this up." Tank drew his large hand through his dark hair.

"Relax, Terry," Tess said starchily. "There was nothing to screw up."

"Tess…"

"When Breezy comes back I'll be going with her."

Tank pulled her against him. His hands wrapped around her back firmly.

"Baby, you're not going anywhere. You're staying with me. I'm sorry if I didn't make that clear." Tank's tone was hard now.

"But…"

"Listen to me. I don't expect anything sexual from you. I enjoy being with you. If it ever comes about that we both want to explore that avenue then I'll be all for it, but for now I really just want you to stay with me. It's not Stockholm syndrome, if that's what you're thinking," he said with a chuckle. "I saw the good in you the first day we met. I'm being selfish, I know. I just can't lose you from my life right now. I can't explain it."

And there it was, in a nutshell. She couldn't explain it either, but Tank was describing what she was feeling. For some reason that made her feel better.

"Terry, I don't know. It's all so confusing. In case you haven't figured it out by now, I have terrible decision-making skills when it comes to men."

"Tess, there's something between us. It may be an adrenaline bond like my brother said, but I'm not taking the risk of you slipping away from me until we figure it out."

"An adrenaline bond? Huh, I didn't think of that."

"So, are we good?"

"How are you going to explain me to your club?"

"I'll tell them the truth; that you saved my life and I'm helping you get back on your feet. How's that?"

"I'll be staying in your cabin?"

"Yup."

"Won't that put a little crimp in your…"

"Nope."

"You really want me to stay with you? No strings?"

"Exactly."

Tess was quiet for a few seconds. She didn't have any money, and truth be told, she didn't really want to leave Tank yet. She was so drawn to him that it frightened her. The problem was that she was more fearful of not being with him. Maybe she was the one with Stockholm syndrome.

"This requires me putting a whole lot of trust in you. I'm not a very trusting person."

"I know, Tess, but for now, I'm asking you to at least give it a try."

"Cara is not going to be happy."

"I want you to be happy."

"I want you to be happy, too, Terry. I hope you know what you're doing."

Tank liked that she now had a small smile on her pretty face.

"I do, Tess. I know exactly what I'm doing."

Tank took Tess by the hand and walked her over to where Lolly and Sweets were patiently waiting.

"Sweets, this is Tess. She saved my life."

"Tess, nice to meet you."

"Tank. You need to go sit down before you fall down. I'm taking your little friend here on a tour."

"Thanks, Lolly. Will you please bring her back to my cabin when you're done?"

"Sure thing. Sweets, help him back to the cabin will ya, Honey? And try to get everyone to give him some space so he can rest."
"You got it, babe."

Chapter 10

Lolly led Tess around the campground introducing her as Tank's friend who had saved his life. Tess had to admit most everyone received her warmly. There were a few men who flirted shamelessly with her and a few women who eyed her suspiciously, but all in all it wasn't bad. Tess loved the camp. It was rustic, yet homey. Children ran all over the place playing together happily. The parents chatted with each other as they watched them from lawn chairs under shady trees. Some men were playing horseshoes and a group of teenagers were playing volleyball.

When they headed back towards the cabins Tess was feeling a bit better about staying. Lolly pointed out her and Sweets' cabin and then she pointed out Grease's cabin.

"Grease was with Tank the night he went missing. He's been a mess."

Tess nodded remembering what she'd heard Toby say.

Lolly climbed Tank's front steps and knocked on the door. A husky, daunting looking man answered the door. He had on jeans with a white tee stretched over a large chest.

"Tess, this is Grease. Grease, this is Tess."

Grease was a big man. He wasn't as tall as Tank, but he was easily over six feet. His width was what set him apart from others. He wasn't fat but he was thick. There was no other way to describe him. He had a full beard, a mustache, and a single braid that hung down his back. He wore a red bandana around his head, and he was scary biker looking.

"I brought her back safe and sound, Tank," Lolly said, peering around Grease. "I gotta run. Tess, it was nice meeting you."

"Thanks for the tour, Lolly."

Grease silently moved away from the door.

"Tess, what did you think of our camp?" Tank asked her. He was sitting on a couch with an open beer in front of him. Another man was sitting on the other side of the couch.

Tess walked inside, looking around Tank's cabin. "I really like it. I met a lot of your family and Lolly said there's a little swimming area back in the woods."

"Yeah, I'll take you there. You'll love it. It's Breezy's favorite place."

"Tess, would you like something to drink?" Grease asked.

"Can I have a water, please?" Tess leaned over the back of the couch and whispered into Tank's ear. "You should be drinking water, Terry. You were dehydrated and you're on antibiotics. Can I get you one?"

Tank smiled at her. He really liked that she was looking out for him. "Grease, get me one, too," he said out loud, winking at Tess.

"Come sit, Tess. You have to be tired, too," Tank said, patting the couch.

Tess sat between Tank and the other man who continued to watch her.

"Tess, this is one of my oldest friends, Joe. He doesn't get up here much, but he's here for the weekend."

"Maybe longer," the man said, looking at Tess.

"Hi," Tess said shyly. Joe hadn't taken his eyes off of her and she felt herself blushing. Joe was so good looking she would not have been surprised if he was a model. He had really short sandy, blond hair and a sexy growth of stubble. He had eyes the color of maple syrup and a charismatic smile. He was sitting so she couldn't tell how tall he was, but his pale green tee shirt clung to large shoulders and a strong looking chest. She could see that his arms were well defined, and his long legs were crossed in a relaxed position.

Grease gave Tess and Tank their waters and they thanked him. Then he sat in a chair across from the couch.

"So, Joe," Grease said, tilting his beer towards Joe. "When do you have to go back?"

"September."

"Joe's a Marine, Tess. He's on leave right now," Tank informed her.

"Were you deployed?" she asked.

"Yeah, I was gone for fourteen months. I'm home for three, then I go back and do fourteen more."

"Are you a member of Tank's club?"

"No, just a friend."

113

"How long will it take to finish your Mom's house?" Tank asked. He then turned to Tess to explain. "Joe's fixing his Mom's house up to sell. She moved to Florida,"

"I should be done in two weeks. Then I'm hoping you'll have a cabin with my name on it."

"You know I will. It's been a long time since we've spent time together up here."

"Yeah, we had some good times."

"Probably won't be trying to rival those now," Joe said, looking at Tess.

Tank saw how Joe was looking at Tess and an uncomfortable feeling settled in his gut. She was sitting too far away for him to draw her next to him without it being awkward, but that's exactly what he wanted to do.

"Tess, Honey, you must be tired," he said, making sure Joe heard his endearment. Joe did hear it and he made immediate eye contact with Tank over the top of Tess's head. Tank didn't look away, message received. Tess was his.

Tess looked up at Tank and mouthed, 'honey?' Tank grinned and shrugged his shoulders as she gave him a perplexed look.

Tank told the men that they were going to rest a bit and then joined everyone outside tonight, so Joe and Grease took their leave. When the door shut, Tess turned to Tank and put her elbows at her hips with her hands facing the ceiling in a 'what's up' gesture.

"I know. I know. I just couldn't help it. Joe was looking at you like you were a Christmas gift and I couldn't stand it."

"You know I don't want any trouble, and if you let your friends think we're together that's going to ruffle some feathers."

"Maybe I don't care about ruffled feathers."

"Terry!"

"Tess, you were with Lolly for all of thirty minutes and the entire time you were away from me all I could think about was what you were seeing, who you were talking too? When you came through that door I just felt... I don't know; relieved. I know it's crazy."

"Adrenaline bond, Terry. It's probably just that and the fact that you were drinking. You're probably just over tired."

Tank stood up and helped Tess to her feet. "When you were with Lolly, did you think of me at all?" Tank's hands rested on her slim hips and Tess placed her hands gently on his chest.

"Yes, I thought about you. I wondered what you were doing and who you were talking to?" She admitted quietly.

"We may not have been together for long, Tess, but the time we have spent together has been telling. I've seen you physically at your worst and compassionately at your best. I want to get to know you without all the bad stuff hanging over us."

"That's sweet, Ter."

"Ter, now?"

Tess giggled. "Sorry I tend to shorten names as an endearment."

"Well, if that was an endearment, I'll take it."

"So, I take it you didn't nap?"

"No, it's been a little hectic."

"Why don't you go in and sleep now?"

"Will you come lay down with me?"

"You're making this hard, Terry."

"No, baby, you're making it hard." Tank was smiling at his double entendre and Tess laughed out loud.

"You are such a man."

"Is that a yes?"

"Will it get you to take a nap?"

"Yup."

"Okay, yes, I will lay down with you."

Tank was beaming and he took her hand and led her into his bedroom.

The room had a king-sized bed in it, a nightstand, and one dresser. There were no photos or any personal, decorative touches. The sheets were white, there was one pillow, and there was a thin, light blue blanket folded at the bottom of the bed.

"Not much of a decorator?" Tess teased.

"Never had anyone I wanted to decorate it for, until now."

"Smooth, Ter," she teased him.

Tank took off his shirt and when he bent to untie his boots, Tess heard him grunt.

"Here let me." She gestured for him to sit on the bed and she knelt down so she could untie and pull off his black combat style boots.

When she dropped the second boot to the ground Tank thanked her and walked to the dresser where he pulled out a tee shirt.

"Here, will you be comfortable in this?"

Tess nodded and left the room to change. When she returned Tank was under the covers. She saw that his jeans were now folded on his dresser. Tank's tee shirt hung on her like his last one had. The man was big.

"I like you in my shirts," Tank said, watching her nervously slip beneath the covers.

Tank was lying on his back. His thick arms were bent so that his hands were behind his head. His position only accentuated his size. Tess hated the bruises that marred his skin, that were now turning varying shades of purple and yellow. After pulling the sheet up to her waist she turned on her side to face him. Tank pushed the pillow towards her, so she tucked it under her head.

"Tess, do you know how gorgeous you are?"

"Terry, stop."

"You don't, do you?"

"Terry, please," she pleaded softly, uncomfortable with the attention.

"See, that's just one of the things I really like about you. Most women eat it up when they hear they're pretty, but you don't want that kind of attention."

"I just think… you know, that you're telling me something to, you know… get something from me." Tank chuckled softly, "Tess, I'm not saying that you're pretty, so you'll have sex with me. I'm telling you because I really thinking you're friggin beautiful."

"Yeah, but I've heard it before and…"

"Okay, stop. I'm not like those other guys."

"I really hope not, Terry. I really, really hope not." Tank took one of Tess's hands and held it. "Time to sleep, Angel. We're having a big cook out tonight and I want you with me the entire night."

Tess smiled at the handsome man sweetly holding her hand. If she let herself fall for him and it didn't work out, it would devastate her. She also was worried for him. She was a criminal in the eyes of the law, and she didn't want him to get in trouble for helping her. Tess heard Tank snoring softly, so she snuck out of the bed, shutting the door softly behind her. It was going to be hard, but Tess knew she needed to keep those walls up around her damaged heart. She would try to keep her distance and that meant not sleeping so close to him. She didn't want to risk waking up wrapped around his gorgeous body again, like she had in the woods. She quietly redressed and lay down on the couch, falling asleep to the natural lull-a-bye of forest sounds surrounding the cabin.

Chapter 11

Tess heard hushed voices in the room and sluggishl'
opened her eyes to find Tank was trying to keep an
excited Breezy quiet as she stood in the doorway.

"It's okay, Ter. I'm awake." Tess sat up on the couch
rubbing the sleep from her eyes.

Breezy practically skipped into the room with bags
hanging off her slender arms.

"Wait till you see what I got you!" she exclaimed
happily.

"What are you talking about?" Tess asked genuinely
baffled.

"Tank asked me to buy you some clothes. Didn't he
tell you?"

"Noooo," Tess replied uneasily.

Tank sank down next to her on the couch. "I just
wanted you to have some clothes of your own."

Tess stared at him and a giant tear slid down her
face.

"Tess, are you mad?" Breezy asked watching Tess's
face closely.

"No, it's just... it's the most thoughtful thing anyone
has ever done for me. Thank you, Terry."

Both Tank and Breezy heaved audible sighs of relief

"Wait until you see everything." Breezy's
enthusiasm was infectious and both Tess and Tank
sat back on the couch and watched as she pulled
one beautiful item after another out of the bags
piled around her.

Tess was soon surrounded with a variety of shorts, skirts, pretty tops, and two bathing suits. Breezy opened yet another shopping bag and pulled out little thong undies and lacy bras. "Breezy! Let's keep them in the bag," Tess squealed embarrassedly, grabbing them from her hand and stuffing them back into the bag.

"Okay, but when you see what's at the bottom of that bag you are really going to thank me." Then she looked at Tank and winked, "or maybe you'll be thanking me."

"Breezy! Sheesh!" Tess giggled as a blush reddened her cheeks.

Next, Breezy pulled out fancy shampoos, conditioners, body lotions, body washes, and other shower essentials. Tess was overwhelmed at her thoroughness.

"It's so much," she murmured, gently touching one of the soft shirts.

"Wait…not done yet!" Breezy laughed.

The next bag contained make up, a brush, a hair dryer, and a three pair of earrings. Then Breezy pulled another bag that had been around the corner of the couch and proceeded to pull out sneakers, sandals, hiking boots, socks, athletic shorts, and shirts.

"I didn't know if you were a jogger. I'm a jogger, maybe we can work out together?"

"I do like to jog, although I'm completely out of shape now. Breezy, thank you."

"Don't thank me. I love shopping with someone else's money. Thank Tank, it was totally his idea and his credit card."

Tess turned to Tank who had been quietly watching the myriad of expressions that had been crossing Tess's face for the last twenty minutes.

"Terry. Thank you so much. I'll pay you back as soon as I can."

"Tess, just seeing you happy and hearing you laugh was worth every single penny Breezy spent."

"Ter," Tess whispered softly. She felt the self-constructed wall around her heart begin to crumble. Tank was a larger than life, badass, alpha male but he was also a sweet, tender, thoughtful man. Tess was in big trouble. How she felt about him in the few days she'd known him rivaled anything she had experienced in her past.

"Priceless," he murmured, still watching her face. The sexual electricity between the two of them sizzled. Tess felt flushed but couldn't look away from him.

Breezy stood up quickly. "Well, I have to get home. Toby and I will be down later for the pig roast. Receipts are in the bags, but I'm pretty good with sizes. See you later!" She skipped out the door leaving them alone. Tess felt emotions she barely recognized bubble to the surface.

"You like everything?" Tank asked gently as he pushed a lock of her hair off her face.

"I love everything, Ter, but mostly I love that you thought of it. For a badass you are incredibly sweet. Thank you so much."

"You are welcome and for the record, you bring out my sweet side." Tank used air quotes when he said sweet making Tess giggle.

Tess swiveled so she was facing him on the couch. Her knees were tucked under her and she placed her hand on Tank's thigh for balance.

"Adrenaline bond aside, you're making it very hard to resist you, Terry." Her eyes misted over and her heart pounded so hard inside her chest that she was sure he could hear it.

Tank gently placed his hand on her hip, relishing the contact. "That's the plan, Angel."

Tess gave him an impish grin. "You're the kindest tough guy I know," she said giving him a playful knuckle tap on his chest.

"I just want to be your kindest, tough guy," he said softly.

Tess pushed to her knees, placed her hand on his shoulder, and gave Tank a timid kiss on his cheek. "Thank you."

Tank didn't let her sink back down on the couch. He held her so they were mere inches from each other's face. Tank had to resist the heady urge to place his lips on hers.

"Baby, I should be thanking you." His voice was husky, and he felt himself begin to harden. Tess felt his warm breath on her lips and she unconsciously

licked them with the tip of her tongue. Tank
groaned at the seductive sight.

Tess became concerned when she heard him groan.
She thought maybe he was in pain.

"Are you okay?"

He didn't want to risk all the progress he had made
with her, so he gently lifted her to her feet and
stood up next to her. He wasn't fully engorged but it
would be noticeable if she rubbed against him. Tess
was staring up at him, worry furrowed her brow.
Tank placed his palm against her cheek. "Yup, I'm
good, promise. Now, let's get ready for the pig
roast." He said energetically hoping to divert her
attention from the bulge pressing against the front
of his jeans.

Tess wanted to shower again. She just couldn't feel
clean enough. So, Tank gave her his room and told
her to come outside when she was ready.

Chapter 12

The camp was buzzing as the club members celebrated Tank's safe return. A pig that had been on the spit all day was sending a mouth-watering aroma wafting throughout the camp. Tables had been set up for all the food, two kegs sat in ice and coolers were packed with soda's and other non-alcoholic beverages. Colorful plastic tablecloths covered more tables that were surrounded with chairs. Children ran around under the watchful eye of their parents and the volleyball court and horseshoe pit were in high demand.

Tank sat in a chair near the pig pit with a bunch of the men. Lolly joined them and handed a few of the men new cans of beer. Tank was still nursing his first one. He knew when Tess came out she'd probably suggest that he switch to water again anyway. Joe was sitting on one side of him and Grease was on the other. Tank was partially listening to Sweets describing the mess the racoons had made in his cabin when he noticed the conversation around him had ceased. Tank turned to look at what the other men were gawking at and saw that Tess was walking towards him. Holy smokes, she was stunning.

He heard Grease say, "Holy Shit, "and Joe swore under his breath. He heard Lolly's deep chuckle and Sweets saying, "My, my, my."

Tess was grinning. Her cheeks were lightly flushed with a rosy glow, and her long, honey blond hair shined in the diminishing sunlight. She was wearing a short denim skirt that hugged her slim hips and accentuated her shapely long legs. Her feet were sporting strappy sandals and he could see she had polished her nails with a bright coral color. Tank raked his eyes back up her body. A tight-fitting light blue tee shirt with a V-neck plunged slightly showing the top swell of her small breasts. Her eyes were beacons of blue, enhanced by dark eyelashes and the shirt's color. As she walked closer, he could see that she had applied a pink lip-gloss and he loved how her face was lit up. She looked happy, really happy and damn if he didn't want to be the one to keep making her happy.

He stood up awkwardly gripping the folding chair for balance since his side still pained him. The men were looking between her and him, waiting to see how he would greet her. Tank knew he needed to stake claim to her now. He took a few steps toward her and when she reached him, her eyes were twinkling, and his heart thudded seeing her smile "Tess, you look unbelievable," he whispered into her ear, after taking her hands in his.

"Thank you," she answered nervously. "Do I look okay for the pig roast Ter?" His smile eased her anxiety and she relished how his gaze caressed her skin, sending a tingling sensation to her girly parts. I was at that precise moment that Tess knew she'd never be able to resist the man in front of her. She had wanted to look good for him and the way he was looking at her she knew she had succeeded. Tank let go of one of her hands and she felt his thumb grazing her palms sensuously. With his free hand he gently tipped her chin up.

"You look fantastic," he answered. Then with a low husky voice he added, "Baby, I'm going to kiss you now."

Before Tess could react, Tank placed one hand on her hip and one hand behind her slim neck and gently pulled her towards his chest. He lowered his head and their lips met for the first time. Tank was hoping she wouldn't pull away and when she didn't, he pulled her flush against him and deepened the kiss.

He knew he needed to break the kiss off before the guys started to raze him. He didn't want to embarrass her, so he ended the kiss. He stared into her blue eyes hoping they would reveal what she was thinking and what he saw almost undid him. Tess was looking at him with a whimsical grin on her face. Her lips were slightly puffy from the kiss and damn if she didn't look even sexier. Tank couldn't resist giving her another kiss and as he pulled away he whispered,

"Thank you, baby."

Tess simply nodded. She looked so joyful in that moment and that pleased him more than anything. Tank took her hand and walked her over to the pit where conversation had resumed. Grease stood up and offered Tess his lawn chair.

"Thanks, Grease," Tank said, still keeping his eyes on the beautiful woman next to him.

"Hi Tess," Joe greeted her.

"Hi, Joe."

"You look gorgeous woman," he said, looking her up and down.

Tess blushed and said thank you. She wasn't comfortable with compliments. She'd been told she was pretty often enough, but for some reason when these men said it she believed it.

Tank remained at her side and switched to water when she raised her eyebrows upon seeing his can. Joe laughed when he saw it, and Tess heard him snicker that 'he never thought he'd see the day.' Tess wasn't sure what he meant by that, but since Tank was smiling it must not have been bad.

The men declared the pig was ready and Sweets rang a triangle bell that was hanging above the spit. Everyone seemed to move at once. Women put out the side dishes and within minutes the entire camp converged on the tables. Everyone got plates and plastic utensils and then they either got in line for pork or they got in line for the side dishes. When they left one line they got in the other until their plates were full.

Tess marveled at how the club members helped each other. Single adults helped parents with children. Children brought food to older persons who were already sitting at tables. It was happily chaotic, yet oddly very orderly. With their plates full, Tank led Tess to a table that Joe, Sweets, Lolly, and Grease were already sitting at. Breezy and Toby joined them as well. Once again Tess thanked Breezy for shopping for her and Breezy and Lolly commented on how nice she looked. Tess was comfortable with the small group of Tank's friends that were around her. She noted the comradery and the way the conversations flowed easily between the good friends. Cara walked up to the table with her plate and squeezed into a space between Tank and Joe. Tess hated the feeling of trepidation that snaked through her.

Everyone at the table greeted Cara warmly, and Cara cheerily returned their hellos. Tank introduced Tess to her, and Cara gave her a beautiful smile and said hello. She too complimented Tess's outfit. Cara was not only gorgeous, but she was nice. Tess could see that she and Tank would have made a striking couple. Tess was at odds with her feelings. She had no reason to be possessive of Tank, yet she was. Cara hadn't seemed upset by her presence, but then, Tess thought, why would she be? As far as anyone knew she was just a friend, right? He had kissed her though and that kiss was not a 'we are just friends' kind of kiss. Tess was so confused. Lolli was holding Tess's attention by explaining the fun events that took place during the summer months at camp. Tess was glad to be occupied. She could hear Cara and Tank bantering easily with each other, and she couldn't stop the jealous sting that jabbed at her.

When Tess turned towards Tank, she saw that Joe was watching her closely. His eyes caught hers and they shared a brief moment of knowing. Joe was aware that Tank and Cara had been immersed in their own private conversation and Joe was letting Tess know that he felt sorry for her. Tess wasn't feeling left out because Lolly and Breezy were keeping her engaged in conversation, but it really bothered her that Tank had just laid a big-time kiss on her and then seemingly just forgot she was there.

Tess stood up to clear her plate and Lolly and Breezy joined her. "You look great, Tess," Breezy said again. "I'm not just talking about the clothes. You, personally, you look good."

"Thanks. I feel good and these clothes are a perfect fit."

"Tank thought she looked pretty good, too," Lolly interjected with her thick voice.

"Oh, yeah?" Breezy asked, knowing Lolly was hinting at something.

"He said I looked nice," Tess said quickly.

"Was that before or after he kissed himself stupid?" Tess started laughing, never hearing that expression before.

"Tank kissed you?" Breezy said.

"He sure did," Lolly answered for her.

"I knew it! I knew he liked you!"

"Yeah, the man looked downright smitten when she walked out of the cabin. Then again, so did Joe, Grease and my Sweets," Lolly joked.

"Lolly, Sweets would never look at another woman," Breezy said with a giggle.

"No, but the man ain't dead, and she does look pretty damn hot, so I know he looked."

"Uh, right here," Tess said, reminding them that they were talking about her and she was right there. The three women helped clear the food while the men put away the tables and chairs. Some of the men had gotten the bon fire started and the children were hunting for sticks to roast marshmallows on. When everything had been tidied, Lolly went to find Sweets while Breezy and Tess sat on a log near the fire.

"Gus is going to be mad that he missed this," Breezy said.

"Tell me how you and Toby met?" Tess asked. Breezy got a whimsical look on her face and launched into the whole story, starting with how she had accidently discovered that her husband had fathered Gus. She told Tess how she ended up in Happy and had met Tank first but had fallen head over heels for Toby. She told Tess how her husband had then been killed in a car wreck and she had taken guardianship of little Gus. When Breezy finished the story, Tess was amazed at what had transpired just the summer before.

"You went through so much, Breezy."

"I did, but it led me to Toby, and I have Gus now, too. It all worked out in the end."

Tess knew she was hinting about her own situation. "I hope you're right."

The fire was crackling and warming the early summer night's air. Toby came over and dropped down in front of his wife.

"Hey, you ready?"

Breezy nodded, "Tess, tell Tank we left, okay?"

"Sure, and thanks again for the clothes."

Tess sat on the log staring into the fire. She hadn't seen Tank in a while, and it made her anxious. Her natural assumption was that he had gone off with Cara and now she was mad at herself for letting him kiss her earlier. She should have known better. He just looked so good and the inexplicable draw she felt towards him was so potent.

"Hey." Tess was startled back from her self-reprimanding by Joe, plopping down on Breezy's vacated piece of log.

"Hi."

"You look very deep in thought."

Tess sensed he wanted to say something to her, and she wasn't sure if she wanted to hear it, especially if it involved Tank being off with Cara.

"No, just relaxing," she answered.

"Where's Tank?" he asked, looking around.

"I don't know."

"Are you really with him, Tess?"

"What do you mean?"

"He kissed you in front of us. He was sending anyone who saw that kiss a message. Hands off."

"Oh." Tess was using a small stick she'd picked up to draw in the dirt at her feet. "Was that what it was? He was claiming me?" Her voice had a little edge to it and she immediately felt guilty for being a snit to Joe. He hadn't done anything to hurt her.

"I'm sorry. I don't mean to upset you, honestly."

Tess nodded, accepting his apology.

"I just want to know because I'm interested."

"Interested?"

"Yeah, in you. I'd like to take you out if you'd let me."

Tess looked up from her dirt doodling. "Joe that's sweet but you don't want to go out with me."

"Yeah, I do. In case you haven't noticed, I've been attracted to you since I saw you walk into Tank's cabin."

"Joe," Tess paused, "I don't know how long I'll be here for. It's complicated."

"You never answered my question," he said. "Are you with Tank?"

At the exact same time that she said, 'no.'

A hard-terse voice behind them said, "yes."

Both Tess and Joe quickly swung their heads around to see Tank standing behind them. His stance was menacing with his arms crossed against his chest. He was pissed. Tess could feel the anger surging off him. Unfortunately for Tank, the effect he probably hoped to project was essentially lost because Cara stood at his side with a toying grin on her face.

Tess looked from Tank to Cara and then stood up and faced him. She spoke using a harsh whisper so only the four of them could hear. "Really? Tank, you must think I'm an idiot!"

Uh, oh. She'd called him Tank. He knew things were about to go south.

Tess looked down to Joe. "I'm not with anyone, Joe," She bit out. Then she walked quickly out of the bon fire area.

Cara placed her hand on Tank's forearm. "Come on baby, let's go."

Joe watched the intimate contact between Tank and Cara, and he sent Tank a nasty smirk.

"Cara, stop." Tank removed her hand and looked at his friend. "Joe, Tess is mine."

"That's pretty Neanderthal even for you, Tank," Joe countered.

"I'm serious, Joe. Keep your distance from her."

Joe ran his hands through his cropped hair.

"Tank, man, where have you been for the last forty-five minutes?"

"Cara and I..."

"Exactly."

"No, we went over paperwork, from the shop."

"Now? Right now, you had to do that paperwork? Shit man even I don't believe you."

"It's true. Cara said..."

Tank turned and stared at the woman by his side. "She said she needed to file the papers tomorrow morning, first thing." His voice trailed off when he realized that Cara had deliberately pulled him away from Tess.

"I do have to mail them off tomorrow, Tank," her voice was silky and her lips pouty as she spoke.

Joe turned and left the fire following Tess's direction. He heard Tank call after him, "don't, Joe." Joe turned to look at Tank and Cara as he continued to walk away. "I like her, Tank, and I sure as hell will treat her better than you do."

Tank watched Joe catch up with Tess. When he saw him place his hand at the small of her back he growled with frustration.

"Cara, did you ask me to sign those papers to keep me away from Tess tonight?"

Cara remained silent.

"Cara, answer me!"

"Well, not completely. They did need to be signed." She placed her hands on his forearms that were crossed over his chest. "Tank, I missed you. I was so worried. I thought we could... you know, catch up."

"Shit!" Tank sat down on the vacated logs. "Cara, I like you... as a friend."

"A friend that has given you a lot of benefits!" Now Cara was pissed.

"You're right, but I thought you liked our arrangement. You never pressed for more and, woman... you got as much out of it as I did."

Cara placed her hand back on Tank's shoulder as she sat down next to him and placed her hand on his thigh. Tank was uncomfortable with how close she was.

"Tank, I love being with you in every way. I was just waiting until you were ready for more. We're good together, you and me. We think alike, we like the same things, the same people." She slid her hand towards his crotch. "And sex is off the charts."

"Geez, Cara," Tank said, stopping her hand from reaching the intended destination.

"It's true, Tank, and you know it," she replied, leaning into him.

Tank paused. He knew this was going to hurt Cara. "Cara, I've never thought of having more with you." Cara froze and he saw her lower lip quiver. She looked like she was going to cry, so he put his arm around her shoulders. "Honey, I need you to keep my business life organized. You're the best office manager ever. I did like having sex with you. Who wouldn't? But that's over. I have to be honest and clear about this, Cara. I like Tess and if I'm going to be with her, there is no you and I, except as friends and someone who helps me run my business. Are you hearing me?"

Cara had tears shimmering in her eyes. Tank kissed the top of her head and stood up.

"I'm sorry, Cara. I never meant to hurt you."

Cara wiped her eyes and smiled up at him. "I know Tank. I just always hoped. You know?" She paused and looked away noticing Tess with Joe. "If she leaves you, Tank, I'll be waiting, you know that," she finished quietly.

Tank nodded and walked off to find Tess. He was in a fine mess, and one of his best friends was probably comforting the one woman he couldn't get off his mind. Tank saw Joe and Tess sitting on the front porch of Joe's cabin. He knew this wouldn't be pretty.

When he got to the bottom of the porch steps, he stopped. "Tess, can we talk?"

Tess shook her head back and forth. "There's nothing to talk about, Tank."

"Terry."

"Tank."

Joe watched the exchange. "Tess, you might as well get it over with. I'll be right here waiting for you, okay?"

Tess hmphed, stood up, and started walking towards the dark woods behind the cabins. She had no idea where she was going, she just knew there were no people back there and except for the flicker of firefly lights, it was black. Black like her current mood.

"Tess, stop, please. Talk to me."

"There's nothing to say." Tess stopped and faced him. "Wait, there is something to say." He heard her voice pitch go higher.

"Why did you have to kiss me? Why? I don't get it?"

"Tess, I kissed you because it's been something I've been wanting to do for a while. I'm sorry if the timing wasn't good."

"Good? It was perfectly timed for you, wasn't it, Tank?"

"Tess, please." Tess could hear how distraught he was. He stopped walking and took her hand gently so she would stop and face him.

"Honey."

"Nope!"

"Tess, this is messed up. Please, I didn't realize wha she was doing."

Tess scuffed her sandal into the ground. She couldn't go through this again. Dan had said he loved her. She had trusted him and look where that got her.

"Listen, Tank."

"Terry," he said softly.

"I think I'll just bunk at Joe's tonight..."

"You fucking will not!" he yelled so loud it scared her. His voice lowered to hushed. "Christ! Tess, please."

"I just need some space, and this way it frees up the cabin for you and Cara."

Tess knew that was a snarky remark, but she couldn't help it.

"Tess, I'm not with Cara. I really did just sign papers."

"I..."

Tank interrupted her before she could finish her sentence. This was spiraling out of control, and he could feel her slip further away from him.

"Tess, please come sit down and talk with me. I'm so sorry that I left you alone. Deep down, you know I would never hurt you."

Tess finally looked up at him. The sadness she saw haunting Tank's eyes were her undoing. He'd been so kind to her, and she'd felt the attraction to him even when he'd been chained in the basement. Her heart and mind were at odds, and she hated what was happening between them. Tank stepped closer to her and against her better judgment she didn't back away.

"Tank…" she whispered a hushed plea.

"Terry," he countered softly.

"Terry," she relented. "I'm so confused." She had to be honest with him.

"I know, but I'm not. Please come back to my cabin so we can talk."

Tess was thoughtful and then she decided she really should just get it over with.

"I need to tell Joe."

"I'll tell him."

"Nooooo. I can tell him, thank you. I'll meet you at your cabin in a little bit." With that, Tess turned and headed back to Joe's.

Twenty long minutes later, Tank heard his front door open and Tess walked in. He shot up from the couch, grimacing as the pain from his battered ribs took hold.

"I was worried you changed your mind," he said, watching her face for any emotional tells.

"I thought about it," she told him honestly. She sounded so unhappy, so defeated, and he knew it was all because of his stupidity. He had promised her that he'd help her and that she could stay with him. He had told her how much he wanted her by him tonight. He knew he needed to go slow with her, but shit, she had looked so damn good walking out of his cabin that he just reacted. Then when he'd felt her respond to the kiss it had rocked him hard. It had been hot, sensual, and potent, and he knew one kiss would never be enough. How he had not seen through Cara's little ploy really ate at him. Worse, why had he left Tess alone? He'd really mucked this up.

Tess sat down wearily on the chair furthest away from where Tank stood.

"Thank you for coming back. Can I get you a water or something?"

"No, I'm good. So, let's get this ironed out, Tank. I can't take anymore shit. I'm so worried about going to jail. Then you kiss me, and then you discarded me. You really suck, Tank!" She wasn't yelling but her voice was laced with indignation.

"Ouch. That was harsh." Tank sat back on the couch, hurt and frustrated.

Tess felt terrible that she'd just lambasted Tank. He deserved to be chastised, but he had every right to do whatever he wanted. She needed to pull back. Tank was not hers.

"Crap," she said regrettably. "I'm sorry. You know you really threw me with that kiss."

"I know and I'm sorry. Well, I'm not sorry I kissed you. I'm very sorry I left you alone for so long and that I didn't see through Cara little ploy."

Tank's frustration was belayed in his blue eyes. They were normally the lighter cadet blue color, but now they were almost a grayer blue, a sad blue.

"I figured that you were with her. You know having…" God she couldn't even say it.

Tank got off the couch and crouched down in front of her.

"No, Tess. I was really signing papers. Do you really think so little of me to think I would kiss you one minute and be with Cara the next?"

"Maybe it's good that this happened. You know, it just illuminates the fact that we really don't know each other that well. I don't know what to think." She answered honestly.

"I'll tell you what to think, Tess." Tank's voice was thick with emotion and she knew he was trying his hardest to convey his feelings.

"Tess, I started falling for you even before I knew how beautiful you were. I want to be with you all the time. When you're not with me, I think about what you're doing. I know we just met, and I know it was under awful circumstances, but I've felt a connection to you that I can't explain. It's nothing I've ever experienced before, and I gotta say, it's a little unnerving. I really like you, Tess. "

Tears tumbled from her blue eyes and Tank knew she'd heard him, that she finally understood how much he liked her.

"Terry..."

"Oh, thank God, we're back to Terry." Tank said giving her a slight grin. Tess choked on a giggle. Tank pulled her down onto his lap, so she was straddling him. Her hands wiped away the tears and she smiled at him. "Ter, this scares me."

"You and me?"

"Yes. I'm running from the law. My heart wants you..."

"It does?"

"It does."

"What's your head say, Tess?"

She laughed sadly, "that I should run for the hills."

"No baby, no running from me."

"I still don't know how to act around you. I really don't want your friends thinking I'm your flavor of the week. I'm not like that."

"No, as of now you're my girlfriend."

"Ter, that's not going to go over well and you know it."

"It will be fine. I won't lie to you. I've been with some of the women here. Cara works as my office manager, and we do spend a lot of time together.

She was kind of a friend with benefits. Tonight, she told me that she was hoping that we would take our relationship to the next level. I told her that wasn't happening, and I told her I liked you."

"You did?"

"I did."

Tess ran her finger through his thick hair and Tank leaned into her touch.

"Joe thinks you're going to hurt me."

"I won't."

"Ter…" her voice was silky soft, sexy, and low. "You may not even like me in a few weeks."

"You're right, baby." Tess stopped playing with his hair, shocked that he would admit to the possibility of not liking her. "I may love you in a few weeks," he added with a grin on his handsome face.

Tess gave him a tiny smile and leaned into him, laying her head on his shoulder, her face tucked into his neck. Tank wrapped his arms around her, holding her tightly to him. Tonight, had been an epic f-up on his part. He was shocked that Cara had been so devious. He was also ticked at himself for leaving Tess for so long. That was on him.

Tank loved that Tess had smuggled into his chest. God he could get use to that. He could hear that her breathing had evened out and then he realized she was asleep. Tank rose to his feet, bringing her with him.

"Ter?" she said drowsily.

"Just putting you into bed, Sweetheart, relax."

"Your bed?"

"Yeah, don't worry, nothing is going to happen until you want it to happen, okay?"

Tess nodded into his neck.

"I really like you, Ter," she said so softly that he almost didn't hear it.

"I like you too, Tess, a lot."

Tank placed her on his bed and took off her sandals. Then he covered her with his blanket, kissed her forehead, and left the cabin to find Joe.

Chapter 13

Joe had moved back to the bon fire and Cara was sitting next to him. When Tank reached them, Cara got up and silently left. Tank didn't care that she was giving him the silent treatment; she was on his shit list anyway.

"Can we talk?" Tank asked Joe wearily.

"Is Tess alright?" Joe was still mad, but Tank understood why.

"Yeah, she fell asleep."

"I like her Tank and she's fucking gorgeous."

"Inside and out," Tank replied. Joe looked at Tank with a puzzled expression.

"So why go off with Cara?"

"I didn't do anything with her, Joe. I really did just sign papers. I didn't realize what Cara was up to."

"Are you that dumb, Tank? Cara is in love with you. It's so friggin obvious."

"I swear I didn't know. I thought she liked our arrangement."

"She's hurting, Tank."

"Shit, I know, but she really pissed me off tonight."

"Talk to me about, Tess."

"Yeah, that's why I came out here. First off all, and hear this clearly my brother, she's mine." Joe started to speak but Tank halted him by putting his hand up. "No, listen, I know what you're going to say. I saw how you were looking at her when she walked into my cabin, but she's mine. I really like her. I'm not going to hurt her, Joe, I promise. I've only known her for one week, one really, really tough week, but what I'm feeling towards her is different. She's special. I can't explain it. When she's near me I'm calmer, happier. When she's not with me I can't stop thinking about her."

"Tell me about what happened to you, Tank. How did you meet her?"

Tank launched into the whole sordid story. Joe couldn't believe what his friend had endured, and he was horrified at what poor Tess had been through.

"Why was she taken, Tank? Why was she there?"

"Okay, listen, Joe. What I tell you has to stay between the two of us. I think I'm going to tell Sweets and Grease, too, but I don't know when. I have to trust someone, and even though I know you're interested in her, I also know you have always had my back. I need you to have it now, Joe, for Tess's sake."

"You're actually starting to scare me, Tank, and that's not easy."

"Yeah, it's bad, my man, and Tess needs us."

"Okay, tell me about it."

"Tess had a boyfriend who she didn't know was married."

"Schmuck."

"Yeah. Well he got into a financial bind, he lost a ton of money and that's when Tess found out that he was married. She threatened to tell his wife. A week later Tess was kidnapped. The men who kidnapped her told her that there is a warrant out for her arrest because her boyfriend's wife was found dead. They told her there is evidence connecting her to the murder and that she stole the money that her boyfriend lost."

"Holy shit! That's so not good."

"She tried to escape a couple times, but she was literally kept in a locked up until we escaped."

"Oh my God." Joe was mortified hearing what Tess had endured.

"Tess would pick the lock in a closet every night to sneak down to the cellar, where I was chained, and feed me water and food to help me keep my strength up. One night, one of the men dragged her in front of me, accused her of helping me and then he punched her so hard she was literally lifted off the ground. I was chained and couldn't help her. I lost it. I was screaming at him that he should hit me instead, but he only laughed. He was a sick bastard and I've never felt so helpless. She still never confessed to helping me which probably saved us because or kidnappers really thought I was walking dead. Tess kept me alive, Joe."

"She knew if she told them that she had been helping you that you probably would have been beaten more."

"Exactly."

"I hate thinking about her being hit." Joe shook off the horrible image.

"Wrecked me, Joe. I felt horrible. So, I guess they got word to kill me. They tried to by tying us together and setting the cabin on fire. We managed to escape and ran for it. We spent one night in the woods, but I was so weak that I just couldn't go any further. I honestly thought I was going to die. I was peeing blood and having trouble breathing, it was bad. Tess left me to go get help. I honestly wasn't sure if she'd come back. She is so afraid about being put in jail. A part of me thought she might run, but deep down I knew she'd come back. It's the kind of person she is, and as weird as it sounds, we formed a bond."

"Sort of a survivor's bond?"

"Yeah, Toby said an adrenaline bond, but the thing is, the more I'm with her the more I like her."

"She's sweet and beautiful. A rare combination, Tank."

"She didn't look like that when I started liking her Joe. You should have seen her. She was dirty and her hair was dark brown and greasy. The first time I saw her, I wasn't even sure she was a girl."

"So, what's the plan, Tank? What are you thinking?"

"First, I have to clear her name. I can't let her go to jail."

"How are you going to do that?"

"The men that kidnapped us are the key to all this. I know where they're from. I heard them talk and they have a distinct accent."

"Did you tell the sheriff?"

"No."

Joe stayed silent for few seconds. "You want to deal with them yourself?"

"Yup. They, beat the shit out of me, stole my cut, tried to kill me in a fire, but worse than that, they hurt Tess. She slept in a fucking closet man. A closet."

"You're going vigilante, man."

"I am."

"That's murder, Tank."

"Only if I kill them."

"Will you?"

"Don't know yet."

"Shit."

"So, can I count on you?"

"I won't murder anyone, Tank."

"I won't ask you to."

"Okay then, I'm in."

"Thanks, man."

"So, what do we do first?"

"First, we set up an escape route out of camp for Tess. If anyone comes for her, she needs to get somewhere safe, fast. That's where you come in."

Joe nodded, "I'll handle that. If shit goes down I'll get her out of here. I guess I won't be heading back to my Mom's right away."

"I appreciate this, Joe."

"I'll always have your back, you know that. Just don't hurt her, Tank. If you start to tire of her, if the novelty of what is between the two of you wears off, I hope you have the balls to do the right thing."

"I will."

"And you probably need to keep Cara away from her."

"Yeah, I'll try."

Tank felt a little better after confiding in Joe. He walked back to his cabin, thinking of the precious woman asleep in his bed. The camp was quiet except for a few of the teenagers still sitting around the glow of the dying fire. The entire winter he had been looking forward to getting to camp. He wanted to fix it up, build the common area, and put in a satellite dish so they could get television. Now, all he wanted was to clear Tess and find those bastards that kidnapped them.

Tank stole quietly into his bedroom and gazed down at the beauty curled up in the middle of his bed. He didn't want to wake her; they'd had a rough night. He needed her to trust him in every way, not just as a man who wanted to make love with her, but also as a man who wanted to keep her safe. Tank grabbed a pair of shorts and bunked down on his couch.

Tank woke up to light tiptoeing. He sat up and saw that Tess was attempting to quietly slip out the door.

"Hey, Tess, where are you going?"

"Oh, I'm sorry, I didn't want to wake you. I thought I'd go for a jog."

"How about a walk and I go with you?"

"No, that's okay. I don't want you doing too much, too soon."

"Actually, I'd really like to take you to the swimming hole, but I can't jog."

"Okay, I'd like to see that, too."

"Can I have a cup of coffee first?" he asked seriously.

"Of course," she laughed, "can I make it for you?"

"That would be great. I'm going to grab a shower."

Tess read the directions on Tank's Mr. Coffee and brewed an entire pot. She had no idea if people stopped over to see him in the morning or even how much of the stuff he drank. She personally liked two cups. The coffee smelled heavenly and Tess remembered from the morning before how he took it, so she added the milk and sugar and walked it towards the bedroom. She thought it would be nice for him to have it when he got out of his shower.

Tess knocked and when she didn't hear anything, walked in. She placed the cup on his lone dresser and turned to leave just as the bathroom door opened. Tank walked out, using a towel to dry his hair. He was naked and Tess froze uncomfortably.

"Tess?"

"I... I... wanted to bring you your coffee." Tess was bright red, but she could not peel her eyes away from the magnificent looking man in front of her.

"Thank you, "Tank said huskily. He knew his dick was rising, and he couldn't have stopped it if he tried. Tess took a few unsteady steps towards the door before Tank reached out and found her hand. "It's going to happen, Tess. I'll wait until you're ready, but Darlin, it's going to happen."

Tess nodded keeping her eyes on his face. Tank dropped her hand and she fled the room.

When Tank emerged from the bedroom, he found that Tess wasn't in his living room. A wave of panic swept through him as he opened the front door to find her sitting on his stoop sipping her coffee. Tank sat down next to her.

"I'm sorry if I made you nervous, you know, inside."

"I'm an idiot, Terry. I shouldn't have gone in your room, I'm so sorry."

"There isn't anything to be sorry about, Tess. Besides, it's not like we haven't seen each other naked before," he chuckled.

Tess colored, "Yeah, but..."

"I know, my body responded naturally. You're a beautiful woman Tess."

Tess gave him a silly grin. "It was a big reaction, Ter."

"Why, thank you, my dear." Tank said using his funny British accent.

They both broke into hysterical laughter remembering the last time he had spoken those same words. They sat for a few more minutes on the steps, drinking their coffees, while Tank pointed out things around the camp he intended to fix up. Tess loved how animated he had become just talking about his plans.

Chapter 14

They finished their coffee and Tank took their cups inside. When he came back out he reached for her hand, which, she shyly placed in his hand. The camp was quiet with most people still sleeping. Tank's cabin was the most remote and closest to the forests edge, so the couple did not see anyone as they headed towards the woods. Tank located the overgrown path in the small field leading to the forest.

The sunlight, filtered through the treetops, made the dew on the leaves and grass glimmer. The air was so sweet that Tess kept taking deep breaths. Tank had to chuckle because he often did the same thing. The thickly wooded area was alive with birds and small animals flitting about.

Tank followed the trail that led them to a stream. They hiked along the bank as it widened, and the moving water became more effervescent. Tank stopped walking and Tess saw they were at a small clearing with a grassy ledge that sat slightly above the creek. He smiled when he saw Tess was appreciating the natural beauty of the place.

They walked to the slight drop off and Tank pointed to a small, carved out area in the sandy bank below where the water had pooled. Tess could see that water flowed slowly into the pools and the water was crystal clear.

"These little pockets of water get really warm, especially in the afternoon. It's kind of our own version of a hot tub."

"Terry, this is wonderful. I love it here. When can we come back to swim?"

Tank had a huge grin on his face and when Tess saw it, she cocked her little hip out and pointed her finger at him.

"What are you thinking? That is a naughty looking smile." Tess was grinning right back at him.

"Well, I was thinking I would love to swim with you, but the water is still pretty cold. My man parts would not be at their best."

Tess laughed, "your man parts?"

"Yes, my man parts," he replied. She looked so adorable joking with him that he couldn't resist her. He grabbed her around the waist hauling her towards him. Tank held her gently but firmly. Tess didn't try to escape his hold and Tank sighed with relief. She felt so perfect in his arms.

Tess met his gaze and she knew he was going to kiss her again, and damn, she wanted him to. She understood he was waiting to make sure she was okay, and she placed her palm on his cheek rubbing her thumb gently on his face.

Tank turned his head and intimately kissed the inside of her palm. This man was so sensual it made her wonder how she'd gone for so long in her life without experiencing the passion that Tank stirred inside of her. She prayed she wasn't making another mistake. Tess stood on her tiptoes and gently pulled him down so she could kiss him. Their mouths met tenderly, and when Tank open his lips she slipped her tongue inside to softly stroke his. Tank groaned and Tess loved that she could affect him so.

The kiss deepened and Tess felt the hard, thick, length of Tank pressing into her. She was so much shorter than him that it was nowhere near where she wanted it to be. Tess could feel her private part simmer with need. Her body was responding to Tank's sensual mouth. Her nipples ached and she pressed against his chest trying to ease their throbbing.

"Ter..." Tess practically moaned his name.

"Are you okay?" Tank's voice was gruff with testosterone.

"I need... I want..."

"Tell me, Sweetheart. Tell me what you want. I swear I'll give you anything." His voice was soft and sincere that Tess felt the remaining pieces of the wall around her heart crumbling.

"You, Ter. I need you," she managed to choke out.

"Tess, Honey, you have me. Don't you know that?" Tank sunk down to the grassy ground and brought Tess with him. He lay back and pulled Tess on top of him.

"Does this hurt you, Ter?"

"No, Angel, it feels great." Tess smiled down at him and then dove in for another kiss. Tank put his hands on her ass and encouraged her to move on him. She rubbed provocatively on his thickness and her audible moans were sweet music to Tank's ear. He could tell she was close.

"Cum for me, baby," he whispered pressing her against his length.

Tess had to stop kissing Tank because she was having trouble breathing. Her body was trembling and even though she could practically feel her orgasm waiting to burst, she knew it wouldn't happen.

"Terry, oh God, Ter, I can't…. I can't…"

Tess froze. The wonderful sensations were ebbing away. Oh, God, please no.

Tess rolled off Tank and curled into a ball. Tank wrapped himself around her and talked to her in a soothing tone. He had no idea what had just happened, but he was going to find out. He didn't think she had cum, but he damn near did, in his jeans no less, like a randy teenager.

"Tess talk to me."

Tess remained quiet except for a few reserved sniffles.

"We aren't going anywhere until you tell me." Tank was wrapped around her protectively. Gently planting light kisses on her neck and cheek.

"I'm… I'm frigid."

"What?" Tank leaned up so he could look down on her face.

"I've never had a… you know."

"Not for nothing, but I think you were pretty damn close just a minute ago."

"I was. That's the problem. I get right to the edge and then nothing. It was happening again. I didn't want to fake it; not with you."

"You rolled off me because you were afraid you weren't going to cum?"

Tess nodded.

"Woman, that's nuts. You should have ridden it out. Maybe you would have."

"I was afraid that if I didn't..."

"What?"

"That you'd see there was something wrong with me."

"Oh God, Tess, there's nothing wrong with you."

"But I've never..."

"Never ever?"

"Not with a man." Tank shot her a look.

"No, I've never been with a woman either," she groaned.

Tank chuckled, "I'd pay to see that."

"Sheesh. Men!" Tess had a small smile breaking on her face. "I'm sorry, Ter. I've just kind of accepted the fact that I'm sexually broken."

"Tess, if I ever hear you say that about yourself again I will paddle your ass."

"Maybe that's what I need," she teased back, giggling impishly.

"Well, it can definitely be arranged," Tank said with a devilish grin on his good-looking face.

Tess laughed outright, "I knew you had some Dom in you."

"For someone claiming to be sexually cold, you know a lot."

"I read romance books," she quipped, raising her hand with a cute little 'what can I say' gesture. Somehow he had made her feel better already. She couldn't believe she had opened up to him.

"Honey, we're going back to my cabin and I'm going to spend this entire day making you cum until you're boneless and begging for mercy."

"Terry, really, it's okay. I love kissing you. I'll make you happy. I promise."

"Darlin, whoever messed you up needs a good ass kicking. Let's just head back and see what happens, okay? No expectations for either of us."

Tess nodded and they headed back to camp. As they walked Tank asked, "so let me just get this straight. You have had an orgasm before, right?"

"Yes, of my own fruition," she replied, humiliated that they were even discussing this.

"I think I'd like to see that, too," Tank's said with a groan. The walk back was slightly uncomfortable for Tank. His hard on was not going to go away as he thought about Tess pleasuring herself.

Chapter 15

When they reached the cabin, Tank told Tess to take a shower and he'd make breakfast. "A shower and food, two of my newest favorite things," she joked. Tank laughed as she left the room. When she returned a half hour later, she was wearing one of his tee shirts.

"Can I wear this?" she asked, as she hopped up on the counter. "It's so comfortable and I need to wash the new clothes."

"Of course, I told you I like seeing you in my shirt," he winked, and a shiver ran through her. That better be a good shiver she thought to herself.

Tank handed her a sweet roll that was still soft and warm. She bit into the delicious cinnamon pastry and the gooey icing slipped down the sides of the breakfast pastry coating her fingers. Tank watched as she licked white sweetness from her lips. She had no idea how sexy she looked at that moment. He felt his body reacting and reached for her hand. Slowly, he placed one finger after another into his seductive wet mouth. His lips closed around her sticky digits, while he slid his masterful tongue expertly around her fingers, cleaning them off. It was deeply erotic, and Tess squirmed on the counter to battle the pulse that had come alive between her thighs.

Tank stared into her doe wide eyes the entire time. Tess found it hard to breath. The sexual air between them was ignitable. She couldn't take her eyes off his mouth as he bathed her fingers sensuously from tip to knuckle. Tess's female bits heated uncomfortably, and she felt moisture collecting in her private parts.

When Tank finished sucking her fingers free of icing, he gently traced her mouth with the tip of his tongue. She copied, with her own tongue tip, the same path Tank had taken, tasting the sweetness that had been transferred on to them. Tess wrapped her arms over his broad shoulders and widened her knees, prompting Tank to move closer to her. Their gentle kiss went from exploratory to frenzied in a few short seconds.

Tank lifted from their kiss and pulled the oversized tee shirt she wore over her head. He lovingly looked at her lithe body.

"You are so beautiful, Tess. You're perfect." Her body still had some bruising and she was still thinner than she should have been, but to him she was gorgeous.

Tess smiled bashfully at him, "no, you're perfect, Ter."

She wasn't as timid as she thought she'd be with Tank seeing her almost naked again. He made her feel beautiful.

With his hands holding her tiny waist, Tank slowly kissed his way down her neck and chest until he reached her round breasts. He ran his tongue underneath one and then the other. Tess gently held his head between her hands. She was unconsciously pushing her chest towards him. In truth, she wished she could reach into her little thong and finish what he'd started because she was so over the top with need that she'd have to fake an orgasm and run into the bathroom to finish herself off.

Tank circled her erect, dark nipples with his tongue's rough tip until she literally couldn't take it anymore, so she guided her sensitive tit into his mouth. Tank latched on greedily and Tess felt the exhilarating swirls of pre-orgasm.

"Oh God, Terry."

Tank continued to alternate between sucking, licking and blowing on her distended nipples, as his hands slowly massaged down her body. When he reached the top of her legs, Tess was on fire. Tank used his thumb pad to rub her clit through her thin panties and Tess let out a whimper that made Tank groan, it was so sensual.

Her thong was drenched and Tank's need to taste her was akin to an unfulfilled craving. His warm mouth released her nipple so it could kiss a trail down to the needy juncture between her thighs. He slowly pulled her thong down her legs. Her female lips were pink and glistening and Tank's heart thudded loving that she was so wet for him.

"Lay back, Tess." Tank's tone was commanding with a deep, sexy timber to it. It was a voice that she would follow anywhere.

Tess lay back on the counter and Tank placed her knees over his shoulders.

"You okay, Darlin?" He asked, softly looking at her eyes that he knew were begging him to bring her to climax.

"Ter," was the only answer he received.

Tank pulled aside the little strip of lace and blew on her pink lubricious lips. Tess's pelvis rocked upwards as she tried to seek relief, and Tank put a hand on her stomach to hold her still. He wanted to do all the work.

"Relax, let me do this for you."

His tongue dipped in for a taste and Tank knew he'd never experienced anything sweeter. He ran his tongue through her creaminess before French kissing her engorged clit. Tess had never felt anything like this before. His wet supple mouth rousting her girly parts was hot and demanding. Tess tried unsuccessfully to press herself into his mouth and moaned incoherently as Tank held her firmly and sucked her hard.

"Oh my God, Ter. Please. Please." Tess was out of her mind she needed to come so badly. Tess felt the ripping orgasm fade slightly and she whimpered that she was once again going to be left unfulfilled.

"I got you, Honey. Relax, I could eat you all day." He placed a sweet kiss on her inner thigh before once again ravaging her swollen, quivering kernel.

His patience eased her, and his talented tongue worshipped her. The pre-orgasmic swirl returned and became a full-blown tsunami of sensation. Tank parted her pink lips with his thumbs and grazed her clit with his teeth before sliding his tongue over her sensitive nub at a maddeningly slow pace. He knew she was close, so he kept up the torturous assault.

"Don't shut your eyes, Tess. Watch me love you." Her eyes locked onto his as he fucked her with his tongue causing her to buck against his mouth. She was so warm and wet he wished he could push his granite hard cock into her softness, but he wanted to send her to heaven first. Tank heard her begin to whimper so he closed his mouth over her distended clit and sucked fiercely.

Tess exploded in a back-bowing orgasm moaning his name over and over again. She came with such force that Tank could feel her ripple around his mouth. He licked her ardently until her orgasm was reduced to small tremors that quaked her little frame.

Tank gently took her knees from his shoulders. He saw that tears dampened her cheeks. What the hell? Tank deftly scooped her up off the counter and carried her to the couch where he kept her cradled on his lap.

"Tess?"

"I'm okay," she said totally embarrassed.

"You're crying, Tess."

"Trust me, Terry, these are happy tears," she said softly.

"Oh, okay. I was worried."

"Thank you. I never knew it could be like that. You know, I almost passed out I think."

"You didn't? Damn, I must be slipping." He had such a great sense of humor. Tess giggled and snuggled into his chest.

"You know that we still have an entire day left, right Tess?"

She looked at him puzzled.

"Well, I'll admit happily that at the moment you are a little boneless, but you haven't begged for mercy yet." Tank stood up with her still nestled in his arms and walked them to the bedroom.

Tank placed her on the bed and drew his tee shirt up and over his head. Tess, propped up by her elbows, admired the way his arms flexed, and his grooved musculature torso repositioned with each movement he made. Tank was gazing at her and when she saw that he noticed her staring, she brightened with a pink blush and looked away.

"Don't look away, Angel. This is all yours."

Tess peeked back up and saw he was pushing down his jeans. Her eyes fell on the bulge in his boxers and when he pulled those off, Tess saw that his manhood was indeed proportionate to the rest of his large body. She'd seen him naked before, but she'd never really grasped his true size. The man was very well endowed.

A light trail of hair ran from his belly button to darker hair surrounding his thick base. His impressive cock stood rigid, reaching just short of his navel. His broad shaft supported a smooth plum shaped head that held a glistening drop of pre-cum. She could see his heavy testicles and her first coherent, and very unlike herself, thought, was that she was going to lick them.

Tess inhaled sharply; surprised at her naughty musings, and Tank chuckled.

"Oh, sweetness. I'd give anything to know what just passed through that beautiful head of yours."

Tess smiled at him coyly. She was normally timid, yet she was so aroused at that very moment that she was imagining all of the carnal scenarios she'd like to experiment with that she'd only read about in her books. The battle that had been waging between her normally timid behavior and the new sensual being Tank had awoken in her ended. Brazenly, she sat up in the bed and slid to the side of the mattress.

"How about I just show you," she whispered huskily. Then she lowered her mouth to Tank's silky-smooth head and licked her way down to his sensitive balls.

"Jesssssus," Tank hissed.

If his legs hadn't been slightly apart, he probably would have fallen over. The full-on sexy assault had taken him totally by surprise. Tank ran his fingers gently through her golden mane of hair, careful not put any pressure on her head. He loved that she was comfortable enough with him to take the lead. Tess's flat tongue lapped up and down his quivering shaft as if it were a dripping cone. Slowly she played with him. Her tongue flicked quickly back and forth across the sensitive skin below his satiny crown and she heard him groan. She hadn't even put him in her mouth, yet she knew he was ready to erupt. "Tesssss." His scratchy voice left no doubt in her mind that she was making him come as undone as he had made her.

"Baby, stop, please, Stop."

Tank tried to step back, but Tess placed one hand on his firm rear, pulling him closer while her other hand encircled his engorged shaft. Tank was panting from trying not to cum like a randy virgin. He watched Tess peer up at him, wink like a freaking sex kitten, and then she took him completely down her throat.

"Holy shit. Tess…. Tess…."

Tess had learned that neat trick with boyfriend number two. He only liked blowjobs and he had demanded she learn how to deep throat. Funny thing, when she had done it with him, she hadn't cared for it, but with Tank it was different, it was sensual. Tess squeezed her thighs together. Her clit was buzzing she was so turned on.

Tess decided to give Tank one of his fantasies and alleviate the pulsing need between her legs, so while she sucked Tank into oblivion, she found her swollen nub with her fingers and began to work herself into a mutual frenzy.

Tank saw what she was doing and moaned out her name. Tess was so turned on that she was ready to cum again. She took her hand off his ass and palmed his heavy sacs gently rolling them between her fingers. While he was still deep in her mouth she swallowed to enhance his pleasure and then let herself go, moaning his name as the lust rolled through her. Tank's body stiffened, his balls drew up tight in her hand, and he grunted incoherently as his salty seed coated the back of her throat.

Tank came with such force that he swayed on his feet. Tess was in the middle of her own lingering orgasm, so she was moaning right along with him. Tess swallowed his essence and then licked his shiny dome before planting a kiss on his head. Tank sunk to his knees, locking his eyes on hers Tess. His large hands gently bracketed her cheeks. He looked at her so tenderly Tess knew she'd always remember that moment no matter what path her life took.

He leaned his damp forehead against hers and they remained like that for a few precious seconds.

Tank then stood up and helped her to move back on the bed. He joined her and pulled the top sheet up to their waists. They lay facing each other. Both of them had their arms bent and tucked under their heads. Tank had his other hand on her hip and Tess had hers on the bicep of his lower arm. They didn't speak as neither felt the need to. Their breathing returned to normal, then Tess fell into a peaceful slumber as did Tank.

When they next woke up, it was to Tess wrapped around Tank with half of her body on top of his. He was on his back and his arms were wrapped around her small body, keeping her close.

Tank leaned down and planted a kiss on the top of her head. "I like waking up with you in my arms, Tess."

"I haven't slept that well in ages," she said, stretching lazily beside him.

"We need nourishment, Sweetheart."

"I am pretty hungry." He pulled her so she lay completely on top of him and wrapped her up in a sweet, encompassing hug.

"One for the road," he whispered and then he cradled her cheek and brought her lips to his. His kiss bespoke heartfelt emotion and Tess returned his fervency by kissing him back passionately. She felt him harden and her body responded accordingly. Tess ground against his steely rod causing them both to groan at the heady sensation. Tank encouraged her to take what she wanted as he held her hips tightly against his pelvis.

Tess rode his length and when she felt herself begin to unravel, she sat up and reached back behind her to gently massage his tightening sacs. Tess shook as the hard climax pummeled through her. Tank erupted; his pearly white semen splattered on his stomach. Tess bent down licking at a drop.

"Tess that was hot," Tank said, after he regained his ability to speak.

"Three times, Terry. Three times." Tess whispered in awe.

"Yeah, well your still not begging for mercy yet, so after we eat..."

"But I want to go swimming and we don't even know how long we slept. It could be early evening for all we know."

"Okay, Angel, but just so you know, three is by no means a record."

Tess turned away from him, hating that he was so practiced when it came to sex.

"Oh baby, I'm sorry. I didn't mean it like that."

Tess lay down on his sticky body and tucked her hands under her chin to prop up her face.

"I know you didn't, Ter, and honestly, I don't know why it bothers me? I know you've been with a lot of women."

"Still, I shouldn't have said that. I swear I just wanted you to know that I wanted to give you more, you know, more than three?"

"Yeah, I know."

"Tess, for the record it is different with you. I'm different with you."

"I'm really different with you, Terry. You make me so, gosh, I don't know, hot, and out of control. I want to do things with you that I've only read about."

"Like what?"

"Oh no, I can't tell you that. It's embarrassing."

"You can't share a fantasy with me?"

"No…."

"Well, you already gave me one of mine. When you got off using your…."

"Stop, ugh, hush, I know what I did."

Tank laughed, "it was freaking hot, woman!"

Tess giggled and kissed him chastely before rolling off of him.

"I'm going to shower, okay?"

"Together?" Tank asked hopefully.

"Really?"

"Yeah." Tank's face looked so optimistic she couldn't resist him.

"Okay."

Showering with a man was another first for Tess. Tank washed and conditioned her hair. She loved how his fingers massaged her scalp. She tried to do his hair, but the shower was small, and he would have had to get on his knees. They soaped each other's bodies, each taking their time, and then the water started to chill. Reluctantly they rinsed off. They dressed into comfy clothes and headed for the kitchen. Tank had on cargo shorts and a tee, and Tess had on yoga pants and a soft tee. She purposely left her bra off for comfort's sake. When they got to the kitchen, they realized that they had indeed spent the entire day in bed. It was dusk and the camp was alive with activity.

She stood next to him looking into his refrigerator. "Slim pickings," Tank said, looking a little embarrassed.

"No, you have eggs and bacon. Oh, and cheese. I love cheese. I'll make us breakfast for dinner."

"Sounds good to me."

Tess found the frying pan and got started on their meal. Tank was sitting at the small table watching her. She was humming a popular country tune as she worked, and Tank realized she must like country music.

"You like country music?" he asked.

At first, Tess was confused as to why he was asking, but then she got a silly grin on her face.

"Oh, you heard me humming?"

"Yeah."

"Well, yes. I do like country music. Do you?"

"I do. I like rock, too, especially the older stuff."

"Yeah, me too. Oh, and I like oldies, Mo Town."

"Me, too." Tank had a smile on his face.

"What?" Tess asked, seeing him smile.

"I want to know all about you," Tank admitted candidly.

Tess cocked her head to one side. "It's kind of strange that we've spent so much time together and kissed and..."

"Kissed?" he teased.

"Kissed... and stuff..."

Tank chuckled and she shot him an adorable look.

"You know exactly what I mean, Terry O'Brian."

"I know Honey, but you are so damn cute right now."

Tess laughed and threw the dishtowel that she had on her shoulder at him.

"So, tell me something else, Tess."

"Like what?"

"What were you studying in college?"

"Business management."

"How close are you to getting your degree?"

"If I were to go full time I would actually finish in one semester. How about you? Did you go to college?"

"I did two years at a local County College. I never really liked school. I went to work for my Dad. He owned the garage I own now. I expanded the business with towing and refurbishing. I also own a Harley Davidson dealership in Townsend and two years ago I bought a RV dealership."

"Wow. You, uh, you have a lot of businesses."

"Yeah, that's why I need Cara. She keeps everything running smoothly. I hate the paperwork."

"You're a successful businessman, Ter. Do you think that's behind your kidnapping?"

"Attempted murder," he corrected, "and I really don't know. It bothers me that I have no idea who hates me so much that they want me dead."

Tank could see that she was almost done so he got dishes and after Tess filled the two plates with bacon and eggs they sat down at the table. They ate in compatible silence, each lost in their own thoughts.

"So why aren't you married yet? If you don't mind me asking."

"I don't mind you asking me anything," he said softly, and Tess's heart pitty pattered happily. "I jus never found the right person."

"Are your parents still around?"

"Yup, they are in Florida loving retirement. They don't like to fly and they're too old to drive back here so we only see them if we go to there. They didn't even make it to Toby's wedding, but we sent them tons of pictures and videos. They were, well are, really good parents. Toby and I didn't get away with much. I was a bit wilder than Toby. He was in the Afghanistan and he has a college degree. He could be a lawyer. He passed the bar."

"Tank, you're accomplished, too," Tess said, sensing that he was comparing himself to his brother.

"Yeah, I guess."

"So how did you get involved with the club?"

"I joined when I was young, early twenties. The club wasn't how it is now. It was into some bad stuff. Toby was so mad at me for joining that we didn't talk for a long time. Anyway, I love riding motorcycles and being a part of a group of people that would do anything for each other. As I got older, I saw that the club was heading down a destructive path. Luckily, the president before me saw this, too. He started to pull us out of some of our not so legal endeavors. When I took over I got us all the way out. Some old timers weren't happy about the pay loss, but I tried to keep everyone working. The more people that join the club, the more people I'm responsible for."

"That's a pretty big job, Ter."

"Yeah. I have help though. Sweets and Grease help me run different businesses. It's been good. We take care of each other."

"I love that about the club. I saw it at the barbeque, everyone was helping each other."

They had finished eating and were perfectly content talking with each other.

"What's your favorite color, Tess?"

"Green," she laughed, "of course! What's yours?"

"That's easy. The color of your eyes," he said softly. Tess blushed but she didn't look away.

"You're sweet, Ter."

"Don't tell anyone," he laughed. "I have a reputation to uphold." Tess giggled at his silliness.

"Do you like sports?" Tess asked.

"Love them. You?"

"All of them. If I had Sunday's off in the fall I would be toes up on my couch watching football all day."

"My kind of woman."

"Ha, you may think that now, but in September, if we're still together…" Tess quickly shut her mouth. What the hell! She chastised herself.

"Tess, when we're still together. Finish what you were saying."

He made her feel so safe, so comfortable. Most men would already be planning their escape route if she had made reference to being together three months from now.

"Well, I was going to say Sunday's are sacred to me. I watch football all day. I tend to order take out and let my laundry pile up. I like watching television, probably too much."

"Me too, Tess. I love watching TV, reading a good book, going out to dinner."

Tess got up and took their plates to the sink. Tank stood next to her and together they quickly did the dishes. Tank asked her a few more questions like if she skied. That was a 'no' and neither did he, so that was good. Did she like animals? She answered that she loved them. When she asked him, he said he tolerated them, but he was too busy for pets.

They were drying their hands on the dishtowel when someone knocked on the door.

"Come in," Tank said, loud enough for the person outside to hear.

Joe walked in and shut the door behind him.

"Hey, he said, looking at the two of them. His eyes lingered on Tess and Tank saw that her nipples were protruding provocatively through her little tee. He quickly stepped in front of her, forcing Joe's eyes to move from her to him.

Tess wasn't sure why Tank had just blocked her from Joe. She hoped the two of them were okay with each other. She tugged on the back of Tank's shirt.

Tank turned and whispered quickly in her ear. Tess nodded and then skirted past Tank and went to put a bra on in the bedroom.

Tank invited Joe to sit and while they were getting comfortable, Tess came back out. Joe sat in the chair and Tess and Tank sat next to each other on the couch.

"You two look happy," Joe said without any hint of sarcasm.

Tess looked to Tank. "We had a good talk. We're good," he said as he placed his arm around her shoulder and then planted a gentle kiss on her head making her to smile.

"I didn't see you today. I just wanted to check in." Joe was looking at Tess.

"Thank you, Joe. That's sweet. I think we've worked things out. We kind of took a really long nap."

"Okay, just checking up, like I said. We're all going to The Pen tonight. You guys coming?"

Tank fiddled with Tess's hair that was along her shoulder. "Not sure yet. I'll talk to Tess about it."

"Ok, I guess if you two come out, I'll see you there." Joe stood just as someone else knocked on Tank's door.

Grand Central," Tank said under his breath, forcing Tess to giggle. "Come in."

Grease opened the door.

"Hi."

They all returned his greeting.

"Tank, man, I tried but your sister in law will not budge."

Joe and Tess looked to Tank. They had no idea what Grease was talking about.

"Damn," Tank said with a good-natured chuckle. He turned to Tess.

"I wanted to take you on my bike for a little tour of Happy. Toby and Breezy have been storing my Harley in their garage since that night at The Pen when I was kidnapped. Breezy won't release the bike to me because she says I shouldn't be riding it yet. I was hoping she'd let Grease drive it here for me, but the woman knows me too well."

"Ter, you really shouldn't be doing too much yet, you know?"

"Yeah, but I just wanted to take you for a short ride. Maybe tomorrow."

Tess nodded and snuggled into his chest.

Chapter 16

The Pen was packed. Harleys and trucks jammed the spacious gravel lot and loud music could be heard from outside the bar. Tank had driven himself and Tess in Sweet's truck. Tess hadn't wanted to come, but Tank was so eager that she didn't have the heart to say no. She wasn't comfortable around a lot of people, and she was still a wreck thinking someone may recognize her and haul her off to jail.

She had taken a little more time than usual with her makeup and clothes. Tank had said some neighboring motorcycle clubs were going to be there. They had all heard he'd been kidnapped, and they wanted to welcome him back properly. Tank knew a proper welcome would be them getting him shit faced and even offering him one of their women. He was starting to rethink coming to The Pen but when he saw how Tess had made a special effort in how she dressed, well, he knew he had to bring her.

Right before they entered the door, Tank pulled her aside and leaned down, so he was looking directly into her eyes.

"Tess, this probably isn't going to be like anything you have ever seen before."

"What do you mean?"

"It's all bikers, babe. Very rowdy and sometimes raunchy."

"Ter, I've worked in bars, I'll be okay." Tank shook his head disagreeing.

"There may be fights. They usually end up with the two guys buying each other beers at the end of the night, but it can get crazy."

"Okay, but you won't fight will you?"

"I don't plan on it, but I'd never back down. I think you know that." He smoothed his thumb over her cheek.

"There are women here, too," he said softly.

"It's a bar, of course there are women." Now she was exasperated.

"Loose women, Tess. Ones that think nothing of blowing a guy in public."

"Ooookayyyy," if he was trying to make her nervous, he had succeeded.

"I've never brought someone with me before so...."

"Some women may hit on you?"

"Yeah, maybe."

"Do you want to be with other women tonight, Ter?"

"Not even a little," he kissed her hard. "I just want you. Just you."

"Okay, then this will be an adventure to say the least."

Tank held the door open and Tess stepped into the dimly lit, very loud bar.

As soon as Tank stepped through the door he was greeted with loud cheers and backslaps, similar to when he had arrived back at camp that first day. A couple of women kissed him, but Tess saw that he was careful about keeping the kisses platonic. She found herself pushed to the side as Tank's friends engulfed him, so she stood back, taking in the boisterous scene.

Tank was looking around the room amidst the friendly chaos and when his eyes finally landed on her; he smiled and headed in her direction. Grease reached her first and took her by the elbow, guiding her towards the bar.

"No way should you be alone," Grease shouted above the din.

"I'm fine, but thanks," she had to shout back.

Tank reached them and placed his hand at the small of her back sending delicious shivers through her. He leaned down so close to her ear that when he spoke his lips tickled her.

"You okay so far?"

"So far, so good," she whispered back.

The night was as Tank had predicted. Crazy. People were dancing and some women were on the bar putting on a bawdy dance show for the fans encouraging them loudly from the floor. There were three frenzied bartenders and Tess watched as they filled drinks orders. The first thing she noticed was that the men didn't seem to have an organized serving plan. They would cross back and forth behind each other, often just barely missing dumping fresh drinks on each other. All three used the register and it was painfully obvious to Tess, who had been working in a restaurant since she was sixteen, that they had no idea how to protect themselves from miscounting money.

Tank had lifted Tess to an empty stool. A bartender placed a beer and shot in front of Tank and a beer in front of Tess. Tank looked at Tess, waiting to see what her reaction would be to him drinking alcohol, so when she picked up her glass and tapped it against him yelling, "Cheers" before taking a big sip of her own, Tank smiled at her broadly. He took a swallow of his beer then bent down and gave her a soft kiss on her lips.

Tess was enjoying herself. One fight broke out and Tank stayed out of it. He had protectively placed his body between her and one of the men that had come crashing their way. When the fight ended, just like Tank had said, the two men sat drinking in a nearby booth, laughing as their women bandaged their cuts and bruises.

A few hours into the night, Tank leaned in close to Tess. "I'm ready when you are," he said nuzzling her cheek with his lips.

She leaned into him, relishing the delicious hum that his kiss stirred inside of her. "I'm ready, too."

Tank and Tess made their way out of the bar. They were stopped a few times and even Tess was included in some of the good-bye hugs and kisses. The ride home was quiet. Tess was thinking about what lay ahead for her when they got back to his cabin. Tank must have been thinking the same thing because as they turned into the camp's drive, he took her hand in his and gave it an affectionate squeeze.

"Nothing is going to happen unless you want it to, Tess."

She smiled sheepishly.

"I know," she said quietly. "I just think... I think I want it to; happen, I mean."

Tank pulled the truck up in front of Sweets cabin and got out of the truck quickly so he could help Tess down. Again, she was struck by how he was so mannerly. He gently took her by the hand and led her inside his cabin. Tess was simmering already. Her skin was on fire and the only remedy would be when Tank finally touched her.

Tank shut the door behind them and turned Tess to face him. Then he lifted her up like she weighed nothing and placed her back against the wooden door. Her crotched was aligned perfectly with Tank's hardness and they both moaned on contact. Their kiss was fuel to the fire, needy and wild. Tank held her ass firmly and thrust against her. Tess's hands were on his thick shoulders and her legs were wrapped around his strong hips as she used her heels to encourage him. She was fast approaching heaven when Tank stilled.

He stopped kissing her and placed his forehead on hers. He was breathing as heavily as was she.

"Honey, I want to take this to my bed, okay?"

Tess nodded. It was going to happen. She was nervous yet so ready.

In the bedroom, Tank helped Tess out of her clothes and when she was completely bare, he sat her on the edge of the bed while he undressed. Tess watched, unable to take her eyes off the perfect specimen of male anatomy in front of her. She'd been with handsome men before, but none were as built as Tank was. She reached out to run her fingers over his V-muscle that trailed into his jeans. Tank stopped undressing and let her touch him.

" You are so handsome, Ter," she whispered.

Tank dropped to his knees in front of her and crashed his mouth to hers. So much emotion rushed through him. This was not just sex with Tess. He felt off kilter and there was a sense that only being inside her would right him again.

As their mouths made love, Tank moved Tess to the center of the bed and covered her with his body. Tess opened her legs and again they aligned perfectly. His steely rod was pressed firmly against her wet woman lips. His thick ridge was snug against her engorged clit.

They moved together, moaning and whispering endearments. He was thrusting through her wetness and she was meeting each push with pelvic pressure of her own. Tank's slick head slid down, nudging at her entrance.

His hands bracketed her face and he kissed her tenderly.

"I want you, Tess. I want to be inside you."

"Ter…." Tess was squirming she was so heated.

"Yes, please," she said her voice thick with lust.

"Are you on anything?" he asked, his voice husky.

"I had a shot in April. It should still be good."

She saw Tank reach towards his nightstand door, and she pulled his arm back.

"No, I need to feel you, Ter. Just you. Please"

"I've never been with someone without a condom. I'm clean, though."

"I haven't either and I was just checked in April when I got my shot."

"You sure you're okay with this?" He searched her eyes for any hint of worry.

Tess's answer was apparent to him when she urged him inside of her by raising her knees up towards her chest, giving him better access. Tank pushed in slowly, stretching her tight sheath. When he heard her gasp and stiffen, he stilled.

"Honey?"

"I'm okay, Ter. I just need a second to adjust."

When Tess started moving underneath him, he knew she was ready for more. Tank steadily sank further into her hot snug channel. She was so tight around his shaft that Tank had to momentarily still to prevent himself from spewing early.

When he was totally seated inside her, he lifted his head, but kept his eyes locked on hers. She was so beautiful, laid out before him, trusting him. Her pale skin contrasted against his sun-tanned tone. Her breasts were a handful in size, and her areolas were an intoxicating shade of dusky rose. Her dark distended nipples were hard and beckoning for attention, so Tank tenderly sucked on each sensitive point leaving them wet and even harder when he pulled away.

He gave Tess a gentle kiss on her mouth and leaned on his forearms creating some space between their bodies. He wanted to see her face, her body, as he made love to her. It was at that precise moment that he realized for the first time in his life he wasn' just having sex; he was making love.

Tess fingered his hair with one hand, while holding on to his bicep with another. She ran her thumb over his lips and Tank sucked it in causing Tess to twerk from the heady sensation. Tank began to slowly work his steel hard length in and out of her wet heat. He alternated his thrusts between hard and fast, or sweet and agonizingly slow.

Tess was beyond rational thought. Her body was ignited and primed for a cataclysmic release. She moved passionately with Tank, circling her pelvis as he pushed in, clenching around him with her vagina walls as he pulled out. Her moans were fast becoming whimpers and Tank felt his balls pull tight He was going to come hard. Tank bent down and latched on to one of Tess's taunt nipples. Her hips began to shake, and her walls were vibrating against him. Tank grazed her nipple with his teeth, and she quaked uncontrollably, her nails digging into his muscled arms. Sweet fluid gushed from her, coating his testicles and Tank thrust deeper and erupted with her, driving his manhood into her rippling core. Tess was still undulating so Tank reached between them and pressed down on her erect clit with his thumb forcing another orgasm through her hypersensitive body. Small tremors continued to shake her, and Tank kissed her tenderly back to reality.

"Tess, that was perfect," he said, peppering her with light affectionate kisses.

Tess wasn't quite able to speak yet. He was laying on her, keeping his weight off her by resting on his forearms. Tess circled him lovingly with her arms and pressed into him kissing his neck.

"Perfect," was all she could murmur.

Tank got out of bed and brought a wet cloth back to wash her. Tess's body was so liquid that she couldn't have stopped him if she wanted. It was an intimate gesture, and except for being slightly embarrassed when he ran the cloth through her lips, she relished the nurturing feeling he was giving her.

When he finished caring for her Tank got back into bed and Tess snuggled into his welcoming arms. They were soon asleep.

Tank awoke when he heard the choppers rolling in an hour later. He slipped from the bed and pulled the sheet up over Tess's shoulder before grabbing his jeans as he left the room.

He put on his jeans and walked barefoot across the grassy front yard to Sweet's cabin.

Sweets and Lolly were sitting on their front stoop. Lolly was leaning back against her big man, between his legs and one step down.

"Hey," he greeted them quietly.

"Everything good, Pres.?" Sweets asked, wondering what would drag Tank away from the woman he figured was in his bed.

"Yeah, just want to talk."

"Need me to leave? "Lolli asked, readying to stand.

"No, Lolly, I want you in on this." She nodded and relaxed once again against Sweets.

Tank sat down next to Sweets and before he started talking, Grease pulled his bike up and shut the engine off. Tank noted that he did not have a female riding behind him, unusual for his large friend after a night out.

"I guess my invite got lost in the mail," Grease said laughing.

Before Tank started talking, Joe's truck pulled up to the cabin next door and the group watched as Joe and Cara exited Joe's truck. Joe looked over to the group and Tank gave him a nod as a way of greeting, before they disappeared inside.

"That's interesting," Lolly said with a grin.

"Hope he knows what he's doing," Grease added, watching the couple disappear inside the door.

Tank pulled everyone's attention from Joe and Cara. Truth was, he was a little nervous about their hook up himself. He knew Cara was still not handling him being with Tess well. She'd said a few snide comments to some of the women at the bar, but luckily Lolly had shut her down. He knew Joe had a crush on Tess, but as long as he was with her, Joe wouldn't move on it. Joe being with Cara, Tank didn't know if it was a good thing or a dangerous thing. His friend had been deployed a long time and Cara was good in bed. Maybe this would help them both.

"I'm glad you're here." Tank said to Grease. "I wanted to talk to all of you anyway."

Grease leaned forward on his handlebars and got comfortable.

"First, does anyone know where Ditch was tonight? I wanted to talk to him."

"No, haven't seen him," Sweets answered, and Grease shook his head no.

"That's strange. Okay, well, I need to tell you something about Tess."

"That you have a major hard on for her?" Grease chuckled.

"I like her a lot, you're right, but there's more." Lolly reached over and patted Tank's thigh, letting him know they were listening.

"Tess was kidnapped from New York City in April." "Shit that's a long time ago!"

"Yeah and she went through a lot. Anyway, she isn't sure why she was kidnapped, but she is pretty sure it had to do with a man she was dating. He didn't tell her he was married. When Tess found out she told him she was going to tell his wife. He threatened her. On top of this, he had just lost a boatload of money in a Ponzi scheme. Tess was kidnapped about a week after she threatened to tell the guy's wife. These men that kidnapped us, I think they are from upper Montana, back woods guys. I recognized their accent. Anyway, one of the guys that kidnapped her told her that there was a warrant out for her arrest for the murder of her ex's wife and for stealing his money. She has no idea if he was telling her the truth or just lying to keep her with him. She told me they were always moving, staying in remote cabins, or camping in the woods. I'm assuming summer cabins because she said they didn't have water or electricity. She tried to escape once, but she was caught. After that she was always locked in a closet at night."

"You have to know she saved my life. She figured out how to jimmy the lock on the closet and at night she'd sneak me food and water."

"That's so f-ed up," Sweets said softly.

"Poor kid," Lolly added.

"Here's the thing. I want to help her. There's no way she killed that guy's wife, and if there is a warrant out for her arrest and this guy has planted evidence she's screwed. I just can't figure out how to help her."

"Did you tell Toby?" Grease asked.

"No. He's the law. That would put him in a compromising position."

"We have to help her," Lolly said.

"You don't have to help her. I want to help her, but I needed you to know what was going on. I'll understand if you want me to take off with her, so the club isn't dragged into anything if any shit does happen."

"Tank, it's us man. We'll always have your back."

"I appreciate that, and right now I need to have Tess's back."

"I think you need to find out why you were kidnapped, Tank." Grease said quietly.

Tank nodded that he agreed.

"I know. It's crazy. At first I thought it was Satan's Army wanting a turf war, but when those cocksuckers took my vest I knew it wasn't any club crap. I want to travel up north and find those guys. I'm hoping to not only find out why I was targeted, but if Tess's boyfriend was behind her being kidnapped. These guys are the key, I know it."

"When are you planning on going?" Grease asked, rubbing a dirt smudge further into his jeans.

"I want to have more of a plan, and I want to make sure Tess is comfortable staying here without me."

"Somehow I don't think the latter is ever going to happen, man," Sweets joked.

Tank grimaced. "Yeah, she is not going to be happy."

"So, a couple weeks then?" Grease surmised.

"Yeah, a couple weeks. First thing I gotta do is get my bike out from Breezy's clutches."

The group laughed and it was then that Tank noticed Tess standing on his front porch looking towards them.

"Oh, oh, busted," Grease said, looking at the woman dressed in a tee shirt that hung to her knees.

"Shit, she's even hot in an oversized tee shirt," Lolli laughed.

"No one's hotter than you, woman," Sweets said, tickling her neck with his lips.

Tank stood up and Sweets clapped him on the back. "We got you Tank, okay?"

"Thanks man." He said as he walked towards his cabin.

Tess stood in the doorway watching him saunter towards her. Dressed only in jeans, the man was sinfully sexy. His bruises had faded to a dull yellow and his gashes had healed into thin pink lines. The man literally took her breath away. His hair was loose and fell to chin level. She could see his smile from where she stood, even though it was dark out. She shivered remembering how he had pleasured her earlier. She had known he was going to be a talented lover. She just hoped she was good enough for him.

"Hey," he said, stopping in front of her.

"Hey."

"Couldn't sleep?"

"When I found you weren't with me, I got worried."

"Worried?"

"Yeah, silly I know. I just wondered where you were."

Tank turned her so they were heading inside, and he shut the door behind him.

"I just needed to talk to the guys."

"Everything alright?"

"It will be, Tess. I promise." Tank made love to Tess again that night. He was so tender and sweet. His lips must have touched every inch of her body, as he loved her. Tess was boneless when he finally let himself cum. For the second time that night they fell asleep wrapped in each other's arms.

Chapter 17

The next two weeks were extraordinary for both Tank and Tess. It was rare that either was without the other. Tank was getting stronger every day, and he began a workout regime that included chopping wood and carrying the heavy logs to different areas of the camp. He finally got his Harley away from Breezy and he and Tess would often take rides along secluded back roads where they would find scenic over views and picnic.

Tank was amazed that he'd only known Tess since Memorial Day. He felt as if he'd known her forever. He now understood the bond Breezy and Toby shared, something he wasn't able to understand before Tess came into his life.

Tess was gaining back the weight she had lost and because she jogged every morning and helped Tank with the wood, her body became curvy and toned. She loved swimming in the creek and she and Tank had even skinny-dipped one afternoon when no one was around.

What was developing between them was on a whole different level than anything she'd ever experienced before. They could talk for hours or not speak at all, yet still feel connected. Unfortunately, the warrant for her arrest was an ever-present, dark cloud looming over her that was never too far from her thoughts. Tess also worried about her apartment back in New York. She didn't have anything of value but there were a few items that she'd hate to lose.

Tank wanted to take her out on a proper date, but they both agreed that it would be too risky. Most evenings they would contribute to group potluck at camp, sometimes they enjoyed quiet meals shared in the cabin. At least once a week they were invited to dinner at Toby and Breezy's. Tess met little Gus and instantly fell in love with the five-year-old. Her heart melted when she saw how great Tank was with him. Breezy's daughters, Mindy and Mandy, had also come home from college and Toby's cabin was filled to capacity, especially when their boyfriends, Two and Bam, were visiting. Tess loved how tight knit they were and a little part of her dared to dream she could have that, too.

Tank and Tess discovered that they shared many of the same ideals and values. They became so in synch with each other that often a mere touch or gesture conveyed what they were thinking. Breezy had laughed out loud when Tess had told her that and Breezy quickly explained that's how it was with her and Toby. She called him her soul mate.

The last few days, Tess sensed that Tank had wanted to tell her something. One night Tess as snuggled into Tank's warm side after their nightly session of lovemaking. It still amazed Tess that Tank was so giving and never failed to make sure she had an orgasm before he found his own release. He brought out a sensuous side of herself that she never knew even existed.

"Ter, is there something you want to talk to me about?" Her fingers intimately caressed his chest.

Tank sighed deeply, "you know me well."

"Is it bad?"

"No, but I know you're not going to like it." Tank placed his hand on hers and she stilled.

Fear gripped Tess and she pulled away from his warm body. Tank hauled her back in close.

"Oh no you don't, Angel. I'll tell you, but I want you right here when I do."

"Oh God, it's really bad," she groaned.

"Tess, I have to leave camp for a bit."

He felt Tess's body tighten next to him.

"I'm going to go find those men, Tess. Grease and Sweets are going to come with me."

"Ter, please no," her voice shook with fear.

"Honey, I have to. I need to know why someone wanted me killed. I'm hoping to get some more information for you, too."

"Ter. No." Tess was weeping softly beside him and he was coming undone see how upset she was.

"Sweetheart. It's going to be fine. Are you upset because I'm leaving or that you're worried about what I might find out? Talk to me."

Tess wiped at her tears.

"Everything, Ter. I'll be so worried. What if something happens to you? I'll miss you. Please, please don't go."

"I'm doing this for us."

"Can I come, too?"

"No, baby, I need you safe. I care for you so much, Tess. If I have to worry about you it might make it unsafe for the guys and me. Please understand, I have to do this."

"When are you leaving?"

"Day after tomorrow."

Tess buried her head in his chest and sucked in a deep breath. She had to be strong. "I'm going to really miss you."

"I'm going to miss you like crazy too. I wish there was a way I could call you, but I can't."

Tess traced his lips with her finger. Her gut was hollow with fear and she wanted to tell him just how much she cared for him, but she couldn't.

They spent the next day getting Tank ready for his trip. He worked on his bike, making sure it was ready for the rough roads he knew he'd be on. Tess sat next to him, handing him tools and they chatted about everything except him leaving. They spent that night making love and pleasuring each other. Neither of them wanted to waste time sleeping, but they ended up falling asleep, completely sated.

When the sun broke through the blinds, Tank turned over to find Tess watching him. He pushed a strand of her long hair back behind her ear.

"Morning woman," he said, in a deep gravelly voice that sent shivers through her.

"Good morning."

"You okay?"

"At the moment," she whispered. Tank knew she was referring to the disparaging fact that he was leaving.

"This is killing me too," he said softly.

"Ter..." Her eyes misted over.

"Come on, baby, up and at 'em, quick shower and breakfast. The faster I go, the sooner I get back," he said, swatting her butt affectionately.

Tess giggled, trying to put on a brave face.

Tank showered while Tess made him eggs, bacon, and pancakes. She couldn't imagine him not being there in a few hours. She knew Lolly was going to be around, and Breezy had already said that she would be inviting her up to their cabin, but Tess already felt alone.

They walked outside, Tank holding his leather saddle over his broad shoulder. She could see Grease was securing his leather bag to the back of his bike and Lolly and Sweets were holding each other and talking quietly.

Tank secured his bag and turned to Tess. He wrapped her lovingly in his arms and kissed her forehead gently.

"Ter?"

"What, baby?"

"I care for you so much that I ache."

"Oh God, Tess, me too." He knew she was afraid to let herself love someone again after what Randal had done to her. He was happy to take what she could give, for now.

"Be safe, okay?"

"I will, Darlin. Try to have some fun while I'm away. Lolly will make sure you have groceries. Breezy will be looking in on you. Please stay in the camp though, okay?"

"I will."

Tess tried to keep from crumbling into a mass of tears. She didn't want Tank's last image for however long he was away to be of her crying. She smiled at her very badass, sweet boyfriend, trying to memorize every detail on his face.

Tank got on his big Harley and pulled Tess in close for an intense last kiss.

"Hey, come on you two, break it up," Grease groaned.

Tess pulled back and whispered, "Miss you." Tank locked his beautiful blue eyes on hers and mouthed back, 'Miss you too.' Then he set Tess safely away from the bike as he started it.

"Let's roll brothers," he told two of his best friends, and Lolly and Tess watched as their men left camp.

The first week, Tess kept herself busy. She cleaned Tank's cabin, learned to make meatballs and froze them, baked cookies and froze them, read a book, picked flowers and even started to weave a dried floral wreath that she found instructions for in a magazine one of the ladies had loaned her. She swam in the swimming hole every day and she even babysat some of the children so their moms could run into Townsend for food and other supplies.

Tess found that the nights were the worst. The first night she cried quietly into Tank's pillow. It smelt like him and she buried her nose in it, wishing for him to stay safe and hurry back.

Joe had come to visit her a few times. She had heard through the ladies' grapevine that he and Cara were still hooking up, but only after they'd been drinking. Joe had confided to Tess that they were enjoying the sex, but she held no appeal to him otherwise. Tess thought that was harsh, but she didn't voice her opinion. Like Tank had said, they were both just scratching an itch, so to speak.

Tess was making another batch of cookies, hoping she wouldn't have to freeze them before Tank returned, when she heard two car doors slam shut outside Tank's cabin.

Tess looked out the window to see Toby and Sheriff Liam walking up the front steps. She saw Joe sprinting towards the cabin and her stomach dropped. Something was wrong. Were they coming to tell her something happened to Terry? Tess's hands were shaking when she opened the door. Had she been identified? Her mind was reeling with negative thoughts.

"Hi Toby, Sheriff. Everything all right?" Her voice was quivering, and Toby felt terrible at how petrified she looked. Tank would have beaten his ass into the ground right then, and rightly so.

"Tess, can we come in?" Liam asked.

Joe jumped up onto the small porch and put his formidable body between Tess and the two law officers.

"What's going on?" His voice was hard, his concern palatable.

"We need to talk to Tess." Sheriff Liam told him, agitated that he was interfering.

"Is Terry okay?" she asked tensely.

Toby looked at Tess who was paling visibly.

"Tess, we haven't heard anything from Tank so I'm sure he's fine." His voice was soft, hoping to ease her tension filled body.

"Why don't you guys wait until Tank gets back before talking to Tess, okay?" Joe's arms were crossed in front of his body and his legs were spread indicating that Toby and Liam would have had to go through him to get to her.

The sheriff was not looking happy and Toby was worried the whole situation was going to escalate into something nasty.

"Joe, Liam's office got an anonymous tip that a fugitive by the name of Tess Green was staying here. If it was Liam that took the call he could wait until Tank gets back, but his entire staff knows. They looked up her name and there is a warrant out for her. He has to bring her to the station."

Tess gasped from behind Joe and he felt her clutch the back of his shirt. After a few tense moments Joe felt Tess move from around his body. She didn't want Joe getting into trouble because of her.

"I am Tess Green, but I didn't do whatever it is I've been accused of."

Tess looked like she was about to pass out, and Joe put his arm around her to steady her.

Liam read Tess her rights and when he went to try to handcuff her as per protocol, Toby placed his hand on Liam's arm and shook his head. Liam put the cuffs back on his belt and walked Tess to his Sheriff's car where he helped her into the back seat. Toby and Joe stood on the porch watching. A few other club members saw what was happening and headed towards Tank's cabin, Lolly was walking towards them quickly. Her head was going moving back and forth between Liam's car and Toby.

"What the hell, Toby?" she spewed, having no problem getting in his face.

"Back off, Lolly. There was nothing I could do. His office got a tip and he had to follow up on it."

"Tank's going to lose it, man," Joe said, running his hand through his short spikey hair.

"Do you know who called it in?" Lolly asked.

"No. Do you?"

Lolly shook her head. "Who else knew about her, Joe?"

Joe was quiet for a few seconds like he was weighing his words.

"I think Cara overheard Tank talking to you guys a couple weeks ago."

Lolly smacked her palm into her other hand. "I will freaking beat the …"

"Lolly, don't invite more trouble. Tank will deal with her if she did snitch. Let's concentrate on Tess." Toby was, as usual, the voice of reason. "I'm going down to the station and act as her lawyer. Let's not speculate any further until we really know what's going on."

"Tank's going to rip me apart," Joe said solemnly.

"I guarantee he's not going to be happy with me either," Toby said grimly.

"Yeah, but I was supposed to get her out of here if I saw that she was going to be arrested. I f-ed up."

"There was no way we could have known, Joe. I'd steer clear from Cara for a bit though." Lolly was trying to make him feel better but he could tell she was really upset.

"Yeah, but I think I'll keep talking to her though. That way if she slips up I'll know for sure."

Toby and Joe shook hands and Lolly apologized for being short with Toby before he took off for the station.

By the time Toby arrived, Tess had just been processed and was sitting in an interrogation room. Her face was ashen, and he could see that she was physically quaking.

"Toby? Why are you here?" Liam asked when he saw his friend.

"I'm going to act as her lawyer."

"Oh, for Pete's sake Toby."

"If she's innocent, and I'm betting she is, she's going to need a lawyer. This saves you from calling into Townsend for a Public Defender."

"Okay, come on, I'm just going in now."

Toby and Liam entered the small room and when Toby saw how cold Tess was, he took off his windbreaker and placed it over her shoulders. Tess smiled gently at him with sad eyes and thanked him

"Tess I'm going to act as your lawyer. Is that alright?"

"Yes." Her voice was barely audible.

Liam started the questioning. "Tess, you've been accused of killing a Lina Randal. You have also been accused of steal twenty thousand dollars, but the evidence against you for that charge is thin, at best."

Tess started to speak, and Toby placed his hand on her arm to quiet her.

"What's the evidence against her for the murder?"

"I don't have to reveal that, Toby. My job is to interrogate and then extradite her back to Manhattan."

"Liam, can you please give me a minute with her?"

Liam stood up and left the room.

"Tess, did you know about this?"

Tess put her face in her hands and then after a few seconds lifted her face and looked at Toby.

"I was told by one of the men that kidnapped me that I had been accused of murdering Dan's wife, but I honestly didn't know if it was a lie to keep me from trying to escape again."

 "Okay, that's good, we can work with that."

"So, you were dating this man, Dan?"

"Yes."

"You had no idea this guy was married?"

"God, no."

"Can anyone verify that?"

Tess thought for a few seconds.

"Well, the ladies I worked with at the bar. They knew how hard Dan had pursued me; sending flowers to the bar, showing up after my shift ended."

"But did any of them know he was married?"

"No, no way. They would have told me."

"Okay, I'll need their names."

Tess wrote down the name of the bar, Mad–hatten, and also the names of three women she worked with. She also gave Toby her bosses name and number.

"Toby, I don't know if this will help but my boss, Tom Finn, he's married and when he was going through a rough patch with his wife, he hit on me and I turned him down. He knows that I wouldn't date a married man. "

"That might help, Tess. Good job. I'm going to let Liam come back in now, and before you answer any questions look to me. If I don't want you to answer it I'll tell him you won't be answering it. Okay?"

"Okay...Toby, thank you."

Toby gave her shoulder a reassuring pat and went to find Liam.

Tess told her entire story to Liam. Toby didn't think it would harm her at all. She gave Liam the same work information that she'd told Toby. When Liam asked if she knew Lina Randal she answered honestly that she did not.

"So, Tess, I've already called the US Marshal's to transport you back to New York. You'll probably leave here within the next twenty-four hours. For what it's worth, I believe you are innocent, but I'll deny saying that, okay?" He gave her a small grin.

"Toby, you should go with her."

"I know, I just have to square things at home. Liam, I expect you to make Tess comfortable here."

"I will."

"And for the record, you better hope Tank doesn't get back before she leaves because all hell will break loose if he finds out she's here, and you know it."

"I'm the law, Toby, so are you. We have to make choices based on that and not on friendship. You know where I stand on this. I wish I'd never gotten the tip."

"Thanks, Liam. I know you're a good friend. It's Tank I'm concerned about."

"Yeah, me too."

Liam had one of his men escort Tess to a cell. She noticed she had an extra blanket, and someone had put a magazine in the small dismal room for her. Toby told Tess he'd be back when she was getting ready to leave and he gave her a brotherly hug telling her to stay strong. He really did feel badly for her. It was a messy situation.

Chapter 18

When Toby got home, he called his FBI friend Special Agent Logan McNeil, who was based in Townsend. Logan had been instrumental when Breezy had fallen prey to her deceased husband's treacherous family's unlawful attempts to take Gus from her. Together, with Logan's connections, they had put the family members in jail and Breezy had retained custody of him.

After an obligatory polite catch up, Toby explained the trouble Tess was in. Logan told Toby that he could get the FBI involved because she had been kidnapped, but he didn't like that she hadn't gone to the authorities as soon as she and Tank had gotten free. Toby explained what she was afraid to because of what the kidnappers had told her. Logan agreed there were extenuating circumstances.

Tess did not get much sleep that night despite Liam's attempts to make her comfortable. The US Marshal showed up in the morning and when she took Tess from her cell, she immediately hand cuffed her. Tess could not have felt lower. She knew Toby was going to try to help her, but not knowing what evidence they had against her ate at her sanity.

Toby arrived as the Marshal was putting Tess in her car. They shook hands and Toby told the Marshal he would be acting as her lawyer until he could obtain one for her in New York. The Marshal was cordial explaining to Toby that she and Tess were flying out that afternoon and would be in the city by nightfall. She gave Toby the address of the station where he would find Tess when he arrived.

The U.S. Marshal never attempted any small talk with Tess while traveling to New York and that was fine with Tess. She was mortified when she had to be put on the plane ahead of everyone else waiting at the gate. People stared at the handcuffs and whispered, making Tess feel so alone and vulnerable. She kept her head down and her eyes remained pinned to the dingy airport carpeting as she was escorted up the ramp and down the small plane's aisle to her seat in the back of the plane. The trip took up the entire day. Tess refused any food or drink. She thought if she ate or drank anything that she might vomit it up. Her stomach was rolling, and her head was pounding by the time they reached the police precinct in downtown Manhattan.

Tess hadn't thought much about the city after she'd been kidnapped. Her life had gone from fast lane to trail ride in one awful evening. Moving frequently with her kidnappers had been difficult. They ate fast food or heated soup or canned chili by leaning the cans near an open fire. The one thing that had always helped Tess through the ugliness of the entire ordeal was that wherever she was, was beautiful.

She loved the thickly wooded forests with the rich scent of pine. She had even liked it when she was allowed to sit by the fire at night, looking into the dark woods, listening to the animal sounds. Lester had taught her how to recognize different animal calls such as bear, raccoon, and wolf. He had pointed out eagles and elk, and once she'd seen a fox with five teeny, tiny cubs.

When she had been with Tank at the camp she had fallen in love with the natural beauty surrounding her on an even deeper level. Tank had made everything seem so new and special. The Montana he introduced her to was even more spectacular. The hot asphalt of the city with it's overpowering mixture of unknown smells permeated her nostrils, and Tess knew she would never call this place her home again.

Tess was processed again, stripped, and searched. She was given a dark blue jumpsuit to wear and placed in a cell with another woman who was clearly whacked out on some kind of drug. Tess didn't even want to touch the bed, but she thought it was safer to keep her back to the gray concrete wall, so she climbed on the top bunk and sat against the cool wall. She was afraid to fall asleep in the presence of the ranting woman in her cell, so she remained awake and vigilant the entire night.

The next morning, a tired and demoralized Tess was led to a small, bleak room with a two-way mirror, a metal table, and two plastic chairs. Her hands were cuffed to chains screwed into the table. She couldn't hold back the tears that filled her eyes and ran down her face, tears that she couldn't wipe away because of her shackled wrists.

Toby and two men wearing suits entered the room and Toby was immediately concerned with how distraught she looked.

"Jesus, Tess." He couldn't keep the concern from his voice.

"Toby...I..." She started to hiccup uncontrollably, as the tears streamed down her face.

Toby knelt down next to her. "Honey, please try to calm down. You're going to make yourself sick." Tess still could not stop crying, but she dialed her emotions back enough so that she could to speak.

"Toby... Toby, I need Terry. I don't think... I don't think I can... I need him." She was sniffling and hated that she couldn't wipe her own face. She couldn't believe how weak and needy she sounded, but the words had just tumbled out of her.

"I know, Honey. As soon as he surfaces I'll get him to you. "

Tess nodded and Toby wiped her face with a hanky he had in his pocket. She gathered herself as best she could.

"I'm sorry Toby," she apologized. "I didn't mean to fall apart like that." Her words were barely audible, but Toby heard her. He knew she was holding it together far better than many others in her situation would be.

"Tess, this is Agent Biggs, the FBI Agent that's been assigned to your case, and this is Mr. Crenshaw, your New York lawyer."

Tess looked at the men numbly.

"Tess, Agent Biggs has an idea that may get you out of this mess but it's not without risk."

Tess looked at Toby who appeared apprehensive, and she realized that he already knew what Agent Biggs was going to propose.

"Tess, we kept it under wraps that you'd been apprehended. No one knows. We think if we send you to talk to Dan Randal, wearing a wire, he might expose himself."

Tess's voice was low, so the men leaned in to hear. "Anything. I'll do anything."

Mr. Crenshaw coughed politely into his hand. "Gentlemen, may I have a private word with my client, please?"

Tess looked nervously at Toby, but then she nodded that she was going to be okay, so Toby and Agent Biggs left.

"Tess, may I call you Tess?"

"Yes."

"I can only guide you in this matter. It is risky, but the alternative is waiting to go to trial and that may not be for months. Do you really want to do this?"

"I have to. I'm innocent. I didn't even know he was married, and when he told me he was I felt sorrier for his wife than angry at him. I need this to end."

"Okay. Your friend, Mr. O'Brian, he's a good person to have helping you. He's going to make sure it's very safe, something about his brother?"

"I'm dating his brother. He's kind of a tough guy." Tess smiled just thinking about Terry and his machismo. It was the first time she'd had a lighthearted thought in days.

Toby and Agent Biggs came back into the room and told Tess that they needed time to set up the ruse, but she needed to be mentally prepared to go when they were. Agent Biggs said he'd get her some clothes other than the yoga pants and tee shirt she'd been traveling in. Before Toby left he tried to talk Tess out of the dangerous plan, but she refused to even entertain the idea of waiting. He hugged her goodbye and told her to try to get some sleep. He watched as she headed back to her cell. Tank was going to really beat his ass.

Tess didn't hear from them again until the following evening. Her deranged cellmate had made bail, so Tess had actually gotten a few hours of sleep. A female guard delivered clothes to Tess through the cell bars and remained outside the cell as Tess changed. The clothes they picked out for her were city clothes; a tight blue skirt, a white button up collared shirt, and a colorful light summer vest. She was given wedge sandals and they'd even given her an empty purse that matched her shoes. After changing into the body hugging, uncomfortable outfit, she was cuffed again and led out a side door where she met Toby. The guard uncuffed her and Agent Biggs signed a paper giving him custody of her.

Tess was helped into a van Tess saw there was a woman inside. She had light brown hair and was dressed professionally. An FBI badge was clipped to her pocket.

Toby handed Tess an energy bar and an iced tea. "You need to eat," he said, concern etched his face. Tess thanked him and ate the bar while Agent Biggs outlined the plan.

"Tonight, Dan Randal is supposed to go to a bar called The Hopper."

"I know it."

"Good, so you know the lay out?"

"Yes, I've been there with him a few times. His friend owns it, he's a real douche."

Toby and Agent Biggs both chuckled at her reference.

Tess shrugged her shoulders. "Sorry, but he really is."

Agent Biggs smiled and placed his hand on her shoulder.

"Okay, so we need you to confront Randal, surprise him. We hope he is rattled enough to say something stupid."

"What if he doesn't?"

"Let's think positive, Tess," Toby urged her.

"Agent Chris here is going to put this wire on you."

Tess was looking at what Agent Chris had in her hand and looked up to Biggs with a raised eyebrow. Agent Chris held a tiny, round, white object in between her finger and her thumb.

"It's not the traditional wire that you see on the TV shows. We've advanced in the technical world. Don't get it wet and try to get him someplace a little quiet."

"So, I go in the bar and what?" Tess asked nervously.

"Pretend you're just back in town and all is well. See if you can get him to talk about his wife or the money. If he says something we can use, we will come in and arrest him."

"You'll be just outside?"

"Yes, and Agent Chris is going in with you to be our eyes inside the bar. She'll head after you, we want him to think that you are alone."

Toby put his hand on her hand. "Stay safe, Tess."

"Okay. I'm a little nervous but I want this to be over."

"Hopefully by tonight, you'll be a free woman," Agent Biggs countered. "If things start to go bad, work the word red into a sentence or just yell it. We'll come running."

Tess nodded and Toby gave her hand a reassuring squeeze.

The van pulled across the street from The Hopper. Agent Chris affixed the small white disc on top of one of Tess's white shirt buttons. The tiny microphone actually reassured Tess knowing that they were going to be hearing everything that she would hear.

"Very James Bond," Tess said, trying to alleviate the tension filled van.

Agent Chris loaned her makeup and Tess quickly applied mascara and lipstick. She had been allowed a shower that morning, so her hair wasn't greasy, and she pulled it back in a messy bun using an elastic band from Agent Chris' hair, who had let her long, light brown hair hang loose.

Agent Biggs looked around the street and then opened the van door for her. Tess slipped out and adjusted her skirt before walking into the bar. Her eyes had to adjust to the dim lighting, and she moved to stand behind one of the old wooden, square pillars that were just inside the door so she would remain hidden for a few seconds longer as she gathered her bearings.

Tess saw the same bartender still working behind the counter and one of the sleazy bouncers standing off to the side keeping a watchful eye on the bar's patrons. Tess turned to look at the other side of the bar and saw Dan sitting at a table with a woman. Dan looked the same. He was facing away from her, laughing with the woman he was with, who had to have had breast implants. Her breasts were so big she was almost resting them on the table. Her hands were all over Dan and Tess sickened, wondering how she could have even thought he was attractive.

Tess watched as Mike, Dan's friend and the owner of the bar, approached the table and whispered something into Dan's ear. She couldn't see his reaction to whatever had been said to him. Tess figured it was some disgusting remark that Mike was notorious for. He'd made so many lewd jokes towards her when she'd been with Dan, and Dan would just laugh and tell him to get his own woman. Mike left the table and she watched him go back to where she knew his office was located down a hallway. Tess was trying to figure out a way to get Dan away from the table and the noise of the main bar area when he solved the problem for her. She watched as he kissed his bimbo and then headed for the bathrooms down the same hallway Mike had gone down.

Tess quickly followed him and as she turned the corner that led to the men's bathroom someone grabbed her from behind and covered her mouth. She gasped as Dan stepped in front of her with a huge smile on his devious face. Tess was desperately trying to get free when she saw Agent Chris rounded the corner. Mike had been waiting for her and slammed a gun down on the back of the Agent's head. Tess watched in horror as Agent Chris crumpled to the floor.

Dan grabbed Tess by her chin, and she knew she'd have a bruise where he was touching her.

"Thought you'd be smart enough to stay away me, Tess."

The meaty hand still kept Tess's mouth closed so she rolled her eyes.

"Ha, still a little firecracker, I see," Dan chuckled.

"Let's move this along, Dan," Mike said. He had picked up Agent Chris and was looking over his shoulder making sure no one else was coming down the hall.

The bouncer held Tess tightly against his body and walked her to door further down the hallway that opened up to a staircase. They were taken to a basement that was used to store the bar supplies.

"You are quite a surprise, my Tess. I thought you'd enjoy living in the mountains." His laugh was evil.

"Lester said you perished in a tragic fire." His voice turned nasty. "You should have never come back here."

Tess tried to bite the grimy hand covering her mouth and had some success. "Bitch!" the bouncer yelled feeling her teeth graze his skin.

"Knock her out," was the last thing Tess heard before something hard came down on her head sending her into darkness.

Chapter 19

Tank, Sweets and Grease had been making the rounds of small upper Montana towns. Tess had told Tank that one night she had overheard the men talking about a bar they frequented. That night, before she'd been locked into the closet for the night, she heard Lester say the name of the bar. She was only able to catch the first syllable, 'Mc'. Tank knew the slight twang he heard when the men had spoken was from upper, northwest Montana. He, Grease and Sweets had been combing the upper regions of Montana, stopping at every hole in the wall, honkey-tonk bar that started with an 'Mc.' There were more than they figured.

They were not wearing their cuts because they were in Satan's Army territory and they wanted to stay as inconspicuous as three large men on loud Harleys could possibly be.

They'd been gone for almost two weeks and Tank knew the perpetual ache in his chest was because he missed Tess. Sweets missed Lolly, too, and although he'd never leave Tank and Grease, he was getting cranky. Grease had been banging a couple of women along the way and was fine with the nomadic lifestyle they'd been leading so far, but Tank knew he'd rather be back at camp, too. Summers at the camp were special. Everyone decompressed and enjoyed the warm weather and camaraderie. They were missing two weeks of the short summer and Tank wanted to get back not only to Tess, but also to his camp.

They'd been passing through towns in a pre-strategized pattern, stopping in small, piece of shit bars that had a 'Mc' preface hoping to get a lead. Finally, in the town they had arrived in that afternoon, in a bar aptly called McDive, Grease had heard one of the drunken patrons bragging that he had a friend that was so bad ass that he had beat up a motorcycle club president. Tank, Sweets and Grease felt a sense of rejuvenation knowing they were in the right area. They also discovered that the bar was a regular hang out for Satan's Amy members but luckily for them one of the barmaids told them they were at a retreat for the weekend. The next night Sweets, who looked the least threatening of the three, went back into McDive alone and played up to a bar whore, plying her with drinks. A couple hours later he made his way back to the crusty motel that they were staying in.

"So?" Tank asked impatiently.

"Can I take a friggin shower first? That bitch was all over me and I can't get her cheap perfume out of my nose."

Grease was laughing. "I am so holding this over your head, Sweets," he teased.

"I'll frigging rip you a new one if you even hint to Lolly that I talked to that whore." He was clearly not happy with his assignment.

"Relax, Sweets," Tank said, hoping to calm him down. "Grease won't say shit. Come on, at least tell me if you got anything."

"I did," Sweets said grinning. "I say we find these guys tomorrow and head home. I need my Lolly." Sweets showered and then told Tank and Grease what he had learned. The woman, once Sweets had gotten her pretty tipsy, said there was a regular customer, a man by the name of Lester, who lived in a rickety trailer a few miles out of town. According to the inebriated woman, Lester had been gone for a few months but when he recently returned, he was flush with cash. When he was flashing his wad at the bar, someone asked jokingly if he robbed a bank and he had replied 'Nope, did a job for my cousin in New York City.'

"Holy shit! We found him! That's got to be him. I bet his cousin is Dan friggin Randal." Tank was smiling ear to ear. Finally, he would get some answers. Wondering why he'd been kidnapped and then left to die in a fire had understandably caused Tank to be a little paranoid. A few times he had lain awake at night, watching Tess sleep, racking his brain for possible suspects. He couldn't imagine anyone in his club wanting him dead. A few old timers wished they were still considered an outlaw club, but they hadn't complained in years.

He hadn't messed with any married women or women that had boyfriends he was aware of. He knew Cara was pissed at him now, but not when all the shit went down. He'd taken the club in a good direction. He provided jobs to many members of his club and even the local Kiwanis Club had invited him to join them.

The only drama he'd been involved in was last summer when two women who were involved with his club, one he had been banging on a very regular basis, had been instrumental in trying to hurt Breezy. Both had received a year in prison for their part in the crime. The only notable change in his life was Breezy giving him the deed to the camp. He kept tossing around that angle. Maybe someone wasn't happy that he now owned that prime piece of mountain property?

That night, when Tank fell asleep, he knew he needed the information that Lester could provide, and he was prepared to get it anyway he had to. The three men had decided to pay Lester an early morning visit. Tess had told him that Lester was usually drunk at night and hung over in the mornings and Tank wanted every possible advantage.

Early the next morning the three men rode towards the remote location that the woman had given to Sweets. Tank was hopefully optimistic that he would very likely be holding Tess that night. He couldn't wait to see her and with any luck, put a little hope back in her future.

They saw the turn off they needed to take and decided to hide their bikes in the woods and continue on foot. They walked on the side of the dirt drive knowing that if a car came by they would have to hide in the woods, but it turned out there was no need. They emerged into a small clearing with an old Silver Bullet trailer sitting in the middle of a weed infested lawn. A shed that looked to be an outhouse was off to the right and it smelled horrible. The men crouched down out of view.

"Tank, look at the trucks in the driveway."

Tank had been concentrating on how to approach the trailer unnoticed, so he hadn't seen the truck. When he looked at them, his jaw dropped.

"That mother f-er."

"What the hell is Ditch doing here?" Sweets whispered.

"Let's go find out," Tank said so fiercely that even Grease jumped.

Sweets grabbed Tank by the back of his jeans and pulled him back down.

"Tank, wait." Tank was so fired up and ready to kick ass for answers, that he fell back onto his ass with the harsh tug Sweets had given him.

" What the hell, Sweets?"

"Listen to me, man. We know that this ass wipe Lester kidnapped you and Tess, right?" Tank nodded. "We now know there is a connection between Ditch and him as well."

"Your point?"

"If you go in there and beat the crap out of them you might get some answers, but you won't be able to tell the law because of your vigilante crap. If we tell Liam, the law can round these guys up proper like and probably even get more answers than we could with our fists. Plus bringing in the law will probably help Tess out more in the long run."

"Fuck me," Tank said, running his hand through his hair, and causing most of it to fall out of the leather ponytail holder.

"Man, I know you want revenge. I can see it in your eye's but think about Tess."

Tank sighed heavily. "I was looking forward to beating him senseless," Tank admitted with a grimace.

"I know, man. But the law can look into bank records and phone calls and emails and stuff. Don't wreck that by going all avenging angel on them. You'd probably be charged and then when Tess is free you'd be in lock up."

"Crap," Tank said exasperated. "I know you're right. What do you think Ditch is doing here?"

"No idea, but the fact that he is tied into this answers at least one of your questions from that night."

"Yeah, the mo-fo roofied me!"

"Let the law find out why. At least now you know the who."

"So, we're just going to leave?" Grease asked.

Tank thought about this for a few seconds before responding. Sweets was hoping he had talked some sense into his best friend.

"I don't want to risk Ditch leaving here. It's only 6:00am. Let's go back to town, call Liam and have him get this town's sheriff on this."

"Good plan," Sweets said, knuckle-bumping Tank. Tank, Sweets and Grease quickly made their way back to their bikes and drove into town. The sheriff's office was housed inside a larger municipal building, so the men found it easily.

Tank used a pay phone to call Liam and Liam told him to right to the Sheriff's office. The sheriff in Norwalk was just coming on duty when they arrived. The deputy at the front desk waved the sheriff over to where Tank, Sweets and Grease were standing.

"Sheriff, these men would like a word," the deputy said. The sheriff nodded, eyeballing the three intimidating men with obvious trepidation.

"Sheriff, my name is Terry O'Brian. I was kidnapped about three weeks ago and two of the men involved are about ten minutes outside of your town."

"Whoa, that's a pretty big accusation."

"It's true. If you would call Liam Ross in Happy he can verify this." Tank was laying on the politeness thick.

"How'd you say you found these man?"

"Me and my friends here were just driving through your town and I happened to see them. One of the men's name is Lester, I don't know his last. The other man he's with is called Ditch."

"Okay, Mr. O'Brian, if you and your friends will wait here I'll give Sheriff Ross a call."

Tank, Sweets and Grease took seats and waited. Tank was hoping Liam was still in the office to take the call. He didn't want Ditch or Lester having time to get away.

The sheriff stepped from his office and motioned to Tank. "Mr. O'Brian, can you come here, please?"

Tank walked into the office. "Your story checks. Evidently the FBI is on this case, too, so I got to roll. I'll get the directions to this guy's place from your friends so we can pick them up. Sheriff Ross wants to talk to you."

The FBI was on this? That set off alarms in Tank and he quickly got on the phone. The sheriff handed Tank the phone and left.

"Liam?"

"Tank, you need to come home."

"Why, what's up? Is everyone okay?"

"No, it's bad. It's a long story but the bottom line is Tess was in New York and she's been kidnapped again."

"What? How the hell? Liam you better be fucking joking man."

"Tank just come home. Toby's in New York looking for her."

"Shit, Liam."

"Tank, come home." Liam disconnected.

Tank hung up and an uneasy feeling washed over him. Tess was in New York and she was kidnapped again. The old Desi Arnez line to Lucille Ball ran

through his head except he substituted Liam's name. 'Liam. You have sum splaining to do.'
Tank left the office, and Grease and Sweets knew immediately that something was wrong by the crazed look on Tank's face.
"Don't know the whole story but Tess is – was in New York City and got kidnapped… again!"
"Holy smokes."
"We gotta go, bros."
They got to their bikes and made it back to Happy in less than three hours for a trip that should normally have taken them four. Tank was running a ton of scenarios through his head and he kept getting stuck on why Tess would have been in New York. Had she left him while he was gone?
Tank pulled into the sheriff's office and sent Grease and Sweets back up to camp to make sure everything was all right.
"Liam," Tank barked, walking into his office and startling him so that he sloshed his coffee over his desk.
"Geez, Tank. Ninja much?"
"What's going on?"
"Sit down, Tank. You want some…"
"Talk. Now." Tank said with a voice carrying an icy edge that caused Liam to grimace.
"We got an anonymous tip here that Tess was a fugitive."
"Liam…"

"Listen, Tank. You want to know everything so just shut up and listen."

Tank glared at Liam but remained quiet.

"One of my deputies took the call. I couldn't deny it or push it off. I served the warrant and brought her down here."

"Oh God," Tank whispered. "She must have been a mess."

"She was. Toby came with me to serve the warrant and he acted as her lawyer. A US Marshal came the next day and took her to New York. Toby met her there." Liam paused for a second.

"The rest is really Toby's story to tell but I'll tell you what he told me. He got Tess a lawyer who was licensed in New York and he also called in a favor with an FBI friend. The FBI asked Tess to confront this guy Randal while wearing a wire."

"Oh no, she did not!"

"She did. They got the evidence they needed to clear Tess but she and the FBI Agent that was inside the bar with her were taken. Randal got away and Toby's been going nuts, along with the FBI, looking for Tess and their agent."

"How could they lose her? Why did Toby let her do this?"

"Tank, you need to calm down. We'll get some answers soon. I'm hoping when the FBI rounds up that man you found that he will shed some light on where they may have taken them."

Tank was visibly shaken. He'd paled and Liam knew from experience that Tank was thinking that Tess might already be dead.

"Don't go there, Tank."

"How can I not? I should have never left her."

"Honestly, Tank, this would have happened whether you were here or not."

"Who tipped you off, Liam?"

"Deputy said it was anonymous."

"Male or female?"

"Tank..."

"You know I'll find out."

Liam nodded. He was sure Tank would find out, too.

"Tank, Toby is going to call you today at 3:00. Go back to camp and come back down later for the call. Maybe the sheriff in Norwalk will have some answers by then."

Grimly, Tank stood up and walked stoically to his bike. His day had gone from awesome to shitty and he knew when he talked to Toby it could get even worse.

Chapter 20

Back at camp, Lolly, Joe, Grease, and Sweets made a beeline for Tank as he stepped off his Harley.

"She's been kidnapped," he said heavily. "She wore a wire to get Randal to incriminate himself and they got the evidence they needed but it went south. They don't know where she is. A female FBI Agent was also taken. Toby's calling Liam at 3:00. I'll go back down for the call."

The small group offered him words of encouragement but even they knew how serious this was. Tank walked inside his cabin and he immediately saw Tess's touches everywhere. It was clean, really clean and there were wilting flowers in a mason jar on the coffee table. A Tupperware full of cookies sat on the counter and a wreath she must have weaving out of flowers and vines sat unfinished on his kitchen table. Tank felt his heart lurch. He walked into his bedroom and saw a romance novel on the bedside table. The cover showed a muscle-bound shirtless man astride a Harley holding a scantily clad woman in his arms. He smiled when he saw it and his throat tightened. Shit, he was a mess.

"Tank?"

Tank hadn't even realized that Joe had followed him inside.

"You couldn't get her away?"

"No man, I had no idea. No one did. They just showed up, I swear."

"I believe you, Joe."

"Tank, I gotta tell you something else."

Tank turned to Joe. He knew just by seeing Joe's face he wasn't going to be happy with what he had to say.

"Tank, I think Cara called in the tip."

"You have got to be fucking kidding me."

"I wish I was. Me and Lolly think she overheard you guys taking that night you were on the porch."

Tank was livid and his body tightened. Joe watched as Tank's fist clenched and unclenched.

"Where is she now?"

"Tank, you have to calm down first."

"What? You think I'd hurt her?"

Joe pointed at Tanks clenched fists.

"Oh, I want to. Trust me, I want to, but I'd never hit a woman. Ever."

"I'm sorry Tank. If I hadn't been thinking with my dick that night she would have never heard anything."

"Yeah, I figured. Don't tell me you like her Joe cause, man, we'd have issues. Not that I care, but she's about to be tossed from her job, this camp, and everything she claimed to care about."

"Want me to get her?"

"No. I'll get her myself."

Tank and Joe walked outside and headed towards the trailer Cara shared with another woman. Lolly and Sweets saw where they were headed and followed.

Cara was outside the trailer sitting in a lawn chair with a few other friends.

When Cara saw him, she jumped up from her chair happily.

"Tank! You're back!" Cara started to put her arms around his neck, but Tank stepped back, forcing her arms to fall quickly to her side.

"Tank? I've missed you," she said quietly. Her friends were watching the entire exchange, as were Sweets, Lolly, and Joe. She had just finished telling her friends that she was sure Tank was going to become her bed companion again and hopefully more.

"Cara, you called the cops on Tess," Tank said without question in a steely voice that dripped with disgust.

"I...I didn't. I would never..."

"You did. You need to pack up and leave. You're fired from your job, you're not welcomed in camp, or anywhere we happened to be. You're dead to us."

Tank turned and walked away. The people around Cara remained stone still and silent. They knew Tank was a tough ass, but none of them had ever been on the receiving end of his wrath. Cara recovered from the shock and ran after Tank.

"Tank!" He didn't stop walking. "Tank!" He continued walking. "Tank!" She was crying now.

Tank turned slowly and faced her. "How could you, Cara?"

"Me? How could I? How could you? You brought that little tramp here and you were my man. You've been my man since last fall. You slept with me. We went out. I love you. She's a criminal Tank, a criminal!" Cara was screaming and her face revealed the hatred she felt towards Tess.

Tank took two steps towards her and she wisely slammed her mouth shut.

"You were a willing convenience, Cara. The fact that you could be so cold hearted to turn Tess in attests as to why I would never, ever, have considered you for more than a suck or bang."

Cara gasped at his harsh words and collapsed onto her knees.

"Tank, please don't do this. I love you."

"I want you gone," Tank said turned away again, and he could hear Cara wailing behind him.

Joe fell into step with him. "Feel better?" he asked sarcastically.

Tank stopped walking and turned to Joe. "I won't feel better until I have Tess back. I don't even know if she's alive."

Joe remained where he was as Tank walked away. Joe had never ever seen his friend demoralize a woman like that. He knew that if Tess wasn't found alive, his friend Tank would never be the same.

Tank showered and even though Lolly brought him a sandwich, he couldn't eat it. He left for Liam's office knowing full well that Toby could be delivering bad news. Sweets tried to accompany him, but Tank needed to be alone. If he found out Tess wasn't alive he didn't want to be around anyone.

Tank sat with Liam in his office waiting for the phone to ring. The second hand on the big old-fashioned clock on Liam's wall ticked loudly. Around 2:45 Liam's phone rang. Tank jerked upright, his stomach pitched, and a cold sweat broke out on his forehead.

Liam answered and then told whoever was on the line to hold on while he or she was put on speaker.

"Go on, Rick," Liam said out loud.

"Mr. O'Brian, this is Sheriff Peters, we met this morning."

"Sheriff," Tank acknowledged.

"We have some news you might be interested in."

"Go on," Tank said.

"My deputy and I brought in a Lester Randal and a Frank Randal; you'd know the latter by the name of Ditch."

"Randal?" Tank asked quickly, not sure if his ears were playing tricks on him.

"Yes. An FBI Agent met us back at the station and we interrogated the men, separately of course. We were able to get some solid information from them. So, first; both of these men are cousins to a man named Dan Randal."

"Son of a bitch."

"A real nasty coincidence actually. Frank admitted to drugging your drink."

"Why?"

"Well, he heard you were going to be building a place on your property that would stop your guys from going to his bar. He had bought it this winter and if your guys stop patronizing it he'd go broke."

"Oh my God, that weasel."

"Anyway, when we told him he was also going to be charged as an accessory for the kidnapping of the women, Tess Green and the FBI Agent, he started talking non-stop. If he were charged with being an accessory to that he'd be eligible for the death penalty. Anyway, he sang like a canary trying to prove he knew nothing about them."

"What about Tess? Is there anything we can use to find her?"

"We think so."

Tank felt a shred of hope filter through his darkness. "Lester is only going to be charged with two counts of kidnapping because he never wanted Tess killed. He liked her and wanted to keep her for himself. The other two men a Rolly Ginder and a Bo Laslow knocked him out so he can claim he had no part with the attempted murders. We've cut a deal with him. He admitted to aiding his cousin Ditch kidnap you."

"This is getting complicated." Liam surmised out loud.

"According to Lester, he was given a good sum of money by his cousin Dan, that we have found a bank transfer for. The money was for kidnapping Tess Green. Like I said, he didn't want her killed. So, we have been talking to Agent Biggs in New York. He's the one that was heading up Ms. Green's case when she was abducted again. We just heard from the District Attorney's office that if Lester can give us any information that will lead us to Ms. Green and Agent Chris, and they are alive, that the D.A. will work a plea deal that would be worth it."

"When will you know more?" Tank asked anxiously.

"Lester is trying to call his cousin in New York as we speak."

Liam leaned into the phone speaker. "Okay. Sheriff Peters, we'd appreciate it if you kept us up to speed."

"You got it." The line went dead.

"It's promising, Tank."

"It's more than we had before, that's for sure."

"What were the friggin chances that Dan Randal was related to Ditch and to this guy Lester?" Tank surmised out loud.

"Is Dan Randal from around here, Liam?"

"I don't know. Good question. I bet the FBI is looking that up, but if not I'll suggest it."

The phone buzzed and Liam picked up the receiver. "Sheriff Ross." He pressed the speaker button and hung up the receiver. "Toby, you're on speaker Tank's here."

"Jesus, Tank, I'm so sorry. I should have never let her do it."

Tank was quiet because he agreed that Toby shouldn't have let her try to entrap Randal.

"Would you have let Breezy wear that wire, Toby?" he said after a brief pause.

"I know. I know. Tess is like Breezy though, Tank. She was adamant. She wanted this to end it and it was a quick way to clear her name. I couldn't have talked her out of it if I tried."

"Did you? Try?"

"I swear I tried to reason with her, but she was adamant."

"What happened?"

"She wore the wire into the bar and followed Randal down a hallway. The owner of the bar had screens to monitor the bar from his office. He recognized her and told Randal. When Tess entered the hallway, they nabbed her. They got the FBI agent as well. Randal and a bouncer named Reese Flynn took off with them."

"Wait. Flynn?"

"Yeah, does the name mean anything to you?"

"Not sure," Tank replied. The fact was that the name did mean something to him, and it was pulling all the loose strands together. Shooter Flynn is the V.P of Satan's Army. Tank realized all these guys probably knew each other.

"Tank, the good news is that we got what we needed on tape to clear Tess."

"Yeah, but the bad news is that you have no idea if she's dead or alive," Tank said solemnly.

"Tank, the FBI is all over this." Toby was desperately trying to be optimistic.

"Toby" Liam interrupted, "has the FBI looked into where Randal's from?"

Tank had hoped Liam would have forgotten that. "Yeah, funny thing, he's from Montana, near Norwalk."

"I understand that you've talked with the Norwalk sheriff's department. You know about Ditch and the men that kidnapped Tess the first time?"

"Yeah, we just heard," Liam answered.

"Are there any leads, Toby?" Tank asked.

"Nothing solid. They are leaning really hard on the owner of the bar, The Hopper, and we're hoping he'll have something new for us. They've been missing for three days..."

Liam knew that the longer someone was missing the less likely they were to be found alive. He interrupted Toby by asking that he be kept in the loop. Then he hung up.

"So now what?" Tank asked.

"We wait. Go back to camp. I'll come get you if I hear anything."

Tank nodded and stood up, trying to appear exhausted. The truth was, he now had an idea as to who might have Tess and possibly even where she was. Tank was going right to the source to find out if he was correct.

Tank mounted his motorcycle and headed out of town, right back to where he'd come from that very morning.

Chapter 21

Tanks reasoning was solid. Shooter Flynn, VP of Satan's Army, and Reese Flynn, from New York City had to be related. He'd bet money that all three Randal's grew up near Norwalk. He also reasoned that all three had a connection to Satan's Army. Tank knew that Satan's Army's home base was near Norwalk. It's why when he and Sweets and Grease had been traveling they had done so Grease and Sweets hadn't worn their cuts. It's also why Ditch hadn't been concerned when Satan's Army was at the bar. He knew them.

Tank had heard rumors years ago, that Satan's Army sold women on the black market. It was one of their biggest moneymakers. Tank figured logically that since Dan Randal was on the run and was as money hungry as Tess said, that he wouldn't kill the women if there was a chance he could sell them. Tank hoped Randal and Resse would reach out to Reese's brother, Shooter, and offer them Tess and Agent Chris. Reese probably didn't even know that the other woman they had taken was a FED. If Shooter did know that Agent Chris was a FED and he refused to take them off Reese's hands, maybe he would know where Reese would have taken them. It was the one thing that helped Tank focus. The one tiny thread of hope he was latching onto. If they were going to be sold that meant they were alive. Please, he prayed, be alive.

Heading towards Norwalk, Tank formulated a plan, one that had many unknown factors. He needed to find the Satan's Army clubhouse and Shooter. It would be risky, but Tank didn't think Satan's Army would knowingly kidnap an FBI Agent. That was something that could bring potential heat down on the club. By him telling Shooter that Randal was going to offer him an Agent, or maybe already had, maybe they would consider this goodwill. If, however, Satan's Army was consciously involved, well then he wasn't sure how he would handle it. Tank wanted to find Shooter and the best way to do that was find their clubhouse. He knew it would be well guarded. He also knew that they wouldn't be stupid enough to have anything at the clubhouse that was illegal. Law enforcement often served warrants on outlaw clubs, hoping to find something incriminating. Tank knew that they had to have a place nearby, where they did their actual business. If Randal had already sold Tess to them, that's the place Tank hoped to find her at.

Tank stopped outside of Norwalk and pulled off the road at a gas station. After filling his tank, he pulled around to the back of the station for some privacy. Tank got off his bike and opened his leather sack, extracting the exhaust wrap he had packed. He had to wait until his muffler cooled down and then, because he wanted to do a good job, it took him an hour to wrap his muffler so that the sound coming from his soft tail was sufficiently lowered.

Tank rode into Norfolk as the sun was setting. He skirted the town looking for anything that might lead him to the Satan's Army Club house. His wrap job was good and the few people he passed on the streets actually saw him before they heard him. Tank got lucky when he rode past McDive. The retreat must have been over because three Harleys with ape hangers were parked outside the dingy establishment. Hoping these bikes belonged to members of Satan's Army, Tank pulled off the road. He had to play the odds, and odds were that these bikes were not recreational, midlife crisis bikes, but outlaw motorcycle club bikes.

He parked his bike behind a business that had closed for the night. He had a good view of McDive's parking lot and the three Harleys. His plan was to follow behind them hoping they would lead him to either the club, where he could have a rational discussion with Shooter, or where Tess and the FBI Agent were being held.

Tank knew if they were going to sell the women, that they'd have to do it quickly, especially if they did know the Feds were breathing down their necks. He was honestly surprised that Satan's Army would risk taking a Fed. The previous Steel Horse Cowboy's President had once told him that their normal M.O. was to take women who would not be missed. Kidnapping a Fed was asking for trouble, big trouble. Tank's body was stiff from sleeping in crappy motels and outside in his sleeping bag for the past two weeks. The seven hours he'd spent on his bike today had also taken its toll. He rolled his neck around his shoulders trying to work out his stiff muscles.

He kept thinking about Tess and how she had looked when he had first met her. How she had kept herself sane for that month and a half of captivity was a testament to how resilient she was. He had to find her. A knot formed in his chest and he absent-mindedly tried to rub it away. She had to be alive. He couldn't believe how fast he had fallen for her. He remembered how Toby had fallen in love with Breezy at first sight. Maybe the O'Brian men just fell hard and fast.

Tank reminisced about the two wonderful weeks he'd had with her. She was witty and had a great sense of humor. She was probably the worst joke teller ever, which only made the jokes seem funnier. When she blushed, he thought she looked adorable. Tank also recognized that she was smart. He had been amazed when she had explained how the bar at The Pen was being run incorrectly. He knew her so well that he joked with her later knowing that she wished she could return to the bar so she could organize the three hapless bartenders. The fact that she had been able to sneak out of the locked closet to care for him still awed him.

He thought back to when he first saw her after her shower. She looked like an angel. Her skin had been practically gleaming from the scrubbing she must have given herself and her hair was shiny and such a beautiful golden color. He loved trailing the soft strands through his fingers, just to look at the different shades.

A loud rumble sound disturbed the quiet night and Tank didn't even have to look up to know it was the Knuckleheads in the parking lot. The three men were patched, and Tank breathed a sigh of relief that he hadn't wasted precious time on a worthless stake out. Tank followed from an inconspicuous distance behind them as they rode out of town. The only worry Tank now had was if he happened to encounter club members coming from the opposite direction; towards him. He had turned off all the lights on his Harley and he was wrapped. No lights and wrapped meant you wanted to be unknown. If they saw that, they would surely turn around to check him out.

Chapter 22

Tank cautiously rode a good distance behind the three men as they sped down the two-lane road. He could hear their bikes and at first he followed them by sound. When they finally turned off the paved road onto an innocuous dirt lane, Tank hung back even further because now he could not only hear them, but he could also follow the trails of dust that hung in the moon's silvery light. Tank could see the small specks of illumination from the Knucklehead's headlights bouncing off the road ahead of him. Tank slowed even further as lights from a structure up ahead came into view.

Adrenaline spiked as he shut off his engine before pushing his bike into the woods on the side of the road. He had to make sure that if another bike came down the road, the chrome on his Harley wouldn't reflect off the headlights. He hated to do it, but he laid his bike down and covered it with leaves and debris from the ground.

Tank walked as silently as possible in the woods along road purposely counting his steps as he made his way toward the lights. The moon was almost full and cast a pale glow, allowing him to see a few yards ahead as he gingerly picked his way through the trees. When he got to the very edge of the clearing, he saw he was at a seedy encampment. He was a few yards away from a rusty, burned out, opened topped oil drum that was most likely used to burn trash in. By Tank's count he was sixty-five paces from his bike. Next to the drum Tank eyed a rock about the size of his fist. He picked it up thinking it could be used as a weapon or a distraction. He had his gun with him, but it was back in his saddlebag. Tank had decided if he was caught the less threatening he appeared, the better.

He wasn't sure if he had found the clubhouse, a residence, or Satan's Army elusive place of business so he scanned the area looking for clues. He saw that there were five choppers, a van, and a truck that was hitched to a large RV camper. To his left was an armed man guarding the driveway's entrance and to Tank's right was a semi-truck with two shipping container on its bed. Tank decided that he'd landed at one of their mobile sites. Club's often moved their illegal camp sites to stay off the laws radar.

A television was on inside the camper and he could hear the laugh track and see the bluish light emitting from under a shaded window. Tank could make out that the guard, who was sitting in a lawn chair at the driveway's entrance, had a semi-automatic assault rifle lying across his lap. Tank soundlessly headed in the opposite direction toward the big rig with the containers. Slowly he inched towards the containers. He froze when he saw a man sitting on a large rock in front of a small fire. The man was leafing through a magazine and he too had an assault rifle perched across his lap.

Sweat trickled down Tank's neck as he crept behind the small encampment. He wondered if Tess was inside the camper or maybe one of the containers. His belly tightened thinking of what kind of condition she could be in. Tank was behind the guard near the fire, but still hidden by the cover of the dark woods. The tree line was only about twenty feet from the truck. Tank cautiously snuck out of the woods and hugged the side of the big rig. He maneuvered himself so that he was directly behind the guard. Before the man could react, Tank slapped his hand over the man's mouth and conked him over the head with the rock. Tank dragged the body into the woods. He could see the man was still breathing, but he was going to have a major headache when he came to. Tank jogged back to the truck remaining in the shadows.

There were no locks on the shipping containers doors, but Tank knew you couldn't open them from the inside anyway. He tossed some dirt on the fire hoping to dim the light it was throwing off. If the women were in the containers and he could sneak them out, he rationalized that would be the best scenario; he didn't relish confronting Shooter or whoever was in charge. Tank found a foothold on the truck behind the first container. He knew the door would creak loudly when he opened it, so he decided he'd get it unlatched and then open it just a crack so he could look inside.

The metal on metal sound the heavy bar made as Tank pulled it up probably sounded louder than it actually was. His heart was pounding, and he now wished he'd brought some back up. He just didn't want to get any of his friends hurt. He knew they would have never let him do this alone if they'd known what he was up to. Tank pulled the heavy door open just enough to stick his head inside. He silently prayed that he'd find her.

"Tess?"

"Terry?"

He couldn't believe his luck. Tank slipped his body inside the container. When his eyes adjusted to the darkness he saw that Tess and another woman were tied to large wooden crates. Their hands were behind them and they were blind folded.

"Terry, is that you?"

"Yes, shush, let me get you out of here."

The other woman was between him and Tess. He assumed she was the FBI Agent and Tank quickly decided getting her untied first might be the smarter move if it came down to a fight. He ripped the blindfold down and looked at the woman he was now untying. She was trying to get her eyes to adjust to light by blinking her eyelids rapidly.

He whispered to her quickly. "Go left into the woods, skirt the camp clockwise until you get to the rusty oil drum, walk approximately sixty-five steps keeping the drive on your right. My Harley is there, but it's covered. Keys are in it."

The woman nodded.

"My gun is in my saddle bag. There are about nine or ten men here. One armed guard near the entrance and the rest are inside a trailer. My bikes wrapped so when you leave no one will hear you."

"Got it," she whispered.

Tank couldn't get the last knot untied so he took his switchblade from his side cargo pocket and cut through the rope. Agent Chris rubbed her wrists and stood up shaking out her legs.

"Go," Tank urged her. The agent hesitated. "I'll get her out," Tank whispered, knowing the woman didn't want to leave Tess.

"Go. Get help," he hissed, prompting her to move. Tank crawled around the crate that was blocking him from seeing Tess.

"Ter..." she whispered with a scratchy voice. He pulled her blindfold down and when her eyes adjusted and she saw him, her eyes misted with tears.

Tank put his finger to his lips telling her she needed to be quiet. "Baby I'm so sorry about this. Let's get you out of here," he whispered.

Tess nodded. She hoped she wasn't dreaming. She had thought she'd never see him again.

Tank cut through her ties and helped her to stand. He took her small, cold hand in his to lead her out. Tank had to stop himself from pulling her against his body. There would be time for holding her later. Right now, they had to get out of there. Tank pushed the creaky door open so he could jump down, and then he reached back up to help Tess. The second she landed on the ground bright lights turned on around them, blinding them.

Tank pushed Tess behind him so her back was against the truck. Tank was shielding his eyes. He could see their booted feet but not their faces.

"You stealing from us? Big mistake," a deep voice stated ominously.

Tank responded with a steely voice of his own. "Can't steal what's already yours."

He heard a deep chuckle and a large man stepped forward, motioning for the men around him to lower the lights so Tank could see him.

One of the men gasped when Tank lowered his hand from shielding his eyes.

The president of Satan's Army stood proudly in front of Tank. The man was huge. He wore his cut with the president's patch and a handgun was in his right hand.

"And why would you think this is your property?" he asked, truly curious and nodding towards Tess.

"She's my woman."

"Married?"

"She's mine, that's all you need to know."

The large man snickered and shook his head. "Well, she's mine now," he said as the men around them laughed.

Tank looked around at the group of eight men. Tess had a death grip on the back of his tee shirt.

Tank's eyes hit upon a prospect. A prospect was someone who was trying to work his way to becoming a fully patched member of a motorcycle club. It was the asshole that had taken his cut.

"Looks like your men have a nasty habit of taking things that don't belong to them." Tank knew he was playing with fire, but he was hoping to keep their attention on him and not the women. He needed to give Agent Chris enough time to get away.

"Now you've piqued my curiosity. What the fuck are you trying to say?"

"Your prospect over there," Tank said, pointing at the man who had beaten him senseless. "Kidnapped me a few weeks ago, beat me while I was tied up, and then took my cut."

"Your cut? Who are you?"

"President of the Steel Horse Cowboys."

"Really? You're the Tank I've heard about?"

"Shooter knows who I am. Ask him."

The president nodded. Tank could see he was thinking.

The president turned to the prospect. "You steal his cut while he was tied up?"

The prospect looked like he was getting ready to bolt.

"Yeah, I can see that you did." The president was shaking his head and Tank knew he was not happy that one of his prospects had broken one of the cardinal rules regarding cuts.

"I don't want any trouble with Satan's Army, but I'm not leaving here without what's mine."

"You're pretty confident you're leaving here at all," the president said stoically. "I heard you had balls."

Tank remained quiet. In his mind he was running through a few scenarios on how to get Tess away from what was probably not going to end well for him.

One of the men stepped up to the president and said something that Tank couldn't hear. The president nodded to the man and the man walked toward Tank and Tess. Tank moved, keeping Tess protectively behind him. The man hoisted himself up into the open trailer.

"She's gone, Red," the man called from the container.

"Now we have a serious problem," the president, who Tank knew was called Red replied.

The man dropped back down to the ground and there were a few moments of silence as Red contemplated their fate.

"If I let you go, I look weak in front of my men and now I have to go through the trouble of getting that woman back before she makes her way out of the woods. You have now stolen from me." Red's voice was ice cold.

"Did you know that woman is FBI?" Tank asked quickly.

Shock registered on Red's face.

Tank knew he had to try to reason with Red. "I know who gave you these women. They're the ones that the FBI are looking for."

Red whispered to two of the men standing next to him. Tank watched as they jogged away. One man jumped into the cab of the truck holding the containers and started it. Another man jumped into the truck with the RV attached and started that. Both vehicles headed out down the small driveway. There were now five men left, all armed.

"See here's the thing, Tank. I took these women off a friend's hands and I can see now that was a mistake." Red looked at a beefy large man who wasn't a prospect and was not wearing a cut. "However, I can't just let you leave without some sort of punishment. You were stealing from me. So, here's what going to happen. I'm a fair man and I've heard you were a brawler, so here's the deal. Bo and Dog are going to fight you. Bo, because he stole your cut and I know you want a piece of him, and Dog, because he was one of the stupid men that brought me the women."

Red turned around with two of his remaining men and started to walk away. He turned back and looked Tank in the eyes, as if sizing him up. Then Red nodded to the man next to him. "Stay until it's over." The man next him nodded and jogged to his Harley.

"Don't leave them any weapons," Red said to the other man.

Red looked to Bo and Dog.

"If you two are able to walk away from this, don't bother looking for us. You are no longer associated with Satan's Army and you'd be smart to stay out of our territory. Bo, I know you're Shooters brother and I've known you for a while, but I know damn well, that you didn't tell him who these women were."

"I didn't know... I..." Bo was stammering.

"Shut it." Bo quieted immediately.

Red looked back to Tank.

"Where's Willie?"

Tank assumed he was referring to the other guard he'd put into the woods. Tank pointed at the area he had dragged him to.

"Is he alive?"

"He was a few minutes ago."

"Christ, that's my sister's kid." Red shook his head. "Tank, if you walk away from this I still don't expect any trouble from you. If I'd known she was yours... Well let's just say she wouldn't be here. I'm leaving my man behind to report back to me. I'd stay and watch myself, but I can't risk it." Tank nodded. Red had given him literally a fighting chance.

The man next to Red, who Tank could see was a Satan's Army lieutenant, walked over to Bo and Dog and took their guns from them and then he picked up the assault rifle that was on the ground. Then Red and his lieutenant walked to their Harleys. Red signaled for the one remaining guard to join them.

Red drove over to the spot Tank had pointed to and Tank watched him pick Willie up and put him on the back of his bike. They took off down the drive, stopping once at the van to take the keys from the vehicle and pocket them.

The man that Red left behind was astride his running Harley, a good distance from the four of them.

Tank could see Bo and Dog were whispering to each other. Two to one was not something Tank hadn't dealt with before, but Dog was a big man and Tank still had to keep Tess safe.

Tank kept his eyes on the men.

"The big guy is the bouncer from the club. He helped kidnap me." Tess whispered.

Tank used that information to fuel his rage.

"Tess, you have to get into the woods and hide," he whispered.

"Ter, no. I'm not leaving you."

"Baby, if I have to worry about you, I won't be able to focus on these assholes. If they got to you, they could use you against me. Please, baby, hide in the woods, for me."

Tess didn't want to leave Tank, but she knew he was right. If he was worried about her he might get hurt. He felt Tess kiss his back and then she ran for the woods. Bo saw her and started to run after her, but Dog called him back.

"Don't worry about the bitch. We'll pick her up and teach her a lesson after we deal with this piece of shit."

Tank moved away from the small fire pit while he shook out his arms and rolled his neck.

"Bring it," he motioned with his hands.

Tank could see that Bo was nervous, but Dog looked very confident. He was a hulk of a man and Tank hoped he got his muscles from lifting. Strong was good, but strong and agile was better. Tank was both.

Dog stepped boldly towards Tank before putting his head down and rushing him like a bull. Dogs hard body slammed into Tank. Tank was prepared for the hit, so he turn sideways using his hands to steer the missile-like body clockwise, sending Dog flying to the ground. Dog was on his knees and Tank placed a vicious kick into his solar plexus. Dog grunted in pain. Bo chose that moment to jump Tank. He landed a solid punch to Tank's cheek. Tank swiveled, grabbing him by the collar, and peeling him far enough away from himself that he could land a punch to his gut. Bo doubled over in pain but now Dog was on his feet again. He came at Tank like a crazed man. Tank was fending off blows as best he could and landing some of his own. Out of the corner of his eye, he could see that Bo was standing again and Tank knew he had to take him out so he could concentrate on Dog.

Bo rushed him and Tank turned away from the fist-flying Dog, surprising Bo. Dogs punch connected with the back of Tank's head, but Tank was able to land an upper cut on Bo, that was so devastating it lifted him off his feet. Bo was out before he hit the ground. Unfortunately, turning his back to Dog gave the man the opening he needed. Dog slammed into Tank's back, taking him down to the ground. Tank was able to twist so that when he landed he was on his back. Tank was a big man, but Dog outweighed him by at least fifty pounds. Dog jumped on Tank straddling his chest. Tank fought to keep his arms free, clawing and punching at anything he could reach. A cut had opened over Tank's eye and blood poured from it, hampering his vision.

Dog continued to pummel him, but nothing was landing squarely, since Tank kept moving his head and blocking most blows with his forearm. Tank could see that Dog was tiring. The man was crazed trying to end the fight. Spit flew from his open mouth with every punch Dog threw the large man inched higher on Tank's chest. Tank held Dog off for as long as he thought his body could handle the blows. Tank was a good fighter and part of that came from knowing how to fight smart. He was waiting for Dog to punch himself out. Finally, when he felt that Dog's blows had lost some of their power, Tank made his move.

He used his palms to push hard against Dog's thick chest and before Dog could land an unblocked punch, Tank used his knees, driving them squarely into Dog's back, forcing Dog to lurch forward. To prevent himself from falling over Tank's head, Dog tried to regain his balance by placing a hand on the ground. Tank was expecting this and didn't hesitate as he drove his fist, middle knuckle slightly raised, into the front of Dog's exposed neck. Dog grabbed for his throat with both hands. Tank pushed Dog off of him, and while Dog was still on his side, Tank scrambled to his feet and sent his size 13 boot savagely into the thug's chin. Dog to crumble to the ground unconscious.

Tank leaned down, resting his hands on his knees. He heard the Harley moving and looked up to see the Satan's Army member that had been left to watch the fight giving him a little salute before driving off.

Tank stood up and slowly headed down the driveway. He was sore and had taken heavy hits. His eye was swelling, and he attempted to wipe some of the blood from his face. Neither Bo nor Dog would be regaining consciousness any time soon, so Tank headed towards the main road without trepidation. He was pretty sure he had done serious damaged to Dog's windpipe. Bo would regain consciousness, but Tank knew he wouldn't go after him without Dog at his side.

Chapter 23

Tank was peering into the dark woods as he walked, looking for Tess, when he heard her squeal. "Tank!" Tank?

Tess flew into his arms and he held her tightly as she sobbed into his chest. She felt so good and the immense weight of worry he'd been harboring melted away.

"You called me, Tank," he said gently.

Tess wiped her tears and he could see that she had a smile on her face.

"I was so scared. I watched from the woods for a few minutes, but then I thought I should go get help, in case CC didn't make it. You were a tank back there, and I'm so glad you were."

"I still want to be Terry to you, Tess," Tank said softly, looking at the woman who had him believing in happy endings.

"You are my Terry. Oh geez, you're bleeding all over the place. Here, can you rip the sleeve off of this shirt for me?"

Tank ripped the sleeve from her button up shirt and she fashioned it over the gash above his eye to stifle the bleeding.

"Are we safe? Did you? Did you?"

"No, Honey, they're alive," Tess snuggled back into his chest.

"Ter. Thank you. I heard them say we were going to be sold."

"Yeah, I figured. Come on let's keep moving. I'm hoping Agent Chris found my bike and is sending help."

When they walked to where Tank thought he'd left his Harley he was relieved to find it was gone. Agent Chris had gotten away. Tank had taken quite a beating and even although he'd been victorious, his body was coming down from the intense adrenalin rush. He needed to sit down before he fell down. They walked to the end of the hidden driveway.

"Tess, I have to sit for a few minutes."

Tess nodded but was immediately concerned and discreetly looked him over for other injuries she may have missed. Tank leaned back against a tree on the side of the road. Tess sat next to him, worried.

"This remind you of anything?" Tank asked with his eyes closed.

"Yes," Tess giggled, "why do we always end up in the woods?"

Tank chuckled.

Tess leaned against him. "Am I hurting you, Ter?"

"No, baby, I've missed you. You feel great."

They sat quietly for minutes. Tank was listening for the sound of cars or bikes. He hoped Red had kept his word and not sent guys back to finish the job Dog and Bo had botched.

"Are you hurt bad, Ter?"

"No, a little banged up is all. I just needed to sit for a second, I promise I'm fine." Tess cuddled into his body. He felt like home.

They could hear an cars engine in the distance, but Tank needed to be sure. He stood using the tree for support and helped Tess to her feet. They could see a car's headlights bobbing on the dirt road coming towards them. They remained on the fringe of the woods wanting to remain cautious, but when Tess saw that it was not only the sheriff's car, but Agent Chris on Tank's Harley, she jumped from the side of the road before Tank could stop her, causing both vehicles to slam on their breaks.

Agent Chris jumped off the bike and the two women hugged. Tank was holding his side as he slowly came out of the woods towards the Sheriff, who had gotten out of his car.

"Sheriff Peters."

"Do I want to know what the other guys look like?" the Sheriff grunted.

"You can go see for yourself. They're hopefully still on the ground down that drive."

"Christ." The Sheriff called for backup and got back in his car heading down the dark lane.

"So, you're Terry?" Agent Chris asked with a grin.

"Yeah, my friends call me Tank. And you're Agent Chris?"

"Yes, my friends call me CC."

"Okay, CC it is."

The three waited by the side of the road. Tank was relieved when neither woman asked how he had found them, and that Tess never said anything about Satan's Army. Tess was glued to his side and CC was telling Tank about what had happened to them after they were kidnapped from the New York bar.

She explained that they woke up blind folded and tied up but were so close together in what they figured was a van that they could whisper to each other. They didn't hear anyone talking so after a few hours they figured there was only the driver. CC said they were in the van for what felt like days. The man let them pee on the side of the road, but they were kept blind folded and their legs were kept tied as well. When he fed them, he would untie their hands and hand them sandwiches and bottled water. He didn't really talk a lot. Once, CC had asked where they were going, and he told them if they continued to ask questions he'd shut them up. Then they were transferred to where Tank had found them. They heard one of the men say they would bring in some good cash. That's how they knew they were to be sold.

Tank gently rubbed Tess's arm grateful she was alive. She looked worn out and her clothes were wrinkled and stained, but she was smiling, and Tank felt his heart swell with pride at her inner strength. Ten minutes later, two more County sheriff cars drove up. CC directed them down the lane. After another ten minutes, they could hear the cars coming back down the drive. The sheriff had Dog cuffed in the back of his car. He motioned for Tank to get in the front seat.

Tank looked at his Harley. "I got your baby." CC told him, and Tank knew she was referring to his Softail. He looked at Tess, and the sheriff told her to ride in the other car.

Tank got in the passenger seat and could hear Dog wheezing, trying to get air into his damaged windpipe.

"When we get to the station, I need you to tell me what happened, okay?"

"There's nothing to tell. I found the women. I had to fight these guys to get them. I won."

"Mr. O'Brian, I know there is more to the story and I can guess who else was involved."

"I'm sorry, Sheriff. I'm telling you what I can tell you."

"Mr. O'Brian, you could help..."

"Do I need a lawyer?" Tank interrupted him.

"No."

"If I have anything to add, my brother, he's my lawyer, will tell you. I'm not trying to be difficult. I don't know this guy," he said, gesturing with his thumb at Dog.

"The other guy is one of the men that kidnapped my girlfriend and me. I'll testify to that in court and I'm sure my girl will, too."

"Okay, that's good. I can work with that. We think this guy is the bouncer from the club where your gir was kidnapped from."

"He is, Tess will confirm that."

Tank turned around to look at the beefy man still clutching his throat. It was a good thing Dog was behind plexiglass because just thinking that the man had put his hands on Tess had Tank ready to beat the piss out of him again.

When they got to the station, Tess flew right back into his arms and damned if that didn't feel friggin perfect.

"Love your Softail, Tank." CC said, handing him his keys.

"No one has ever driven it before. You're pretty small for such a big bike, how'd she handle?"

"Like a dream. I'm thinking I need one." Tank smiled at the whimsical look on her face.

"The sheriff wants to see you ladies," A deputy told them once they entered the building.

Tank spoke to them before they went in.

"Ladies, I told the sheriff that Bo was one of the men that kidnapped Tess and me, and that I didn't know Dog, but Tess said he was the bouncer at the club and had a hand in kidnapping you. I don't know if you know more than that."

CC gave him a quizzical look, shrugged her shoulders, and went into the sheriff's office.

"Honey, I'm not telling you to lie, but it would be in our best interest if you left Satan's Army out of this.

I don't think CC knows who was holding you guys, but I know you heard."

Tess looked at Tank thoughtfully. "I trust you, Terry. Honestly, we were blindfolded the whole time."

"Good. Say that, but if you could avoid mentioning Satan's Army, I'd appreciate it."

"Red said he would have never held me if he'd known I was yours. I believe him, Ter."

Tank pulled her close and before he settled his lips over hers, he whispered to her softly.

"Missed you so much, woman."

Tess breathed in his leathery scent and moaned gently through his tender kiss.

When they pulled apart, Tank needed to adjust his tightening groin and Tess was looking at him with her sexy blue eyes. Her grin that suggested she was feeling the sexual pull herself.

It took an hour to debrief the women. As Tank had thought, Agent Chris just thought Dan Randal was behind the kidnapping. She identified Dog as the bouncer from the bar and she also added that his voice was the only one she had heard when they were traveling. Tess reiterated the same information, so the Sheriff was satisfied.

It was after midnight when they left the station. The sheriff had called an EMT to meet them at the station and while the sheriff debriefed the women, Tank was attended to. After the EMT closed the gash in Tank's head with a butterfly bandage, he declared Tank was battered and bruised but didn't need to go to the hospital unless he started feeling woozy.

The two women came out of the sheriff's office and walked over to Tank who was waiting for them in the reception area.

"If I need to talk to either of you, will you make yourself available?" The Sheriff was addressing his question to Tank and Tess.

"We'll be at my camp in Happy. Call Liam if you need us."

"Do you need me to find you a place to stay tonight?"

"No thanks," CC said, declining the offer. She had called her boss, Agent Biggs, and relayed what had happened. He told her to sit tight, that he had a local Agent on the way to pick her up. "My ride will be here shortly."

"Tess? Tank?"

"No thanks, Sheriff. I think we're going to get a bit down the road and then find a hotel. "

"Not much out there."

"We'll be fine thanks."

"CC, what did Agent Biggs say?" Tess asked anxiously. She was hoping that the FBI had gotten something useful from the wire she'd worn. Tank already knew the answer, but he knew it would be better if she heard it from someone in an official capacity.

"I'm sorry, Tess, I shouldn't say anything right now. I have to be debriefed and I'm not the lead agent. As soon as information becomes available, we'll get word to you."

Tess looked crestfallen. She was thinking she should probably let Sheriff Peters know she was a murder suspect.

Unable to keep the good news from her new friend any longer she looked at the Sheriff who gave her a curt nod.

"Well, there is one thing I can share with you though." She winked at the sheriff who had a goofy smile on his face. "The wiretap paid off. We got enough on tape to clear you of any wrongdoing. Your lawyer has been working to have the charges dropped, probably as early as tomorrow morning. Oh, my bad, this morning! Congratulations, Tess you did it! You cleared your name!"

"Oh my gosh! Terry did you hear that? Yes!" Tess fist pumped in the air. "Thank you CC" Tess hugged her and then jumped into Tank's arms. Tank was chuckling at Tess's exuberance and CC was beaming, delighted that her new friend had successfully cleared her name.

They said their goodbyes and Tess couldn't stop smiling. She was free! She couldn't believe it was over. The constant fear that she'd been carrying around was gone, leaving Tess feeling euphoric.

Tank walked Tess to his bike. "Hon, I don't have a helmet for you but as soon as we see a place that sells one, I'll get you one. I'll drive slowly. You okay with that?"

"I know you'll be careful. I don't want to wait until stores open either. Let's get out of here."

Tess had to ask Tank to rip her tight skirt up the seam so she could sit astride his softail. Tank gave her his leather jacket from his pack, and they headed out.

Tank's body was still sore, and he was tired and hungry. He could feel Tess coming off her little high and he didn't want her falling asleep behind him, so he pulled off the road and helped Tess off the bike. Tess didn't question what he was doing. She was so tired she was having trouble keeping her eyes open. Tank pulled to the side of the road and shut off his bike.

"Honey, I'm too tired to keep driving and so are you. When I was away, we camped out; I still have the stuff in my bags. Would you mind if we make camp here? Just for a couple hours."

Tess wrapped her arms around Tank and pressed her face into his back. I'm tired too, Ter. If you got a blanket or two it will feel like the Hilton compared to what I've slept on the past week."

Tank guided his bike into the woods and Tess followed him. When he felt they were far enough into the woods he unpacked his sack and handed Tess water and a granola bar. He spread a tarp on the ground and laid a double sized sleeping bag on top of it. Then he tied another tarp to four nearby trees, so it was positioned like a lean to.

"Look at my clever little boy scout," Tess teased him.

Tank smiled. He loved that she was feeling so happy. Tank drank down water from another bottle, wolfed down his granola bar, and they both went their separate ways to pee. When they met back at the sleeping bag, they undressed, keeping only their under clothes on and snuggled against each other in the warm bag.

"This is not what I was planning for our first night back together," Tank whispered against her hair. He heard her giggle and her warm breath tickled his neck. Tess was lying partially on top of him while he was on his back. Her face was resting comfortably on his shoulder, tucked into the nook of his neck.

Tess felt his body responding to her and she teased her fingers down his tight torso, encircling his swelling appendage. Tank hissed when she fisted him, and he bucked slightly into her hand.

"Baby," he groaned sexily.

Tess worked his shaft using the small drop of fluid that leaked from him as a lubricant. Tess felt Tank skim his hand down her side and slip his fingers inside her damp panties.

"Ahhhh," was the only sound she could make when he seesawed through her wet lips.

They made love with their mouths as they kissed each other passionately. Their hands feverously worked to bring each other to climax. Tess's hips were moving as Tank's fingers entered her and his thumb strummed her swollen clitoris. Tess was pumping hard on his thick shaft and twisting softly when she reached his satiny head. They were both moaning their approval. When Tank ran a finger across her spongy g-spot, Tess detonated, grinding wantonly into his hand. She moaned into Tank's mouth as her body convulsed out of control. Tess's tight channel clamped down on Tank's fingers and he felt his own orgasm take hold in his balls before cum shot from his pulsating stalk into Tess's hand. His warm cum dotted his chest and pooled in Tess's hand, but neither cared. Their heartbeats were pounding harmoniously as they slowly recovered from their sensual reunion.

"I really missed you Ter. I missed us." Tess sighed between soft, tender kisses to Tank's neck.

"Me too, Angel." He whispered into her neck before leaning up on his elbow. "Let me get us cleaned up."

"No." Tess stopped him from moving by sliding on top of his body. She stared into his questioning face and gave him a wicked smile. Then she rubbed her cum coated hand on her hip and very slowly and very erotically dragged her breasts back and forth, mopping the pearly drops of his cum from his torso. "I want to wear you," she murmured sexily into his ear.

"Holy fuck, Tess, that's so hot," Tank chocked out.

"I read about it in a book."

"The one on my nightstand?"

"Yeah."

"I think I like this book."

Tess giggled. "It's about a hot, motorcycle club president. I thought it was very après pros."

Tank kissed her lovingly.

"I have so many question, Tess, but I'm so tired."

"Me too, Ter. I have to tell you something though."

Tank didn't like the sound of that.

"You can tell me anything, you know that."

"Ter, I don't know if I should go back to your camp."

"Honey, why wouldn't you want to come home with me?" Tank held her on top of his body, stroking her hair. She lay with her head on his shoulder. Tank was worried that she might want to move back to New York.

"I think someone in your camp told Liam I was there. I don't want to cause you any trouble. I can…"

"Don't even go there, Tess." Tank's voice was low, and Tess knew she'd hurt him.

"Tank, I want to be with you. I do, but not if it's going to cause a problem in your club."

"No, Honey, listen to me, please. We know who called Liam. She's been dealt with."

"She?"

"Cara."

"Oh Tank, I'm sorry. I know you considered her a friend."

"Tess, what she did was spiteful. The club has been good to her. When she did that to you, she showed her true colors. Which reminds me. Want a job?'

Tess laughed out loud. "What?"

"You're a business major, almost a graduate I might add. I need someone to keep the club's affairs in order."

"Are you serious?"

"Very."

"Oh Ter, that's so nice, but..."

"What?"

"Well, what if we break up? Won't that be weird seeing each other every day?"

"No, Tess."

"No? That won't be weird for you?"

"No. We aren't breaking up." Tank kissed her on her head. "Now, let's get some sleep, Angel."

Tess felt all warm and wanted. She snuggled into her handsome motorcycle man's side and fell asleep.

Chapter 24

Tess felt Tank moving beside her in the snug sleeping bag, and when he rolled out of the warm cocoon of the bag, she opened her eyes drowsily. He kissed her forehead, "go back to sleep. I want to clean my bike."
When Tess looked at him like he was speaking a different language, he explained further.
"I had to lay my bike down in the woods yesterday and cover it with leaves. I also wrapped my muffler. I want to take the wrap off. I'll wake you when I'm done, okay?"
Satisfied that Tank was not losing his mind, Tess snuggled back into the bag and dozed off. When she awoke again, she saw that Tank was applying a clear liquid on his muffler with a rag. Tess noticed that his bike was shining in the forest's filtered sunlight.
"Perfect timing," Tank said, as he watched Tess stretching.
"Ter, the khaki colored design on your tank, it's not something I've seen on other bikes."
Tess was referring to a slightly raised adornment that was shaped like the sun, on top of his black tank. Tank leaned over and shined the khaki colored ornamentation.
"It's the sun. It was designed from a piece of armor off of a tank called Chobham armor. Toby brought it back from Afghanistan. He gave it to me as a gift when I became president of The Steel Horse

Cowboys. He was proud that I was going to be taking the club down a lawful path. He knew it wasn't going to be easy. He gave me the piece of armor as a gift and told me how it was a piece from a tank that had saved his life. The tank took a major hit and was out of commission; the army was breaking it down for parts. Toby salvaged a piece, this piece. He said there was nothing tougher than a tank and he said if anyone could take the club legit, it was me."

"That's a wonderful story, Ter."

"Yeah, my big brother is all right. He really understood what I was going through. So, I took the piece of armor to a guy I know in Helena that does incredible work with hard metals and had him create something that I could put on my bike so I would always see it."

"I get the symbolism of armor from a tank and your nickname is 'Tank' and you are definitely a tough guy, but why the sun?"

"That's easy. I love summer!"

Tess laughed. "This one maybe not so much, huh?" Tank walked over to Tess who was still laying in the sleeping bag and knelt down.

"Have you ever heard the saying, 'every cloud has a silver lining'?

"Sure."

"Baby, you're my silver lining." He gave Tess a kiss that set her toes curling.

"Mmmmm, that was a nice way to start the day, Ter," Tess said after Tank ended the kiss. "How did you sleep?"

"I slept pretty well, but I'm looking forward to being in a bed tonight," then shot her a wink, which made her laugh.

Tess dress quickly and then relieved herself behind a nearby bush. She was starting to feel that cloying sense of being dirty again. It was one of the horrible memories that continued to plague her dreams. A posttraumatic residual effect that she knew she'd be dealing with for a while.

She hadn't been raped and she'd slept in closets or sometimes tied to immovable objects, but that awful feeling of not being clean made her skin crawl.

She did realize that she had only worsened how unclean she was now feeling because of her wonton act last night, but she just couldn't resist. The moment had been perfect for her to do it. She was not only dirty but sticky too. The surprised look on Tank's face had been priceless and well worth the little discomfort she was feeling.

Tank quickly broke down their little campsite and they got on the road again. The sun was climbing into the pristine, Montana sky and it was warm enough that Tess didn't need Tank's leather jacket. She wished she had sunglasses though, because the flow of air was making her eyes water and she had to bury her face into Tank's back instead of enjoying the sun's rays. Tess felt the motorcycle slow and when she looked up, Tank was pulling into a combination gas station and convenience store. After they both washed up in the restrooms, Tank bought them coffee and fried egg sandwiches, which they promptly ate. They walked around the little store area and Tank showed Tess where the helmets were, there were four that she could choose from. She selected a green one and Tank had known that if he'd been given the choice, he would have chosen that one for her too. He also bought her a pair of sunglasses, which she appreciated. She hadn't asked him to buy them, but he had known she needed them. Tank steered her to a section of the store that had boots. He had wanted to replace her wedge sandals with motorcycle boots, but Tess insisted she was fine. She hated that she had no money of her own and Tank, knowing how proud she was, recognized this. Tess went to use the restroom again before they left. There was a woman inside brushing her teeth and Tess begged a dab of toothpaste from her so she could brush her own teeth using her fingers. When Tess went out to find Tank, he was standing near his bike and the boots that she had liked best, but didn't want Tank spending money on, sat on the seat.

"Ter, thank you. I love these, I really do, but I can't let you keep buying me stuff."

"Well, for the record, I enjoy buying you things. Would you have bought these if you'd had your own money?"

"Yes," Tess laughed. "You know me so well."

"Let's just say that these boots are your signing bonus."

"My what?"

"You're going to work for me, right?"

"Uh, yeah, I guess so."

"Tesssss."

"Okay, yes, I am."

"Well, in honor of accepting your new job, the company has thrown in a pair of boots to sweeten the deal. You're part of a motorcycle club now. You need boots, woman!"

Tess had her fingers perched under her chin and her other hand was crossed over her waist. Her little eyebrows were crunched up and her lips were pursed as she thought about what he'd said. Tank waited for her to react. Then she unfolded her arm, let out a happy whoop, and launched herself into his arms.

"I'll keep the boots if we can we seal the deal with a kiss? Cause then that's the best offer I've had in a long time."

Tank chuckled and kissed her silly. They broke apart, smiling, a few seconds later but only because a car speeding past on the highway honked at them, reminding them that they were standing in the middle of a parking lot. His kisses did that to her. He laid his warm full lips onto hers and she couldn't think straight. Every female part in her body clamored to life when he looked at her and touched her. When he kissed her, she wanted to crawl up his body and never let go.

"Thank you, Ter. I love them!" She sat down on the ground and slipped off her sandals, which Tank put in his pouch. He watched as she tugged on the black, silver buckled, low cut motorcycle boots. They were a perfect fit, mid – calf height, black, shiny, yet very feminine, and Tess loved them.

"You look sexy, Tess," Tank said quietly, raking his gray blue eyes over her body.

"I feel a little ridiculous in a torn skirt and a grimy top with awesome new boots."

"You don't look ridiculous, baby. You. Look. Hot." Tank's voice lowered and Tess recognized the sexy look he was sending her way. The slight bulge in the front of his jeans sent tingles through Tess.

"Christ, we gotta go now," he said quickly, gingerly settling himself on his bike and extending his hand backwards to help Tess on.

"Thank you, Ter, for everything," Tess whispered quietly into his ear as she got on behind him.

Tank tuned his head. "Your welcome, Angel. Now strap on that helmet because we are going home."

Two hours later, after another restroom stop, Tank and Tess drove up Happy Mountain and into his camp. Everyone that was around heard Tank's bike coming down the drive and ran to greet them as they got off the large Softail in front of his cabin. This time not only was Tank greeted with pats and hugs, but Tess was, too. A warm feeling of belonging surged through her.

"We've been so worried," Lolly said speaking for everyone.

"Toby said you'd been kidnapped again?" one of the other women said.

Tess couldn't answer because the questions kept coming. She heard Sweets tell Tank that if he ever went off alone like that without telling him, he'd find another club. She cringed until she saw Tank smiling at his best friend.

Tank held up his hand and the small crowd around them quieted down.

"Listen, I promise we will tell you everything, but we're really beat and hungry…"

'And dirty…" Tess interjected, causing everyone to laugh because it was almost a joke as to how Tess relished being clean.

Tank continued, "let us clean up, eat, and take a nap. Then tonight, after the kids are asleep, we'll tell you what happened. Deal?"

The group murmured their approval and Tess saw the relief on many of Tank's member's faces, knowing he was home safe. It warmed her to see how much he was loved and respected him.

"Tess, go hop in the shower. I'll join you in a minute. I have to tell the guys something, okay?"

Tess nodded and Lolly gave her another hug. "I'm glad you're back, Tess."

"Thanks, Lolly. I am too." Then Tess took off to enjoy the shower.

"Want me to leave, Tank?" Lolly asked.

"Yeah, only because I don't want the other women to feel excluded, but Sweets can tell you in private what I tell him, okay?"

"No problem." She gave Tank a hug. "Welcome home, Prez." Lolly then went to her cabin.

"Tank, what the hell were you thinking going off alone like that?" Grease said. He couldn't keep the disappointment from his voice.

"I'm sorry, I know the rules, shit, I made the rules. But this is why I wanted to talk to you. When we tell our story tonight, I'll be leaving out the fact that Tess and Agent Chris were being held by Satan's Army."

"Shit man, you fucking didn't?" Sweets groaned.

"I did."

"Tank, we can't war with them. We're..."

"Stop. Listen. Turns out Red, their president had no idea that Tess belonged to me and that the other woman was FBI. The vice president of the club is Shooter Flynn."

"Shit," Grease exclaimed.

"Turns out Flynn and Randal all grew up together. The bouncer at the club in New York City, where Tess and Agent Chris were taken from, is tight with Dan Randal, Tess's ex. He's also Shooter's brother."

"Wow, that's nuts," Joe piped in.

"So anyway, Tess and Agent Chris were being held in shipping containers on the back of a truck. I broke them out. They were going to be sold on the black market, but Red said if I fought Dog, the bouncer, and Bo, one of the assholes who had kidnapped me and the one who took my cut; if I fought them and won, I could walk away."

"Shit, we should have been there," Sweets said in a hushed voice.

"No, man, it turned out perfect. If you guys had been there it would have been considered club business. As it turned out, it was simply me wanting my woman back. Red respected that. He was pissed at Dog for bringing him an FBI Agent and a club's president's woman, and he was really pissed at Bo for taking my cut. He told them not to come around Satan Army territory ever again."

"So, I take it you won."

"Yeah," Tank replied, shrugging his shoulders.

"Someone got a good hit on you though," Joe said, pointing at his bandaged eyebrow.

"Yeah…"

"But you should see the other guy?" Grease finished for him chuckling.

Tank nodded and they all laughed.

"So anyway, I think we're good with Satan's Army. Tess didn't mention them being involved when she talked to the Sheriff in Norwalk and Agent Christ doesn't know. They were kept blindfolded the entire time so they only recognized and can identify Dog because he was involved in the kidnapping and because he was the only one that took care of them. I just wanted you guys to know the real story. Sweets, you can tell Lolly, but make sure she understands it's not something to be shared, okay?"

"Got it."

"So, is everything good here?"

"Yup. Everyone was just pretty worried about you."

"Cara?"

"Gone. I called Gino in Townsend, from Pete's, and told him to change the locks and told him that she no longer worked for us."

"That was smart. I do have a favor. Can someone ride up and tell Breezy that we're back? I'm sure she's frantic. I'm not sure if Toby's back from New York yet."

"I'll go," Grease said.

"Thanks. Could you call Liam from their house and tell him that Tess is at camp? Tell him, in case he hasn't heard, that she's been cleared of all charges."

"That's great!" Sweets said pounding Tank gingerly on his back.

"Yeah, the wiretap paid off."

Tank was still pissed at Toby for allowing Tess to meet with Randal. He appreciated that Toby had acted as her lawyer and gone with her to New York, but if that been Breezy, he knew his brother would have found another way.

"Tell Breezy if she wants to hear what happened to come down tonight."

"Got it, boss."

Tank was getting ready to head back inside when Lolly called him. She was carrying a large platter. "This should hold you over till tonight. The camp is having potluck tonight. Tell Tess to bring the cookies she put in the freezer and that will be your contribution, okay?"

"Thanks, Lolly. You're the best."

Tank put the platter on the kitchen table and walked into his bedroom to find Tess was drying her hair. She was dressed in running shorts and a tee shirt.

"I was kind of hoping you'd still be naked and wet," Tank said with a chuckle.

Tess blushed. "Everything all right?" she asked, referring to Tank's meeting on the front porch.

"Yeah, I just wanted to tell the guys what really happened. Tonight, we will be telling the rest of camp what we told Sheriff Peters."

"You don't have to worry about me, Terry, I understand."

"I know you do, Angel. My woman's smart."

"Your woman," Tess said with a giggle, "so caveman. Why do I like it?"

"I'm glad you like it, Tess," he said, coming up to her and wanting to wrap her in his arms.

Tess threw out her palm to stop him from getting closer. "Oh, no you don't, my man. I'm wonderfully clean. Go shower."

Tank laughed, a wonderful, booming laugh that sent happy buzzes through Tess.

"Okay, I'm going." Tank started to undress. "Lolly made food, it's on the table. Go ahead and start. I know you're hungry."

"I am, thanks."

Chapter 25

Hours later, Tank and Tess emerged from his cabin with cookies in hand. They had stuffed themselves on Lolly's meatball sandwiches, made love, talked about their last two weeks, made love again, and then, completely sated, fell asleep enfolded in each other's arms.

The camp was a flurry of activity getting ready for the potluck dinner. Tank gave Tess a gentle kiss before she left his side to put the cookies on the dessert table.

Gus came sprinting to Tank, who scooped him up and threw him in the air, catching him and tickling him until he tapped out. Breezy and Toby walked to him, hand in hand. Gus had already scampered away, and Tank clenched and unclenched his fist upon seeing his brother.

"Tank, I know…" Toby knew Tank would still be pissed.

"You don't know shit, Toby!" Breezy had never seen Tank this mad, and she subconsciously stepped closer to Toby.

"Tank!" Breezy admonished him.

"No, you listen. I appreciate that you acted as her lawyer and went with her to New York, but I know damn well had that been you in jail," he pointed at Breezy, "Toby would have never, ever, let you walk into that bar with a wire on."

"Tank I…"

He interrupted Toby again. His palm shot out as if warding off his apology.

"She could have been killed. I could have lost her because you gave her that dumb ass option."

"Tank…" Breezy tried to let him know that Tess was right behind him.

"I said listen," Tank spoke harshly, quieting her. "I love her. I have never met anyone like her, and it kills me to think I could have lost her. I can't imagine life without her. She's my happy. Do you get that? She's. My. Happy."

Tank saw that Breezy was smiling and that Toby had a shit-eating grin on his face. That was definitely not the reaction they should be having with him bitching them out. He saw Breezy was looking behind him, so he turned around. Tess stood behind him and he knew she had overheard everything he'd said.

"Tess?" he stammered.

She didn't answer and his first thought was that his public and bold declaration had panicked her.

They'd only known each other a month.

Tank saw Toby steering Breezy away from them and he returned his focus to Tess who hadn't moved.

"Tess. I'm sorry. I…"

"Why are you sorry?" she interjected nervously.

"I…"

"Did you mean what you just said?"

Tank was afraid if he said yes that she'd run for the hills, but he never wanted to lie to her. For Tank, being truthful in a relationship was of paramount importance.

Tank sighed and shoved his hands in his jean pockets. His dark hair fell across his handsome face and Tess watched his eyes change from their normal shade of beautiful gray blue to a stormy gray.

He looked up from the ground and found her eyes with his. "I meant every word, Tess. Every damn word."

He watched her anxiously, hoping she wouldn't turn away from him. Instead, a tiny smile started at the corner of her perfect pink lips and slowly widened. Tank's heart thudded inside his chest.

"Why do you look so nervous?" she asked quietly.

"I thought you might think it was too much, too soon."

"It is quick, Ter, but it's not too much."

Tank had her in his arms before she even finished talking.

That night turned into a welcome home celebration. A few hours later, the potluck dinner had been cleared and the younger children, after roasting marshmallows, were tuckered out enough so that the parents didn't need to coax them too much to get them home. Toby had tucked Gus into a tent set up in the RV area, with three of his buddies. With the youngster bedded down for the night, Tank and Tess told their stories to the twenty adults sitting around the crackling fire. Toby interjected bits of information that neither of them had known.

Evidently, Toby had been turning New York City upside down looking for Tess. The FBI had launched their own search and Toby was given a few leads to follow up on his own. Breezy was livid when she heard where he'd been poking around the notorious NYC docks. Tank knew his brother was going to get an earful when he got home and would need the alone time that Gus' impromptu sleepover at the camp afforded, to get back into his wife's good graces.

The fire dwindled to glowing red and orange embers as the night's activities came to a close. With Tank and Tess's story now told, the group around the fire pit had been reduced to Tank and Tess's closest friends. They talked quietly with each other and enjoyed the peaceful sounds of the wood's nocturnal creatures and the soft breezes rustling through the aspen trees.

The glow from the remaining bits of wood cast the pit with a soft shadowy light. Tess was leaning back against Tank's warm chest, relishing the precious feeling of belonging. Tank was talking to Grease while he unconsciously caressed her neck and shoulders. Throughout the evening they had rarely been apart, and when they were together their bodies sought out contact, hand holding, arms around each other, and now back to chest.

Loud, rumbling, gravel-churning sounds echoed from down the driveway. The men looked at each other knowing it was the hum of bikes, large, raucous bikes.

"Anyone coming in tonight?" Tank asked looking at his friends.

Sweets shook his head and the men around the fire pit quickly stood up. Tank pulled Tess up from the ground. He glanced towards the nearest cabin hoping to send the women there, but the choppers emerged into the clearing of the camp and Tank knew they'd never make it.

The lead chopper slowed and the six other choppers behind him did the same. Tank knew that bike and he knew its rider. Red was leading a group of Satan's Army right into his camp. They were all wearing their cuts. Sweets pushed Lolly behind him and Toby had already placed Breezy behind him. He knew this wasn't going to be good.

Tess felt someone hold her arm and she looked up as Joe gripped her, not so much that it hurt but enough that she couldn't move. She didn't understand why until Tank walked towards the men on their choppers.

Tess wanted to call him back, but the look Joe gave her told her to be silent. Even Lolly shook her head at her knowing Tess wanted to make him turn back. Tank approached the bikes cautiously. Sweets and Grease remained at the fire pit, but they were ready for whatever went down. Tank had given them the signal to stand down so that's what they were doing, at least until it got crazy. Then they were all in.

"You lost, Red?" Tank asked.

"You do have balls, Tank, big, nasty kahunas. I like that."

Tank looked behind Red and saw his nephew at the end of the line of choppers with a bandage around his head. The nephew gave him the finger and Tank chuckled, shaking his head.

"We're not lost, we're here on business," Red admitted.

"We got no business, man." Tank was tense and the slight bulge under Red's cut alerted Tank to the fact they were openly carrying. If Red pulled the gun he was a dead man.

Red reached back to his black leather saddle and pulled something from the silver studded bag, throwing it at Tank. Tank caught it in the air. It was his leather cut.

"Now we got no business, Tank," Red said seriously, knowing it was not what the other club president had been anticipating. Red laughed loudly seeing the surprised expression on Tank's face.

Red kicked his Knucklehead into gear and his men followed suit. Tank stood there holding his cut. He never thought he'd see it again. Grease and Sweets walked up to him quickly and he held up his cut so everyone could see it.

"I guess he wanted to return it," Tank said, with a sheepish grin.

Grease started laughing and Sweets let out a holler that sounded like Tarzan. The men were all clapping each other on their backs. They'd been ready to fight, and they were telling each other which Satan's Army guy they were eyeing up to scuffle with. There reverie was cut short when Toby solemnly informed them that Satan's Army had been carrying and the fight would have been very one sided. The somber news jolted the group back to reality.

Breezy and Toby stood near the pit. Tank could see that Breezy still looked unnerved and she had her forehead pressed into Toby's chest while he whispered quietly to her. Sweets, Lolly, and Grease had settled back near the waning fire. Sweets still had a hold of Lolly's hand.

Tank looked to Tess who had her back to him as she talked to Joe. He realized seeing Red again had probably scared her silly. If she needed reassurance that everything was all right, he wanted to be the one to give it to her, not Joe.

When Tank reached Tess, Joe politely walked away. Tank placed his hand on her shoulder, and she rested her cheek against the top of his hand. Tank pulled her back against him so her back was to his front and he leaned down to whisper in her ear. "Baby, you okay?"

Tess reached both hands up and circled them around Tank's neck. Her ass pressed into his groin as her back bowed slightly. Her lips found his and she felt him harden against her. Tank flexed his hips into her and groaned audibly.

Tess released him from the kiss.

"Tess," Tank was struggling to keep his emotions in check. "Tess, Sweetheart, what you do to me, Darlin..."

"Terry, I ... you..."

"Talk to me, Darlin." He had no idea what the hell was going through her beautiful mind.

"If you ever walk up alone to outlaw biker dudes again..."

"You'll what?" he whispered into her ear, with a little sexy drawl.

"I'll tie you up so..." Tank didn't even let her finish. His hands encircled her waist, holding her close.

"Is that in a chapter in your book?" he said between little kisses. Tess laughed out loud and he knew he had made her relax again.

"If anyone is doing the tying, Sweetheart, it will be me," Tank continued. His voice dripped sex and Tess melted against him.

He swung her up into his arms and kissed her hard.

"Night everyone!" he called over his shoulder as he walked them towards their cabin.

Tess waved and they heard their friends and family laughing as he carried her to his cabin.

Chapter 26

August blew into camp with a huge thunder and lightning storm that took out the lights. The miserable weather that followed the storm kept the camp's residents inside. Tank took Tess into Townsend using Sweets truck so he could show her where she'd be working. He had never mentioned his home and Tess didn't want to presume anything. She was comfortable staying in Tank's cabin with him, but she naturally assumed she would need to find an apartment when they left camp.

As they rode into Townsend, Tess was quieter than usual. Tank kept glancing towards her. He was worried she was beginning to regret telling him she'd work for him. He realized he had tossed the offer out at an unconventional moment, but in his mind, it was a perfect solution. He sure as hell didn't want her going anywhere.

Tess was thinking about her future and she was beginning to feel a little like the weather, gloomy. She loved the cabin in Happy and didn't want to even think about leaving it at the end of the month. Together, she and Tank had worked on personalizing it. They bought furniture and pictures for the walls, kitchen items, and throw rugs. The cabin smelled fresh from handpicked flowers that Tess had arranged in large blue and green mason jars that she found at the local flea market. Her other find at the flea market was a set of blue and green ceramic bowls that she placed sweet smelling pinecones in, adding to the rustic décor that she an Tank both liked. Tess discovered that she had a knack for DIY projects. when Lolly and Breezy had seen the wreath that she had fashioned from small vines and dried flowers, they promptly commissioned her to make them each one. They told her they would gladly pay her, but Tank knew she'd never take any money from them.

Tank had been working on projects at the cabin as well. He had combed through the woods bringing home large, flat rocks that he used to make a stone patio with. Grease had helped him to install a sliding door in the living area that lead out to it. Toby had shown up the day it was done and gifted Tank with a set on Adirondack chairs. It soon became their favorite place to relax.

Tank broke through her thoughts when he reached over and placed his hand on her thigh.

"You're making me a little nervous, Tess. What's keeping you so quiet?"

Tess smiled at Tank and placed her hand over his. "I'm sorry. I don't mean to be so glum. I'm just thinking about stuff."

"Care to share? You know you can tell me anything, right?"

"I know," she paused and sighed sadly. "I'm just thinking about when the summer is over. I don't want to leave camp."

Tank chuckled. "I feel that way every summer, Babe. This year though, I'm hoping it will be easier."

Tess looked at him, puzzled. "Why will it be easier? I would think with all the things you've done to fix your cabin up that it would be even harder to leave."

"You're right. The cabin really feels like a home now and with the prefab going up next week, I am going to be sad that summer is over. But, Tess, this time when I go back to Townsend, you'll be with me and I love that."

Tess blushed and Tank chuckled.

"Are you worried about the job?" he gently pressed her.

"Not really. It's my first real business-related job and I'm ready to tackle it. I do want to finish my degree though."

Tank nodded. "I know you do. We can look into where you can take classes. Maybe they can even be on - line."

"I was thinking that, too." Tess paused; she knew what she was going to say next would not make Tank happy.

"Terry, I have to go back to New York and clear out my apartment." Tank sighed. He knew she had been thinking about that and he hated the thought of her going back there. It didn't help that Liam had told them that they couldn't find Dan Randal and that Tess was the lynchpin regarding the state's case against him.

"I know you do, and I want to go with you..."

"Ter, you don't have to. I have this covered. I emailed CC and she's going to help me. It actually works out perfectly. She's got a little vacation time coming. Camp will still be open. So, after she helps me move, she'll drive with me back here. I'm hoping she can take her vacation time at your camp. I know I should have asked you first."

"You already planned when you're leaving?"

Tess knew Tank was hurt that she hadn't discussed this with him.

"Yes, I heard back from CC yesterday when Lolly and I drove to Pete's. Are you mad?"

"No, I know you need to get your things from back east. I have to tell you that I'm a little hurt you didn't even tell me you were planning it."

"I'm sorry. I knew you'd want to come with me, and I didn't want you to feel obligated to help me and leave camp, especially since there are so few weeks left. With the pre-fab coming I figured if I organized it and had it all set that it would be easier on you."

Tank was quiet and Tess knew she had thrown him with her plans. She unbuckled her seat belt and slid over to him.

"Ter, don't be upset." She slid her hand through his hair and the other lay over his heart. Tank pulled over to the side of the lightly traveled road.

He unbuckled his seatbelt and placed his arms around her.

"Tess, I'm not upset that you are going to be going back East. Well I am, but what I'm most upset about is that you didn't talk to me about it. I love you. I don't want any secrets between us."

"I'm sorry, Ter, I really did keep it to myself because I knew you'd want to come with me."

"I do want to come with you. Randal's still out there and that worries me."

"I'll be with CC, I'll be safe. You need to stay at camp at make sure that everything goes right with the new cabin."

"You're going next week?"

"Yes. I'll be back as soon as I load what I want to keep into the van CC rented for me."

"She rented you a van?"

"Yes, I'll pay her back."

"You really organized this?"

Tess nodded, "I didn't want you to have to worry about anything."

"Tess, when it comes to you I'll always worry." Tank had a small frown marring his face and Tess ran a fingertip gently over his lips. His lips parted and he pulled her finger into his warm mouth.

Tess moved to straddle his lap and Tank pulled her to him with one hand on her hip and the other behind her slender neck. Their lips collided with such need that they both moaned. Tess could feel him beneath her and after a few seconds he lifted her slightly so he could adjust his hard length.

Tess had both hands in Tank's thick hair, keeping him anchored to her lips. Tank's hands roamed her back and slid around her side to caress her breasts. Tess groaned into his mouth as she dampened. Tank ended the kiss and placed his forehead against hers. "Baby, I want you. I always want you, but we're on a public road."

Tess was breathing heavily. The thick bulge pressing against her female bits was begging to be stroked. Reluctantly, Tess slid off Tank's lap and as she moved to go back to the passenger seat, Tank held her arm. She looked up to him and he reached around her finding the middle seatbelt and fastened her in, so that she was sitting next to him.

"Love you, Tess," he said, after giving her a gentle kiss. He kept his arm around her as he restarted the truck and pulled back on to the road.

"Love you, too, Ter," Tess said softly, leaning her head on his chest.

The remained quiet until they got closer to town.

"Tess, I need to tell you something, okay?"

"Uh oh, I don't like the sound of this," she replied anxiously.

"Honey, if you and I are going to have a future, I need you to always be honest with me, no keeping anything from me, ever. It is something I feel really strongly about. Can we agree on this?

Tess sighed heavily, and Tank didn't take that for a good sign.

"Do we need to have serious talk, Tess? It sounds like you don't agree with me."

"No, it's not that. I like full disclosure. I've never been in a relationship where secrets haven't chopped away at it. I don't want to keep things from you. It's just… It's just that I'm so afraid if I tell you how I'm feeling or what I'm thinking, you'll rethink us."

"Rethink us? I don't understand."

"Well, I know we are dating."

Tank chuckled. "You think?" he said sarcastically. Tess lightly punched his arm.

"Ter, I don't know what to expect when you… when we move to Townsend in September."

"Okay, I'm still lost."

"Ter……." Tess groaned frustrated. "Where will I stay? Are you going to help me find an apartment? Will we still see each other as much as we do now?"

"Okay… okay… I get it."

Tess nervously clasped her hands in her lap. She had no idea what Tank was going to say. She wasn't used to being so transparent with her fears and concerns, especially with a boyfriend. She had learned the hard way to keep quiet and let the man take the lead. This way she wouldn't embarrass herself by revealing her hopes and dreams.

"This is my fault, Tess. We should have talked about this. When you started to have these questions, you should have asked me right away. That's the way we need to be. I know it's a scary prospect to tell someone your fears and personal thoughts, but it's worse to keep it bottled up, hoping the answer might present itself. You might not like what I have to say..."

"Exactly!"

"No, Tess, listen. Even if you don't like what my answer is, or vice versa, we will discuss it."

Tess nodded.

"So, Sweetheart, full disclosure from now on?"

"Yes. I promise."

"Okay, now let's talk about what you're concerned about."

Tank saw Tess cringe and he wished they were someplace that he could hold her.

"I love you. I would, of course, hope to continue dating you. I hope you want the same thing."

Tess remained quiet and he knew her mind was going a mile a minute.

"I would like you to stay with me, at my house, when we move back here."

Tess wasn't sure how to tell him what she was thinking. She knew it would hurt him.

"Tell me what you're think, Tess? Be honest."

Tank had pulled into a parking lot that Tess saw was adjacent to a small brick building with a sign that read O'Brian's over a side door. He cut the engine and turned to face her.

"Okay. Honesty. Here goes." She sighed heavily before continuing. "I'm very concerned that if I live with you and work with you, you'll get tired of me and then when you want to break up with me, I'm going to be left with no place to live and maybe, even without a job. Ter, you have to know I've been down this road. I have to be smart here."

"I get that, Tess, and I told you once before that I don't plan on breaking up with you, but I do get your concerns. Would you like me to find you an apartment?" It killed Tank to suggest that, but he was trying to put her feelings ahead of his.

Tess looked away from him, her emotions were raw, and she felt vulnerable. Tank reached for her hand.

"Yes... and no," she continued. Her voice wavered with uncertainty.

Tank cocked his head indicating he was puzzled with her answer.

"I don't want to break up with you, and I am very much afraid of losing everything, again. But Ter, I'll miss you if I have my own place. I love being with you. I'll worry that..."

"Honey, I've never told anyone that I've loved them before, just you. If you're worried about other women you don't need to be."

Tess nodded, sniffling. She hated being so emotional. Tank recognized this was difficult for her and he wanted today to be fun.

"How about we shelve this discussion for a bit? I know what you're thinking, and you know how I feel. Maybe it will resolve itself." Tank brought her hand to his mouth and kissed the back of her hand.

"I love you, Tess. That's the most important fact you need to get through that smart brain of yours."

Tess smiled up at him and nodded. "I love you, too, Ter."

Tess wiped her face and when she opened the car door Tank was there ready to help her down. When she touched the ground, Tank pulled her close.

"We're sealing this with a kiss, Darlin. Full disclosure. No secrets. We talk out any questions we have and remember that we love each other. Sound good?"

"Sounds scary..."

"Tess..."

"But good, Ter, really good." They kissed tenderly and Tank begrudgingly released her before he ended up carrying her off to his office. He did have plans for her that involved being in his office. Things he'd been fantasizing about, but right now was not the time.

Chapter 27

Tank unlocked the door on the side of the building and escorted Tess into a small warehouse area with engine parts, rows of tires, and boxes upon boxes of inventory.

"This is where we keep the automotive parts. The garage bays are on the other side of the building along with a storefront that stocks items such as car mats, wiper fluid, everything that customers might want for their car can be purchased here. I'll show you that later."

He led her down a hallway and opened a door. Inside was a desk that was completely laden with papers and unopened envelopes. Tess looked at Tank.

"Yup, my office. The guys have been putting things on my desk that need my attention. You can see why I need someone with your expertise," he sighed wearily, thinking about tackling the papers on his desk.

Tess looked around the rest of the room. There was a file cabinet and a window that was in dire of need of cleaning, but other than that it resembled his cabin, very utilitarian with no personal embellishments.

Next, Tank walked them a little further down the hall and opened another door. This room didn't have a window, or the clutter. The desk was free of papers and there was a file cabinet against the wall with a lock and keys dangling from it. On a bookshelf there were large buying guide manuals organized by year. There were a few pictures on the wall but the one that caught Tess's attention was on the desk. It was a picture of Cara with Tank standing behind her, holding her intimately in his arms. They both had huge smiles on their faces. Cara was looking at Tank with adoration and Tank was looking down at her with a carefree and very content look on his handsome face.

Tank saw what Tess was looking at and swore as he took the picture off the desk and tossed it in the nearby garbage can.

"That should have been cleared out of here, Tess." Tess couldn't say anything that wouldn't have sounded trite and bitchy, so she kept her mouth shut. A niggle of doubt pierced her happy bubble.

"So, this will be your office. I'll get you a new desk if you want, and you can decorate or change it any way that you want."

"What exactly will I be doing?"

"I'm hoping you can be the manager for all three business'. Not a secretary. We need someone to manage the accounts, be in charge of advertising, organizing our banking and payroll, things like that. I know it will take some time for you to get use to everything, but we really could use some professional help here. I know you'll do a great job Tess. Do you think you could be comfortable here?" Tank said gesturing to the office.

"Thank you for your confidence in me and yes, I'm sure we can make the office work." Tess wasn't sure how comfortable she would ever be in that office now that she'd seen the picture of Cara and Tank that had obviously been taken in there.

They left the office and Tank showed her a small meeting room that was located further down the hallway and where the bathrooms were located. Then they walked back through the warehouse and Tank brought her in the back entrance of the garage area. Men were working on cars and trucks in a couple of the bays. Another man stood up from behind a desk and greeted them.

"Tank, I didn't know you were coming down."

"Hey, Gino. The weather has been bad, so I decided to bring Tess in to show her around."

"Tess, this is Gino, he manages the garage and tow service."

The man appeared to be in his thirties. He had dark short wavy hair and looked every bit like an Italian man with the name of Gino. He was about 5'8" and he wore green dickies and a blue, button up, grease stained, shirt that had O'Brian's embroidered above the shirt pocket.

Tess shook Gino's hand.

"Nice to meet you. So camp is good, Tank? You get that cabin up yet?"

"Next week. You have to come when we christen it."

"Oh yeah. I won't miss that blow out," Gino said enthusiastically.

"Everything all right here?" Tank asked, hoping he wouldn't bring up Cara. He already knew that damn picture had gotten under Tess skin.

"Pretty good. Changed the locks like Sweets asked. I've seen her around a couple of times, Tank." Tess knew he was referring to Cara. "She talks to the guys at the bar. Heard she's still asking about you."

Tank blew out an exasperated breath. "When we have our next meeting, I'll bring the guys up to speed. I won't dictate who they hang with, but they have to understand she will never be welcomed at club events again."

Tank reached for Tess's hand.

"Tess will be managing things from here on out. Can you find her a set of keys?"

"Sure thing." Gino turned to leave.

"Gino?"

He turned back to Tank.

"I know you and Cara were close. I'm sorry."

"Yeah, my wife was happy though. She never liked her. Thought she flirted with me."

Tank chuckled, "how are Mary and the kids?"

"They're great. We booked a vacation to Cabo in October. We're going to take the oldest one out of school for a few days. Can't wait."

Gino was all smiles talking about his family and Tess empathized with his wife regarding Cara.

"That's great, Gino. You'll have a blast. I've heard it's a great vacation destination. I'm going to drive Tess to see the other businesses. I'll talk to you next week."

"Okay, Tank. Enjoy your last couple weeks of vacation," Gino said merrily.

Tank walked Tess through a side door and into the storefront. A middle-aged woman came flying around the corner and flew into Tank's arms.

"Boss, what are you doing here?"

Tank gave her a friendly hug. "Angie, this is Tess, my girlfriend. She's going to be our new business manager."

"Yeah, I heard we were getting a new one. Nice to meet you, Tess."

"Tess, Angie is Old Knockers' daughter." Tess had met Old Knockers at the camp. He had a small RV and he loved telling stories about the old days.

"And how is my dear dad?"

"Ornery as ever," Tank chuckled.

The two caught up and then Tank led Tess out the front door. They rounded the corner of the building and walked to Sweet's truck.

"Well, what did you think?" Tank asked.

"It seems well run, Ter. You have good people running your business'"

"Yeah, it's the only reason I can get away in the summers. Gino and his family are ski bums. They ski almost every day. It's perfect. He uses his vacation time in the winter. I bet his kids had something to do with Cabo. His wife likes the snow as much as he does."

Tank helped Tess into the truck's cab, and they drove through the town of Townsend. He drove her past his Harley Dealership and right next to it was his RV Dealership. They were not huge, but there was good inventory displayed outside. Tess noticed that both places were also named O'Brian's.

Tank turned down a road that took them away from the main area of town, and a few minutes later he turned down a more rural road. The houses had thinned out and Tess watched as the woods became denser. It took about ten minutes before Tank turned the truck into a very small dirt lane.

"This is my driveway."

"You have a house?" She hadn't really thought about where Tank lived during the winter months.

"You'll see," Tank said with a smile. Tess could tell they were climbing in elevation. At the end of the lane, the woods opened into a clearing, and in the center of the clearing was a large A frame.

"Oh, Terry, it's beautiful," Tess exclaimed.

The A frame had a porch that extended the width of the front of the house. There were two long windows on either side of the door and two more windows above them. Tess noted that a second floor had been added, extending towards the back, but not wrecking the original A frame appearance.

Tank unlocked the door and ushered Tess inside. He flipped the lights on since the gray clouds outside were keeping the natural light out.

Inside, Tess saw that the entire downstairs was open. There was a kitchen, dining area, and large living room. A stone fireplace with a large mantel took up a good portion of the back wall. A sliding glass door next to the fireplace led out to a wooden deck. Tess looked out onto the deck and saw there was a hot tub along with a grill.

"You're going to love the hot tub, Tess," Tank said, with a very mischievous smile.

"I'm sure I will," she replied giving him a wink. They walked up stairs that led to the second floor. Tank showed Tess a small bedroom off to the left that contained one window. It was one of the windows she'd seen from the front. The next door he opened was a bathroom that was the other window she'd seen from the front. Tank opened a door on his right revealing the master bedroom. Tess saw that the entire back of the A frame had been blown out allowing for the large room. Two large skylights were cut into the V shape of the ceiling over the king - sized bed that allowed for natural light to illuminate the room. A large sliding glass door led to a private deck that was wide enough for two chairs and a table. The deck looked out over the back of Tank's property.

"I love sitting out here. It's so quiet," Tank murmured.

"It's beautiful, Tank. Your home is beautiful."
Tank's home was furnished, but not really decorated. A few pictures were scattered about. Tess could see they were of him and Toby at different stages of their lives. One picture looked pretty recent. It was of Toby, Breezy, Mindy, Mandy, Gus, and himself.

"That's at their wedding last November."

"Everyone looks so happy."

"It was a good day."

There were pictures of Tank's friends in the club, mostly hanging around their Harleys. One picture was of an elderly couple and Tank explained it was of his parents.

"So, what do you think?"

"I love your home, Terry. It's so you."

He agreed with a grin, "sometimes during really bad winter storms I lose power for a few days. I have a generator that runs my refrigerator and the septic, but I use candles for light. I even like those days."

"I think I'd like that once in a while too," Tess said. Tank nodded because he knew that she would, and he envisioned the two of them happily snuggling together as they waited for the power to return.

"I like not having a ton of people around. It gets hectic at work and the club is always holding some event on weekends. Sometimes I just need a little down time."

Tess smiled, "well, you already know how I feel about my sacred football Sundays."

Tank pulled Tess into his chest and tilted her chin up with a finger.

"I really want you to rethink moving in here with me, Honey."

"Ter, it would be so easy for me to say yes and…"

"Great!!"

"But… like I said, working next to each other all day and then coming home here. Ter, if you started to hate me because I was suffocating you I couldn't bear it."

Tank sighed, "I can't see that happening, but I'll respect your decision whatever it is."

Tank reached around her and picked her up. Her ankles naturally hooked behind him as she wrapped her arms around his neck. Their mouths met softly, and Tank walked them to his bed. When he sat down, Tess remained on his lap. She could feel his hardness and Tess rocked against it, trying to alleviate the need building inside of her.

"Jesus Tess, I always want you. You're like a drug," Tank pulled off her shirt and helped her pull his off. She unhooked her bra and Tank bent down, licking her erect nipples. Delicious shivers ran through her small frame. They looked down at their jeans and then when they looked back up at each other they started laughing, knowing exactly what the other was thinking. Tank stood and placed Tess on her feet so he could stand up and they both took off their jeans and underwear.

Tess stood before Tank completely naked. It always amazed her how comfortable she was in front of him. Tank raked his eyes over her body and an unbearable angst swept over him. He needed this woman like he needed air. His cock ached from the want pulsing through it and he felt a surge of emotion press into his chest that rocked him.

"Ter, are you all right?" Tess asked, seeing an unusual expression pass over his handsome features.

Tank reached for her, bracketing her slim hips with his large hands and walked them backwards to his bed.

"Ter?"

Tanks voice was husky when he spoke. "I'm going to love you so well, Darlin."

"You always love me well, Ter," Tess whispered softly against his neck. "I wish I knew how to love you better."

Laying on the bed Tank held his weight off by using his forearms. He stilled and looked into her eyes.

"Baby, what are you talking about? I love making love with you."

"Ter, you are the best, most considerate lover any woman could ever want. I wish I knew how to please you more."

"Darlin, you do know I cum every time we're together don't you?"

"Yes, but I want to be your best. I know you've been with…"

"Don't Tess. Making love with you gets better every time. You get me so ramped up, sometimes I'm afraid I'm going to cum like a teenager, before you do."

Tess wrapped her legs over his strong hips and urged him to enter her.

His slit wept as he pressed into her hot tight channel. There was no foreplay. He wanted in and she welcomed him with gentle moans that formed his name. The passion they were feeling played out in their eyes that were locked on each other. Tank worked into her with gentle thrusts and Tess met each claiming thrust with one of her own. When he was fully inside of her, he stilled and dropped his forehead to hers.

"I will always love you, Tess. I know I will."

"Ter...."

He kissed her deeply then drove into her trying to reach depths that she would never forget. Tank masterfully worked her into a delirious incoherent mass of sensations. He gathered her hands holding them above her head against the pillow as he plunged into her warm, glove like sheath. Tess's velvet walls began rippling around his shaft and his balls pulled tight, a precursor to him ejaculating. Tank pulled completely out of her heat and Tess groaned in frustration. He circled the base of his cock with his fist and held tight, thwarting off the orgasm that was ready to rip from him.

Tess had a slight sheen of sweat covering her body. Her core was on fire, her breasts ached, her release had been just moments away. Tank slid down her body and stopped only long enough to suck on each nipple leaving them painfully hard.

He took her hands, which he had pinned above her and brought them down by her sides before pushing them underneath her behind.

"Keep them there, baby," Tank said, softly looking up at her. Tess nodded.

Her arms underneath her pushed her chest out and tilted her pelvis upwards. Tank settled between her open bent legs. He used one hand to part her sensitive wet lips and then he licked her back into a crescendo of sensations that was a note away from the grand finale.

Her body was primed for release as Tank continued to trail his tongue around her exposed bits. Then he drove his tongue into her simmering channel and Tess moaned as his fingers began circling her clit and her virgin rosette hole. It was so intense she started to shake as the orgasm began to build. Tank pulled away from her lips and Tess couldn't stop the aggravated "Terry!" that escaped her mouth.

Tank knelt between her legs and watched Tess as the orgasm that she'd been chasing faded away. Tank smiled and winked before he turned her over and placed pillows under her pelvis. He placed her hands above her head again and told her to keep them there. Tess shuddered but it was from anticipation and not fear.

Tank massaged her rear and proceeded to give her tight, heart shaped flesh tender kisses, licks, and gentle bites. His fingers moved closer to her engorged, sensitive crux and Tess whimpered and wiggled hoping to hurry him there. He gave her a quick slap and then massaged the pink mark away. Tess moaned and Tank sucked in a breath hearing her erotic sounds. She was absolutely perfect Tank thought, just submissive enough to make life interesting.

"Has anyone ever had you here?" he asked softly, leaning over her back to whisper in her ear as he pushed a finger to the puckered edge of her rosy opening.

"No," she whispered back.

"Someday I'll have it, my Angel. Not today, but soon. I want all of you. You're mine, Tess."

Tess was out of her mind from all the synapses firing throughout her overly stimulated body. "Yours, Ter. I'm yours."

Tank pushed her legs together and knelt, so his knees were on either side of her. He pressed his eager cock into her tight channel at an angle that allowed him to penetrate deeper than she ever thought possible. She sucked in a deep breath as she adjusted to his length that filled her completely. "Ter," she moaned. Her body was quivering uncontrollably. Tank slowly set a rhythm that she matched with her hips. He reached around her thigh and stroked her taut clit. Tess was on the verge of a cataclysmic release. Every nerve and fiber in her body was clamoring for release and Tank held the key. He rubbed the wetness that was seeping from her core before erotically spreading her juices, rimming her rosette. Tess was beside herself; the need for release was chocking her.

"Ter, now, make me cum now!"

Tank gently pressed his thumb inside of her as he simultaneously rubbed her clit and hammered his large granite hard length into her hot passage. Every molecule in her body reacted simultaneously and she exploded as wave after wave of undulating orgasmic pulses pummeled her body. Tank drove into her with ferocious passion, and as he found his own release he rubbed her sensitive pearl with vigor, and she exploded yet again. Tess screamed his name and then gripped the hand that was strumming her clit with her own, grinding it unabashedly against herself. She detonated again, this time with such ferocity that she groaned huskily, not even sounding like herself.

Tess was trembling from the three tumultuous orgasms that had racked her body. Tank fell on top of her. Their bodies were moist with sweat and they lay panting as they came back to earth.

Tank recovered first and started kissing her cheek. "Tess, that was the best ever."

Tess nodded and squirmed and Tank lifted so that she could turn around and face him. "You are the best lover, Ter. Three times, Ter. Three times."

"I love you, Tess. I'd give you four…"

"Ter, I don't know if my heart can handle four," she giggled. "Did you spank me?"

"I did," he was grinning wolfishly. "You were trying to hurry me."

Tess giggled. "I was?" she answered coquettishly. Tank chuckled and she heard him mutter, 'minx.' He then wrapped her in his arms and kissed the top of her head contently.

Chapter 28

The next week passed way too quickly for the two of them. Tess didn't want to leave but she knew she needed to take care of things in New York. Tank was miserable as he drove Tess to the bus station. She couldn't fly because she had no picture ID on her. Her pocketbook had been tossed when she'd been kidnapped and that had her license in it. She'd never needed a Passport, so she was going have to look into getting a duplicate license when she was in New York. Liam had issued her a temporary ID she could use while she traveled.

When the bus pulled in, Tank was debating whether or not he should just buy a ticket and go with her. He was unsettled with her leaving, even though he knew she had everything organized and was going to be with CC most of the time.

"Tess, I don't like this," he said, holding her against him and memorizing how she felt in his arms.

"Ter, I'll be fine. It's a three-day ride. I'll be careful and as soon as I can I'll be back. I'll call Breezy and Toby's house when I get there, okay?"

"And when you're heading back, so I know."

"And when we are heading back." She repeated. "I promise. Ter, you will be so busy with the prefab that time will fly, you'll see. Everything will be fine."

Tank grunted and shook his head.

"I won't be fine until you're back in Happy," he mumbled gloomily.

"Oh, my big, sweet, bad ass motorcycle prez. Look at you; being all sentimental." Tess gave his arm a squeeze and Tank held her tighter.

The driver was calling for tickets and Tess pressed a palm against his sad face.

"Tess, please be careful," he said, holding her hand against his face.

"I will, Ter. You be safe, too. I'll miss you."

He took her hand from his face and kissed her palm. "Miss you, too, woman."

"Stay out of trouble, my man."

"You know I will," Tank said, kissing her tenderly.

Tess leaned back and looked him directly in his eyes.

"Ter, I trust you. I've never trusted anyone before and with good reason, but I really, really do trust you."

"Thanks, Tess. That means a lot to me. I know what you've been through."

The driver yelled last call for tickets and Tank gave her an intense kiss that had her heart pounding.

When he released her, he took one look at her face and chuckled.

"Mission accomplished," he said smugly.

Tess laughed, "you are such a man."

"Your man, baby, and don't forget it."

Tess boarded the bus. When she found her seat and looked out the window, she saw that Tank was still on the walkway. She watched him through the tinted glass as the bus began to move. Tess's heart ached as the bus rolled away.

Three days later, when the bus finally got to the
Port Authority in New York City, Tess was a jumble
of nerves and her muscles were stiff from sitting for
so long. She had to change buses a couple of times
and there had been one long layover in Chicago.
When she emerged onto the busy New York City
streets, the cloying smells of exhaust fumes, nearby
food carts, and crowed streets turned her stomach.
Tess took a taxi to FBI headquarters and told the
man at the front desk who she was there to see. A
few minutes later, CC emerged from an elevator. CC
was all smiles when she saw Tess and she looked
her up and down commenting on how Montana life
must be agreeing with her making Tess grin like a
loon. Special Agent Chris Chris knew it wasn't just
beautiful Montana that had her new friend, Tess
grinning ear to ear, but also her handsome
boyfriend.

CC steered Tess downstairs to the parking garage
and she took Tess's bag from her, throwing it into
the trunk. The two women took off towards Tess's
old apartment. Tess asked to borrow CC's cell phone
and she used it to call Toby and Breezy's house.
When no one answered, she left a message on their
answering machine letting them know she had
arrived in New York safe and sound.

As they drove to Tess old apartment, CC explained
that she had already spoken with the landlord, so he
was expecting them. She also told Tess that because
she had not paid rent or been seen for two months,

he had put all her belongings in the basement as requested by the detectives that had been working on Tess's case.

When they reached her building, the landlord, Mr. Tobias, greeted Tess as if she were a long-lost daughter. Tess thought this was strange, he had only spoken to her a few times and that was when she had brought him her rent. Mr. Tobias showed them down into the basement and unlocked a caged in area that contained her furniture, a few boxes, and garbage bags filled with miscellaneous items.

"So, how do you want to proceed here, Tess?" CC asked, poking around the dusty area.

"Well, first let's look for anything that I can use that has my name on it, like a bill, so I can get my license. Then while you're at work tomorrow, I'll close out my bank account and then come here go through all this stuff and decide what I'm taking back with me."

"Sounds good."

They spent a half hour untying garbage bags that were stuffed with personal items. There was no organization as to what was in each bag. Whoever had stuffed them must have grabbed anything within reach and jammed them into the heavy-duty, dark green, plastic bags.

Finally, they had found a couple of bills, Tess's voter registration card, her birth certificate, social security card, and her college picture ID. CC said she thought they had enough, so they locked up the cage. Mr.

Tobias was at the top of the stairs and they handed him the key and told him that Tess would need to get back in tomorrow.

Next, CC drove Tess to get her license. The lines were ridiculously long, and the entire process took an hour and a half, but finally Tess had her license. It was closing in on five o'clock when they left the DMV, so they stopped at a tavern near CC's apartment and ate dinner.

After dinner, CC parked her car in a garage, and they walked to a nearby charming brick building. Tess noticed right away how much nicer CC's neighborhood and apartment was compared to hers. Her furniture was high end, and everything was color coordinated. CC's fun personality was evident in the whimsical and clever way she had decorated it. Tess did not begrudge CC for having the nice place, in fact she was happy for her friend. When Tess and CC had been kidnapped, they had spent many of those terrifying hours talking. Tess discovered she and CC had a lot in common. Neither had family and they had both worked their way through college. CC had been left an inheritance from her parents, whom had been killed in a small plane wreck when she was in high school. Her grandparents had raised her and then a few years later, when CC was in college, both her grandparents died within months of each other. CC had always wanted to be an FBI Agent and as soon as she graduated from Fordham with a bachelor's in criminal law, she applied to the Academy. She was accepted and the FBI had been CC's family ever since.

Like Tess, CC had been in a few relationships with men, but none ever felt right. Men resented her job, especially when she would have to leave at a moment's notice. One man didn't want her wearing her gun when he was with her. Another idiot tried to get her to spar with him and when she quickly restrained him, he had huffed out of the gym calling her a lesbian.

CC told Tess she hadn't been on a good date in a year and was beginning to think she was destined to be alone. The problem with that scenario was that CC really wanted to be a mother someday and she was hoping to become one the old-fashioned way; by being a wife first and then a mother.

The two women chatted about they had been doing since they'd last seen each other in Norwalk, and after watching Sleepless In Seattle, Tess settled in on the couch for the night. She fell asleep wondering what Tank was doing. She knew with the time difference he was probably still up and about. She hoped the prefab had come in on time since she knew that would keep him busy. Tess had told Tank how much she trusted him, and that was true, however she didn't trust other people, namely other women. She knew with her not being there it could be the opening some women had been waiting for. Cara was out of the picture, she was pretty sure about that, but Tank had history and that history included many women. She hated the insecure feelings she had, but with her history with men she knew she had good reason for them. Tank had never given her reason to distrust him, but still she'd been burned before. Tess slept fitfully due to the trifling qualms that kept creeping into her dreams.

The next morning CC dropped Tess off at the bank and told her she'd meet her back at her apartment around two o'clock. They would pack what Tess wanted into the van CC had rented and head for Montana. CC had already mapped the trip out and they figured with them sharing the driving they could manage the thirty-four-hour drive in hopefully three, maybe four days.

Tess made quick work out of the mess in the caged area. She packed a few personal mementos, a quilt that she had bought, clothes, and her jewelry, none of which was worth much. She put unwanted items back into bags and placed her clothes and other soft items into another bag. She packed kitchen items and a small flat screen into a box along with some DVD's she liked. She wanted her bed frame, but she wasn't taking her mattress or box spring. The only other pieces of furniture she wanted included her dresser and nightstand. She also packed one lamp, and her bike. She wasn't taking her living room furniture because, like her mattress it had become home to a family of mice.

When CC pulled up to Tess's apartment, Tess had already hauled most of the items she was taking to the first-floor foyer. CC helped her with the heavier things and even Mr. Tobias lent them a hand.

The last item to be loaded was the dresser. Tess was on the street and CC was in the van as one pushed and the other pulled it, trying to move it far enough inside the cargo hold so the doors would close.

A car with tinted windows crept unnoticed up the tiny street behind them. When it stopped, adjacent to where Tess stood outside the back of the van doors, the passenger side window rolled down. Tess thought it was going to be someone asking for the parking spot, instead she saw a very smug looking Dan Randal sitting behind the wheel.

Tess stopped pushing the dresser, an icy fear paralyzed her, rendering her immobile. She could vaguely hear CC telling her to keep pushing because the dresser still wasn't in the van far enough. An unrecognizable pudda-pudda - pudda sound pounded loudly in her ears and Tess realized it was her heart hammering wildly. Randal pointed a handgun at her, blew her a kiss with his other hand and Tess knew her life was over. A blaring whoop whoop sounded from behind them. Tess almost fainted with fright. Flashing lights accompanied the distinguishable police horn. Randal quickly lowered his gun and sneered at her. The officer used his loudspeaker telling him to keep moving, because he was blocking traffic. Randal pointed his hand at her, like he was firing a gun and laughed maniacally as he drove off.

Tess leaned heavily on the dresser that was partially hanging out of the cargo doors. She was starting to hyper ventilate and she couldn't speak. CC looked over the dresser and noticed how pale she was.

"Tess? What's the matter? Did the police car scare you?" CC had heard the horn and the officer tell the motorist to keep moving.

Tess was staring wide eyed at CC. Her body began to quake, and CC realized something was really wrong. CC used her hip to nudge the dresser over enough so she could fit around it and she jumped down to street level.

"Tess, breathe slowly. In through your nose, out through your mouth." CC had her hand on Tess's shoulder trying to comfort her shaking friend. She still wasn't sure what had happened.

It took a few minutes before Tess was able to speak. She was so unsteady that CC made her sit on the curb.

"Tess, should I call an ambulance?"

Tess shook her head back forth. She was looking down the one-way street with a frightened look on her face. Finally, she was able to talk.

"Dan. I just saw Dan," she croaked out.

"What? Just now?"

Tess nodded. "He pulled up, rolled his window down and pointed a gun at me; he was going to shoot me." Tess starting to hyperventilate again, so

CC talked to her calmly helping her to regulate her breathing. Finally, Tess was finally able to tell CC what happened.

"He was going to pull the trigger, I know it, I felt it. A cop pulled up behind him and told him to move his car because he was blocking traffic. Dan lowered the gun, gave me the creepiest smile, used his hand like it was a gun, pointing it at me and then took off."

"Oh, shit. Not good, Tess. We have been looking everywhere for him. Get in the van. I have to call this in."

Tess scrambled into the passenger seat while CC put her shoulder against the dresser and was able to push it in enough to close the doors. She then got in the driver's seat and pulled out her cell.

Tess listened as CC talked to Agent Biggs. Tess tried to describe the car but all she remembered was that it was a midsized, dark sedan with dark tinted windows. CC hung up and started the van.

"Tess, I want to get you out of here. Are you going to be all right?"

"Yes, let's go, please. I'm fine, I was just so sure I was going to be shot." Tess let out a nervous giggle. "Wow, your life really does flash in front of your eyes."

CC chuckled, "Yeah, tell me about it."

CC drove them out of the city and through the Holland Tunnel. She kept peppering Tess with questions hoping to get more information. She also wanted to keep Tess talking because she knew it would channel her energy and keep her from focusing on the what if; like what if Randal had pulled the trigger.

After they had driven a few hours, CC pulled into a rest area. They used the facilities and bought coffee. CC called Agent Biggs again and then Tess asked to use the phone to call Toby and Breezy's to let Tank know she was on the road.

The phone was ringing and Breezy answered. "Hello?"

"Hi, Breezy, it's Tess."

"Oh, Tess, great timing. Tank just walked in."

Tess heard a lull and then she heard Tank's deep voice. "Tess?"

"Hi." Tess missed him terribly and the whole 'almost got shot thing' had her voice quivering.

"Baby, you on your way home?"

"Yes, we just left. I'm hoping we'll be there sometime on Friday."

"Tess, I can't wait. It feels like you've been away for weeks rather than days."

"I know…" She was fisting her jeans and CC smoothed a hand over her shoulder, knowing that Tess was trying to not get emotional.

"Is everything alright? You sound a little off."

"No everything's fine, really. I just miss you, Ter."

"Tess, the pre-fab is up, the plumber is almost done, and the kitchen appliances go in tomorrow. I can't wait for you to see it."

Tess could hear how excited he was, and she didn't want him to worry, so she decided to end the conversation before he caught on that she really was upset.

"Ter, I have to go it's my turn to drive."

"Oh, okay. Drive safely. I cannot wait to see you."

"Me too, Ter. Me too."

Tess hung up and handed CC her phone. "Couldn't tell him, huh?"

"No. He's so excited about the new cabin he's putting up at camp. It would only worry him, and I am fine, now. I'll tell him face to face, so he can see that I'm okay."

"Are you okay, Tess?"

"Yeah. It was scary, really scary. I guess it just wasn't my time."

"Thank God. I would not want to be the one to have told Tank that something happened to you while you were with me. Talk about scary." Tess laughed at CC's fake shiver.

The women started driving again, placing themselves further and further away from the sweltering, noisy city, and Dan Randal. CC was being vigilant as they drove and at rest stops. She didn't tell Tess, but she was purposely keeping her close. They stopped in Indiana to sleep since both women were tired, even though they'd been sharing the driving.

The next day they stopped less often and made it into Minnesota. They found a Marriot right off the highway and after eating a decent dinner, climbed into bed. CC had been regularly checking in with Agent Biggs and Tess heard her say, "Oh, man," with a hint of concern in her voice. CC hung up and looked over to Tess in the other bed.

"What happened?" Tess asked. "Did they find Randal?"

"Uh, no."

"What CC?"

"Well, Biggs told Toby about your run in with Randal so..."

"Oh crap, that means Terry will know. He's going to be livid that I didn't tell him."

CC remained quiet so Tess explained further. "He has a really big issue with trust and no secrets. Crap," Tess said again.

"There's more," CC said. "They got a hit on Randal. He used a fake ID and got on a plane headed for Idaho."

"Damn, that's not good either."

"Well, the good news is that I know he's not following us, on the road, I mean."

"You've been worried?" Tess asked.

"A little" CC replied with a shrug. "Let's get some sleep. You may be with your man this time tomorrow."

"Yeah, maybe," Tess replied nervously.

"Come on, Tess, he won't be that mad."

"You don't know him CC. He's going to be really, really mad."

"Well, it's not like he could have done anything."

"Yeah but…"

"No, it would have only worried him. You were only thinking of him. He may be upset now, but he'll understand."

Tess was praying she was right. If things went south with Tank, she knew she'd steer clear of men for the rest of her life. He had literally ruined her for other men.

"CC can I use your phone again?" Tess asked quickly.

"Sure." CC tossed her cell.

Tess dialed Toby's house and nervously listened to the phone ringing.

"Hello?" Breezy's sing song voice answered.

"Uh, Breezy, hi, it's Tess."

"Oh, Tess. Hi. Is everything all right?"

"Yeah, I'm hoping to get there late tomorrow. Breezy, is Toby there?"

"Yes, sure. Tess, Tank's here too." Breezy's voice sounded a little nervous.

"Oh, uh, okay, maybe I better talk to Terry then."

"Ok, hold on." Tess could hear some noises on the other end, but the unmistakable sound of a motorcycle starting up came through loud and clear. A few moments later Tess heard "Hello, Tess," and she knew it was not Tank.

"Oh, Toby, hi. I'm sorry to bother you."

"You're not bothering me, Tess. What's up?"

"Toby, did Tank just leave because he knew I was on the phone?"

CC had rolled over and turned the light back on. She could tell Tess was upset.

"Tess," Toby said, "he's just upset, he'll calm down."

"He knows, about Dan?"

"Yeah, he was here when Biggs called."

"Crud," Tess said softly.

"You're going to be here tomorrow?"

"Well, that had been the plan."

"Had been?"

"Toby, your brother just left your house knowing I was on the phone. I think he's made it pretty obvious that he doesn't want to talk to me."

"Tess, listen, he's just hurt you didn't tell him."

"I know. I figured. I just didn't want to worry him, and he was so happy about the prefab. I didn't want to bring him down."

"He's kind of got this thing about honesty."

"Yeah. Well, I was going to tell him when I got there, but bad news travels fast I guess."

"Don't worry about this, Tess. By the time you get here tomorrow, he'll be back to normal. Okay?"

"Yeah, sure Toby. Thanks."

"See you soon."

"Bye, Toby." Tess hung up. She kept her head down. She didn't want CC to see she was ridiculously close to crying.

"Tess?"

"He's so mad he didn't even want to talk to me."

"Ouch."

"CC, maybe I need to rethink where to go?"

"Tess, you're going to see him tomorrow. Just talk to him. If he's still being a jerk, then dump his ass."
Tess chuckled sadly. "Way easier said than done."
Tess reached over and shut off the light.
"Night, CC"
"Night, Tess. Don't worry, okay?"
"Yeah. Thanks for being a good friend CC."
Tears silently slid down Tess's cheeks, wetting her pillow. She had the night to decide what to do. She hated that CC was going to be involved in this. She had taken a two-week vacation to help her and Tess knew she was looking forward to relaxing at Tank's camp. CC was a country girl at heart and was excited to swim in the stream and hike. She had been telling Tess how she was going to beg Tank to let her ride his Harley again.

Chapter 29

The women got up early and were on the road before dawn. Tess hadn't slept much, worried about how Tank was going to receive her. She voiced her negative thoughts to CC, jokingly saying that if she and Tank were done, at least she didn't have anything to pack since everything she owned was in the small van. CC tried to keep her spirits up throughout the long, final day on the road, but she knew her friend was hurting. Selfishly, she really hoped Tess and Tank were going to be okay because she had really been looking forward to spending some time at the camp and simply relaxing. She hadn't had a real vacation in years and the fact that there was no cell service, internet, television, and the closest phone was at Toby's or down at the General Store in Happy, was going to be a welcomed change to her normally plugged-in lifestyle.

They finally arrived in Happy and Tess directed CC up the mountain pass. CC was just as enamored with the beauty surrounding her as Tess had been. They pulled into Tank's private camp drive and Tess's nerves became visible as her hands began to shake. She had missed Tank so much and now she was a wreck at the thought of seeing him. It was just past four o'clock in the afternoon and as they came to the clearing, Tess saw the large prefab cabin to her right. She was glad Tank hadn't put the large building near his cabin. She had liked the privacy his cabin afforded.

The first thing Tess noticed was that Tank's motorcycle was not in front of his cabin. Lolly and Sweets were outside on their stoop and Joe was with them. Tess noticed Grease's motorcycle was in front of his cabin, but she didn't see him. The two women climbed out of the van after parking it in front of Tank's cabin. Lolly walked to the van to greet her.

"Hi, I'm so glad you're back," she said as she gave Tess a warm hug.

"Lolly, this is CC, CC this is Lolly."

The women shook hands and they headed towards Lolly's cabin so Tess could introduce CC to Joe and Sweets.

After the introductions were made, Tess declared she needed a shower and Joe offered to take CC's bag and show her to the cabin next to his that Tank had made available for her.

Tess walked into the cabin that she loved so much and because of all the unpleasant thoughts she'd been having, felt like she was an intruder. She tried to clamp down her fears, but her women's intuition was niggling her and she had come to trust her own intuits.

After showering, Tess walked back outside to where she found CC and Joe enjoying a beer on Joe's front steps. When she reached them, Joe handed her one.

Tess thanked him and leaned against the handrail. Tess screwed off the cap and took a long swallow of the cool liquid. The cabin door next to Joe's opened and Grease walked out with his arms around a curvy redhead. When Grease saw that it was Tess, he and the lady walked to them.

"Hey, Tess. You made good time," Grease commented.

Tess nodded. "Grease, this is CC my friend from New York." Tess didn't want to say anything about the kidnapping in front of a stranger.

"Nice to meet you, CC"

"This is Janet," Grease said, nodding to the woman who was draped around him, clearly wanting to display ownership. Tess noticed Grease didn't mind though.

"So," Tess began apprehensively, "where's Terry?" Joe shrugged his shoulders and shook his head, so Tess looked to Grease.

"I saw him last night. We went to Happy Endings for a couple of beers."

Grease's woman spoke up. "You mean that handsome big guy?"

Grease looked from Janet to Tess clearly anxious. Janet continued, "he was with my friend Beth and they were all over each other. Knowing her, he's probably still in her bed."

Tess saw how Grease had tried to get Janet to stop talking but she must have thought he was just giving her a good hug. Tess's hands began to shake, and she tried to cover it up by taking a swallow of beer. Joe was clearly pissed, and CC was trying to send eye signals of support to Tess.

Grease knew he had to say something. "Well, now, Janet. We left before them, so we have no idea if Tank's left with Beth."

Janet was delighted to be dishing out dirt. She obviously had no idea that Tess was Tank's girl.

"Now, sugar," Janet continued happily, "I was with my Beth in the little girl's room and she said that big handsome man was giving her the vibes, if you know what I mean? And she was definitely taking him up on the offer."

Tess thought she might throw up and immediately excused herself from the group. Joe quickly jogged after her.

"Tess. Tess, stop."

Tess continued towards Tank's cabin, so Joe just fell into step with her.

"Tess, I don't think Tank would…"

"Yeah, Joe, he would. I lied to him. Well, I didn't tell him something. He's mad. I know he values honesty in a relationship. I screwed up. It's over."

"Tess, Honey, you don't know that."

Tess was fighting the tears.

They stood on the steps to Tank's porch.

"Joe, I have a huge favor." Her large blue eyes were rimmed with tears and Joe wanted to pound Tank into the ground for hurting her.

"Name it, Tess."

"It's a lot really."

"Name it." Tess could tell Joe felt sorry for her and was equally mad at his best friend.

"Joe, I need two things. I'd like to store my things in your Mom's garage in Townsend, just until I know where I'm going."

"Done," Joe said.

"And I want you to keep CC here. She needs this vacation. Tell her that you've arranged some place for me to keep my things and that I'm going to drive there and come right back. Tell her there are guys there who will lift out the heavy stuff, so she won't try to come after me."

"But you're not coming back, are you?"

"No. I have to drop the van off, and I'll rent a car. I'll email you as soon as I'm settled and let you know when I'll be back for my stuff."

"Tess, I leave for Afghanistan in two weeks. Why don't you just stay at my house in Townsend?"

"Oh, Joe, that's so sweet. I don't know if that would be the best thing for your friendship with Tank though."

"I'll worry about that. The keys to the house are under the potted plant on the front porch. Can you remember this address?"

"Yes."

"27 Lathrop. Stay the night there, Tess. Think about things. You won't be able to rent a car until tomorrow anyways. You haven't talked to Tank yet. It could all be a colossal mix up."

"Thanks, Joe. I appreciate this. Please don't tell anyone especially, Tank or CC where I am. CC would want to be with me and... well, just help her to have fun here, please?"

"I will, I promise. Tess listen, stay at my place as long as you want. I just got back from there a few hours ago and there's even food in the fridge."

"You're a good friend, Joe. Thank you."

Joe gave her a hug and walked back to his cabin.

"Is she all right?" CC asked.

"No." Joe glared at Grease.

"I'm sorry, man," Grease countered.

"I don't know why you need to be sorry, Grease. That hunky man was clearly not sending out any indication that he was off limits. Seems to me..."

"Shut it, Janet," Grease hissed. Janet looked as if she'd been slapped and her face reddened in embarrassment.

Janet stalked off and Grease muttered 'shit' under his breath before following after her. Joe and CC watched them get on Grease's bike and leave camp. Then CC heard a car door slam shut and looked up to see the van moving. She quickly stood up and Joe put his arm on her to restrain her from chasing after the van that was already heading down the driveway.

"You better move that hand, Joe, before I remove it for you." CC was pissed.

Joe put his hands up in an 'I surrender' gesture knowing CC wasn't catching the van now anyways.

"What the hell? Where's she going?" CC was scowling at Joe.

"She's just going to put her things in my garage in Townsend."

"Is she coming back?"

"I don't know. Tonight, she'll most likely sleep at my house. You know she's upset. If Tank comes home and he brings that Beth woman with him that would hurt her even more. This is a good solution."

CC sighed. "Well, shit. This is not how I thought my first vacation in two years would start out."

Jo chuckled. "So, tell me about yourself, CC? Like, is that your real name? CC."

Joe made her smile. The man was handsome with a capital 'H'. He was big but not overly muscled. His short blond hair screamed military and he had the most amazing smile. She liked how he had immediately hopped off the porch to make sure Tess was all right. In CC's book, good character was everything.

"No. My real name is Chris, and my last name..."

"Oh no, don't tell me it's Chris as well?"

CC laughed. "You guessed it."

"Wow, your parents must have quite a sense of humor."

"Yes." CC smiled thinking about her fun-loving parents. "They did."

"Did?" Joe asked.

"They've passed."

"Oh CC, I'm sorry. I didn't mean..."

"Joe, no worries. I have great memories and at least I had my parents while I grew up."

"You're thinking about Tess now," Joe said solemnly.

CC nodded. "That girl has been through too much. It just doesn't seem fair. Did you know she is only a few credits shy from getting her college degree?"

Joe nodded. "Tank told me. He's really proud of her. He told me she's amazingly resilient and he says she's wicked smart."

"She is. If she didn't like business so much I'd steer her towards the FBI. We need smart, tough woman like her."

"Like you?"

CC blushed, "just saying."

"No need to be modest. Tess talked you up plenty before she left. You know, I think you might be one of the few people she considers a friend."

"Yeah, it's strange. We got so close when we…"

"I know about the kidnapping CC"

"Okay, well, we were bound and blindfolded for days and all we did was talk. We shared how we grew up and some girlish dreams."

"And what girlish dreams do you have?"

She laughed out loud, loving how Joe had completely made her feel at home despite her just arriving.

"I'm going to take the fifth on that, Joe."

They each drank another beer and then Joe invited CC inside where he fixed them hamburgers. He told her he would take her down to Pete's the next day so she could stock her fridge.

After they ate, Joe took CC into Happy to get an ice cream cone. He knew she was tired and still concerned about Tess. He hoped she didn't ask him to drive her into Townsend. He had promised Tess he'd keep her here, but he was worried, too. He decided he'd call his home tomorrow from Pete's. He didn't know if Tess would answer the phone, but he would give it a shot.

When CC and Joe got back from getting ice cream, Joe saw that Tank's Harley was in front of his cabin. He was livid with him for tossing Tess aside. Tank had promised him that he wouldn't hurt her, but he had. Joe knew if they had words it was going to turn ugly. Tank was bigger than him and strong as an ox, but Joe had military training and had held his own with men bigger than Tank.

He parked his truck near his cabin. He saw that CC was looking at Tank's bike.

"He's back," she said quietly.

"Yeah."

"Do you think he knows she came and left?"

Joe looked at Sweets and Lolly's cabin and saw that their truck was gone, and that Grease's bike was still gone. "Maybe not. No one's here that saw her."

CC nodded, "I really don't want to be the bearer of that news, but I owe him my life."

"Yeah," Joe breathed heavily. "I'll go with you."

They got out of the truck and headed towards Tank's cabin. Before they reached his front steps CC stopped and looked at Joe.

"Joe." She had her hand on his forearm successfully stopping him from taking another step and damn if that contact didn't send a zing pulsing through him. "If he has a woman with him I might take a swing at him." Joe could tell CC was dead serious.

He placed his hand on top of hers and smiled. "Get in line, Darlin."

CC's heart did a little flip when he called her 'Darlin'. This man was seriously heart melting. She took a calming breath and walked up the steps, knocking on the door.

They heard feet walking towards them and the door opened.

"C.C!" he exclaimed happily when he saw her. Then it must have dawned on him that she was with Joe and not Tess.

"Where's Tess?" he asked, clearly puzzled.

"Tank, can we come in?" Joe asked.

"Yeah, sure. Where's Tess?" He asked again. Joe could tell he was uneasy.

CC faced Tank. "She left, Tank."

"Left? Why? Where is she?"

Joe watched as his friend sunk into a nearby chair.

"Tank, you were with a girl last night. Tess knows."

"What?" Tank sprang up from the chair.

"Grease's girl told Tess that you and her friend, Beth, hooked up last night."

"But I didn't."

Joe looked at CC, so she took over. "Tank, why didn't you talk to Tess when she called last night? She knew you were at Toby's and that you chose not to talk to her."

"Oh, God!" Tank ran his hands through his hair, clearly upset. "I was pissed that she had lied to me."

"She didn't lie, Tank!" CC was just as agitated.

"She told me everything was all right."

"It was! She didn't tell you about Randal because she didn't want to worry you. She was going to tell you when she got here. She told me you were so happy about the new cabin and she didn't want to ruin your good mood."

"Shit!" Tank was pacing.

"Where is she?"

Joe and CC looked at each other, neither knew what to do. It was either break Tess's confidence or lie to Tank.

Joe looked at his best friend and sighed. "Tank, I'm going to ask you this and I want an honest answer."

Tank nodded.

"Tank, were you with another woman last night?"

"No. No way."

"So, where have you been?"

Tank walked over to his leather sidesaddle bag and pulled out a box. He brought the box back and opened it. Inside sat a beautiful diamond engagement ring and two wedding bands.

"They're beautiful, Tank," CC said quietly. "But I don't understand why you didn't talk to her when she called Toby's?"

"Crap. I was mad. I'll admit it. No, I was more than mad. She should have told me. Then last night I was at the bar and that woman, Beth, was all over me. She sat on my lap and before I could remove her, Grease and the woman he was with walked past us. I pushed her off my lap and told her I had a woman. A woman that I loved."

Joe and CC watched as Tank paced the floor nervously.

"I knew then, right then, God, it was so clear, that I'd never love anyone the way I love Tess. Honestly, I knew she just didn't want me to worry when I heard what happened and that's why she didn't tell me. And yes, I was furious, but I also know that's one of the reason's I love her so much. She will always want to protect me, even when I want to be the one protecting her."

"Well shit," Joe said softly.

"Tell him, Joe," CC said.

Tank looked up from the ring box he was holding. "Tell me what?"

"She's at my house in Townsend."

"You son of a bitch." Tank took two steps towards Joe and CC stepped between them.

"Don't waste your time, Tank. Joe was being a good friend. Where have you been since last night? If you don't mind me asking," CC asked tersely. CC believed Tank, but she'd been fooled before and the detective in her still had questions.

Tank ushered them outside and pointed out the sun on his bike's gas tank that had three grooved out slices.

"I had the rings specially made. I made the band for her engagement ring, her wedding band, and my wedding band from the armor sun on my bike. I drove home to Townsend and slept there so I could to take my bike to my garage in the morning. I had Gino cut the strips off the sun and then I drove to Helena and bought a diamond. I had to take the armor strips to a guy in Helena that works magic with metals, and he forged the bands. Then I took the band back to the jewelers and I waited there all day while he finished the ring. I wanted to have it with me for when the right moment came up."

"Wow, that's nice," CC admitted.

"Yeah, Tank, that's pretty romantic."

Tank shrugged. "What if she doesn't believe me?" His voice was laden with concern.

"She will," CC said. "She loves you, Tank."

Tank grabbed his leather jacket and his bag and walked out the door leaving Joe and CC following behind him. They watched him tear down the driveway.

"Wish I could be a fly on the wall for that little reunion," Joe chuckled.

"Poor, Tess. What she's been thinking this whole time. I hope she did stay at your house, Joe, because if she's already gone we are going to have one big crazy man on our hands."

Joe nodded. "Yeah. Come on, I need another beer."

They walked back to Joe's cabin.

Chapter 30

Tess was exhausted by the time she unloaded the van and put everything in Joe's garage. She had practically dropped the dresser on the driveway lifting it down, but she didn't even care. She then drove the van to the U-Haul place to drop it off so she wouldn't be charged another day. She had told Mr. Tobias she would send him an address to send her deposit so she asked the manager, who was flirting with her, if she could call New York and that she'd gladly pay for the call. Tess called Mr. Tobias and left him Joe's address. She asked that the check be made out to cash. Tess knew she would be leaving Joe's in the morning. She decided she'd leave him a note and tell him to use the check as payment for letting her store her stuff at his place.

The manager at the U-Haul tried to talk her into going out for drinks with him, and after more than one, 'no thank you', he finally took the hint. After the van had been processed, Tess rode her bike back to Joe's. She couldn't shake the awful feeling of loneliness that had settled over her. She knew Tank had a right to be upset that she had lied, but to hook up with another woman, that she couldn't forgive.

By the time she got back to Joe's it was after nine o'clock and she was so tired all she wanted to do was sink into a comfortable bed. She took the spare

347

key out from the hiding spot and unlocked the front
door. She was bone weary and sweaty from moving
everything into the garage and then cycling the two
miles back to Joe's, so she jumped into the shower.
She threw on a tee shirt of Joe's that she dug out
from his dresser. She had left her clothing bag in the
garage and was too tuckered out to go downstairs
and get it. Tess climbed into a bed in the guest room
and fell asleep immediately.

Tank was flying down the mountain. It was after ten
at night and he knew if he wanted to get to Tess
alive he'd better slow his ass down. When he
reached the edge of town he could see the lights on
at Happy Endings. His decision to not talk to Tess on
the phone the night before was coming back to
haunt him. He knew it had been childish. He had
driven into camp and Grease had been on his way
out for a drink, so Tank joined him.
Since Ditch's arrest The Pen had closed down so
Tank had talked to the owner of Happy Endings and
as long as nothing crazy went on Tank and his club
could go in for drinks. Tank knew as soon as the new
cabin was ready, his club members would rarely
leave camp. However, some of the younger guys
liked to check out the ladies and Happy Endings was
proving to be a fun place for them. The Pen had had
plenty of women, but Tank noticed that the ones
that visited The Pen had been too willing and too

wild. Some of his guys liked the sure score, but most of them liked the flirty chase too.

As Tank neared the restaurant, an elk jumped out of the woods landing in the middle of the road right in front of him. Tank held fast to his Harley's handlebars as he expertly maneuvered his large bike around the oblivious animal. Unfortunately, his rear tire skidded uncontrollably on the road's gravelly edge causing his bike to veer sharply into the roadside ditch.

Tank tumbled off his Harley into the small trench on the side of the road and his bike twerked uncontrollably before coming to rest nearby. Tank sat up, slowly shaking out his limbs and waiting for a telltale pain to indicate he was injured. He felt warm wetness running down the side of his face and knew he must have cut his head. He quickly went to his bike and turned the engine off.

It was too dark to see how badly his bike was damaged, so he restarted it and used the lights to check it out. The only real damage was that his rear tire was punctured, Tank could see the gaping hole where it had blown. He couldn't see what had caused the damage, but he assumed it was pretty sharp.

Tank turned off his bike again and began pushing it towards the restaurant.

Well, he thought sarcastically, if there was a silver lining it was that the blowout had happened near the restaurant.

Tank pushed his bike to the rear of the restaurant and looked around to see if there were any cars he recognized. As he made his way to the front doors, he noticed Sweets' truck sitting in the lot. Tank walked inside and as he moved towards the bar, knowing that's where Sweets and Lolly would be, he heard a few hushed gasps. He had forgotten about the blood on his face.

Sweets was standing next to Lolly, who was on a stool, and when they saw him, Tank saw the concern that surfaced on their faces.

"Jesus, Tank what happened?" Sweets asked.

Lolly didn't even give him a chance to answer. "Tank get your ass back to the restroom so I can check you out. You're scaring the customers."

Tank followed Lolly and Sweets followed Tank back towards the restrooms. Before they reached the bathroom the manager came jogging towards them.

"Tank, I told you man I don't want any trouble here."

Tank held up his hand. "Relax, Randy, I crashed my bike just up the road."

"Oh, okay. You're pretty bloody."

Lolly was looking at the manager and before she could say some snide comment to the man, Sweets stepped in.

"Say, Randy, do you have a med kit we could borrow?"

"Yeah, yeah, sure." Randy was tripping over himself trying to undo the unwarranted accusation he had thrown out. "Here, go use my office. Do you want me to call an ambulance? The sheriff?"

"No, no," Tank shook his head. "Just need to get cleaned up, is all."

The manager showed them where the med kit was and left them alone. Lolly washed up Tank's wound and then applied a butterfly stitch.

"What happened?" Sweets asked again.

"Dodged a damn elk and punctured my rear tire in the ditch."

"You're lucky you didn't really mash that head of yours. I'm keep telling you boys to wear helmets."

Tank and Sweets smiled. Lolly had been trying to get them to wear helmets for years.

"Where were you headed, Tank?" Lolly asked, after she applied the last strip.

"You didn't hear?"

"Hear what?"

"Tess is back."

"Yeah, we saw her and the new girl at camp. That's why I'm wondering where you're going?"

"Grease's girl told her I was with a woman here last night."

"Ohhh," they both said together.

"I was pissed she didn't tell me something last night and came down here to blow off some steam with Grease. Some girl was all over me and they saw her on my lap."

"You were gone all day," Lolly said gently, looking to Sweets for back up.

"I wasn't with her, Lolly," Tank said loudly, totally exasperated. "I ran an errand today."

"Okay, I hear ya, relax. What can we do? And it still doesn't explain what you're doing here."

"Tess left camp. She's at Joe's house in Townsend. I'm heading there now. Well, I was." Tank smacked his palm against the chair he was sitting in.

"Want us to drive you, Tank?" Sweets asked.

"I can't ask you to do that," Tank replied, even though it was exactly what he wanted them to do. Someone knocked on the door before pushing it open; Toby's head appeared. "Having a par..." He never finished his sentence.

"What the hell, Tank? What happened?" Toby asked, seeing the steri-strips and the bruise starting to form on the side of his brother's face.

"Relax, Toby, just a little accident. I'm fine."

The door pushed open wider and Tank saw Breezy's head appear.

When she saw her brother-in-law's face she ran towards him. "Tank!"

"Oh, brother," Tank muttered. "I'm fine, all right? Can everyone back off a little? My tire blew. I landed in a ditch. I scratched my face. End of story." Tank was clearly irritated.

Sweets saw how upset his friend was and knew it had nothing to do with smashing his face on the road.

"Hey, Toby, can you give me and Lolly a ride back into camp when you're ready to leave? I'm going to give Tank my truck."

"Sure."

"That would be great," Tank said enthusiastically. They left the office and Randy intercepted them as they entered the bar.

"Can I buy everyone a round of drinks?"

"Not for me," Tank said. "I want to get on the road."

"We'll take you up on that, Randy," Toby said.

"Ladies, why don't you find us a table? We're just going to help Tank secure his bike in the truck bed."

"Good idea. I can take my bike to the garage and fix the tire."

Sweets drove his truck to where Tank had parked, and the three men hefted the large Softail up into the bed. Sweets brought out straps that were behind the front seat and they secured the motorcycle to the hooks on the sides of the truck bed. Sweets tossed Tank the keys and said good luck to him.

"Why's he need luck?" Toby asked, as he drove away.

Sweets chuckled. "Because your idiot brother acted like a child and refused to speak to Tess the other night at your house. Then last night he was being pawed at by a woman and Grease's flavor of the week told Tess."

"Holy smokes."

"Yup. Tess is at Joe's in Townsend. That's where Tank was headed before the blowout."

"This is getting interesting," Toby kidded.

"He really loves her, Toby. Like wham, ton of bricks, real honest to goodness loves her."

Toby chuckled. "Yeah. I know the feeling." Sweets laughed and slapped him on the back good-naturedly.

Chapter 31

It was close to one in the morning when Tess was awakened out of a sound sleep. She sat up in bed and it took a moment for her to recall where she was. The heavy miserable feeling of losing Tank took hold of her and she let a forlorn tear escape unchecked. The stealthy creeping of shoes walking on a wooden floor had Tess sitting up quickly in bed. Tess knew Joe wouldn't come to Townsend and leave CC alone at camp. He promised to take care of her. No one else knew she was there. Tess scrambled out of the bed and silently stole behind the open bedroom door. The footsteps were now climbing the newly carpeted steps. Tess felt her heart thumping madly and she clamped a hand over her mouth to try to quiet her breaths that were obtrusively loud. A dark figure stopped in her doorway and peered into the room. The intruder was using his cell phone as a flashlight. The light cast a small glow on the prowler and Tess could not stifle the gasp that left her mouth. Dan.

She heard him chuckle as he stepped around the door. The same gun he had pointed at her days ago was aimed at her yet again. She wanted to bolt but he jammed the nozzle of the black gun into her side causing her to wince. Dan wrapped his other arm around her shoulder clamping her mouth shut with his hand and whispered into her ear.

"You best keep quiet, my Tess. If anyone else steps out of these rooms they're dead. You understand?" Tess nodded, even though she knew no one else was there, she didn't want Dan to know that. Dan walked her down the hallway looking into each of the other two bedrooms and when he found them empty, he eased up on his hold.

"Well, isn't this nice. Just you and me, like old times."

He took his hand from her mouth but kept the gun firmly planted into her side.

"What do you want, Dan? You should be running. When you're caught…"

"That's just it, Darlin. I will be caught someday, but when I am, you won't be around to testify."

Tess was terrified and her body stiffened as her heart pounded uncontrollably in her chest. She wasn't sure why he hadn't pulled the trigger yet, but she knew whatever he was going to do he already had all planned out.

Dan walked her down the stairs towards the sliding door in the kitchen. That's when Tess saw that the small window above the kitchen sink had been jimmied open.

Dan stopped in front of the window, closed it, and then relocked it.

"We don't need to draw any unnecessary attention here do we, Darlin?"

"What are you talking about?' Tess hissed.

Dan shoved Tess ahead of him pushing her out the already opened sliding door. He then turned and closed the door. His grip on Tess was surprisingly strong and the urge to run was overpowering, but the cold metal nozzle that was now digging into her spine held her in place.

"I'm saying I'm going to make it look like you hung yourself." Dan pointed at a rope he had already hung from a tree in Joe's back yard. Tess backed away from the tree. Her panic level soared, and her eyes widened as pure fear surged through her. She heard him chuckle. "Yeah, that's the look I've been wanting to see. Let's go, my Tess." Dan placed his hand back on her mouth and pulled her tightly against him. He was trying to walk her towards the noose and Tess was fighting wildly.

Tank arrived at Joe's and looked for the van. When he didn't see it, his insides clenched. He kept telling himself she had to be there, praying for her to still be at Joe's. He walked to the front door and reached under the plant for the key. Tank smiled knowing that everyone and their mother knew where Joe hid his house keys. Tank let himself in and just before he began to climb the stairs he saw a flash of light in the back yard. Tank remained in the shadows and when he got to the kitchen he looked through the kitchen window and his blood ran cold.

Tank moved to the side of the window so he could see into the backyard and not be seen by anyone outside. What he saw scared him more than anything ever before in his life. A man was holding Tess to his chest, trying to get her to a hangman's rope a few yards away. Tank saw that Tess was struggling vehemently against him. Tank froze. His immediate thought was to run out back and save his woman, but he checked himself knowing he had to be smarter.

Tank snuck back to the front door of the house then quietly opened the truck's door. He had no idea if the man holding Tess had an accomplice. Tank rummaged quickly through his saddlebag and found his gun buried at the bottom of his sack. He drew back the top bolt and checked the chamber, and then released the safety. Tank crept around to the back using the side of the house for cover until he reached the back. He and Joe had played in that yard all the time growing up. Tank knew every bush, every tree and he now used it to his advantage to get a close as possible to Tess.

The man had almost gotten Tess to the low hanging noose. Tank could see the terror in her eyes. He had worked his way so that he was about fifteen yards from them. The man was alone, and Tank didn't see a gun. The only thing he could think of was to confront the man and hope Tess was smart enough to run so the man couldn't use her as a shield.

Tank heard sirens in the distance, he didn't know if they were coming to them, but he knew he couldn' wait any longer. Tank stepped out of the shadows and leveled his gun at the man.

"Let her go," he demanded with a steely voice. Randal pivoted, holding Tess to him, and that's when Tank saw that he was holding a gun to her side. Tess reached up and clawed at his face, but th man held her tight.

"You bitch!" Tank heard him say as he used his gun hand to wipe at the bloody grooves her nails had left. The man's face contorted in rage. He then pointing the gun at Tess's head and started laughing.

"Is this your new love, my Tess?"

Tess didn't answer.

Tank tried to step closer to them, but Randal levele the gun at him and told him if he moved another muscle he'd shoot Tess. He then re-aimed the gun at Tess. Tank halted, not wanting to do anything to incite the crazed man further.

The sirens were getting louder and Tank hoped a neighbor had called in a disturbance.

"Is he?" Dan hissed.

Tess looked at Tank and the love he saw in her eyes shook him to his core.

"Yes, I love him," she answered quietly looking vulnerably at Tank. Tank realized the man was Randal.

"Well then, let me help put an end to this love affair."

Randal pointed the gun at Tank and right before he pulled the trigger Tess grabbed his outstretched arm and jumped in front of the gun.

The booming sound from the lone gunshot echoed off the nearby mountain and Tank heard himself scream. He watched helplessly as Tess crumpled to the cold ground. Randal was laughing as he aimed his gun at Tank and fired. The bullet never found its mark as Tank threw himself to the ground and fired off two shots that slammed into Randal's chest, throwing him backwards.

Tank dropped his gun and ran towards Tess who was covered in blood. Pandemonium hit the backyard as three Townsend deputies, followed by the sheriff and another man, descended on the deadly scene. They ran into the yard, guns drawn, after hearing the gunshots.

Chapter 32

Tank was barely registering what was happening. He had to be forcibly removed from Tess's side and he knew he was yelling at whoever would listen that she needed help. Tank had tried to press against the wound that was located on the right side of her chest, but he couldn't stop the bleeding. His hands were covered in her blood. He was being led away in handcuffs and he saw the sheriff begin to administer CPR to Tess. Tank howled angrily, trying to run back to her, but the two deputies held him tightly between them. One man was on a walkie-talkie and another deputy was tending to Randal who Tank knew was dead.

Tank was placed in the back of a squad car and handcuffed to a pole that stretched across the back. The man that had been on the walkie-talkie came over to the squad car and leaned in to talk to him through the door that hadn't been closed.

"Are you Tank O'Brian?"

Tank was going into shock; he couldn't shake the image of Tess lying on the ground covered in blood. Tank nodded numbly.

"Is the woman, Tess Green?"

Tank nodded again.

"Want to tell me what happened?"

Tank didn't answer. His throat had dried up and he was on the verge of losing it emotionally. A whoosh-whoosh-whoosh sound permeated the air and Tank

watched as a helicopter landed on the street. Two
men jumped out and ran to the backyard carrying a
flat mobile stretcher.

"Are they taking Tess? Is she...? Is she...?"

Tank's eyes had misted up and he felt a lump in his
throat that threatened to choke him.

"We're air lifting her to County." Tank knew that
was the hospital in Helena.

"She's still...?"

"She's got a pulse."

"Oh, God." The anguish in Tank's voice tore at the
man.

"Tank, I'm a friend of your brother. I'm Agent Logan
McNeil. Can you tell me what happened?"

The two men from the helicopter, along with the
sheriff and a deputy, jogged quickly through the
front yard, all four of them supporting the stretcher.
Tank saw a small, lifeless form belted onto the flat
board.

"Oh, God. Tess," Tank whispered. He followed the
men with his eyes as they placed Tess on the
helicopter, shut the door, and took off.

"Tank, I know you're upset but I really need a
statement from you."

"I hope that fuckers dead" Tank said venomously.
Agent McNeil tapped his pen against his notebook.
"He is."

"I shot him. He was aiming at me and Tess jumped
in front of the gun. Oh my God, she wanted to save
me and..."

"She'll be at the hospital in less than twenty minutes." Agent McNeil told him wanting to give the big man some hope.

"Tell me what happened. Exactly."

Tank sighed deeply and told the FBI Agent why Tess was at Joe's. Then how he had crashed his motorcycle driving into Townsend and that's why he was at Joe's so late. Tank explained how he wasn't even sure if Tess was there, so he let himself in and was looking around, hoping she was, when he noticed movement in the back yard. Tank told him what happened next and when he finished, Agent McNeil saw that tears trailed down the grieving man's face.

McNeil stood up after patting Tank's large shoulder compassionately. He shut the door and left Tank alone in the car.

A few minutes later, the sheriff came to the car with Agent McNeil. They opened the door again.

"Tank, I'm sorry about your girl."

Tank looked up at the two men. He thought they were telling him that she had died en-route.

"She's...?"

He couldn't even get the word out. It stuck in his throat and he sucked in a deep breath knowing his life was never going to be the same.

"No. No. I'm sorry. I just meant that I'm sorry she got shot."

Tank blew out the breath he'd been holding.

"I just got word the helicopter landed a few minutes ago and Miss Green was still holding on."

Tank nodded. The sheriff reached inside the door and unlocked the cuffs from the bar and then unlocked the cuffs from Tank's wrists. Tank didn't comprehend what was happening and he just continued to sit in the car.

The sheriff opened his front door, reached in, and handed Tank a small packet of baby wipes that he'd take from the glove compartment.

Tank mumbled a thank you and began cleaning the dark pink stains from his hands.

The sheriff waited until Tank was done before speaking. "Tank, the shooting, as far as we can tell, was justified. There will be more questions and I'm going to keep your gun, but you're free to go."

The words slowly began to make sense and Tank stood shakily from the car.

Agent McNeil steadied Tank as he swayed slightly. "Tank, I called your brother." Tank nodded. He couldn't think straight. His chest ached and he couldn't seem to get a good breath.

"I need to get to, Tess." Tank didn't realize he had even said that out loud.

"I'll take you. We'll make it in half an hour tops," the Sheriff offered.

The Sheriffs voiced pulled him out of his dark thoughts.

Tanks body was still in shock and Agent McNeil asked him if he had a jacket.

Tank told him his stuff was in the truck, so McNeil trotted over and pulled out the jacket and saddlebag that were on the front seat.

"Put the coat on, man."

Tank took it from him and put it on.

"I'll call Toby and tell him where you're going."

"Thanks." Tank nodded.

The sheriff motioned for Tank to get into the front seat and after making sure Tank was buckled in, he turned on his lights, flipped on the siren, and headed to Helena.

The sheriff was concentrating on driving. He was pushing one hundred on the paved two-lane highway. There were no cars on the road as it was still the middle of the night. The sheriff explained that he was keeping his lights flashing and the siren on to keep any animals away from the road.

"How did you know to go to Joe's house?" Tank asked.

"We got a call from Agent Biggs. Agent Chris had mentioned to him that Tess had said her landlord was acting off; friendly. They taped his phone and discovered Randall had paid him to tell him if he heard from Tess. Tess had called her landlord telling him where to send her rent deposit. Randal knew exactly where she was."

Tank blew out a deep breath. He wanted to kill the man all over again.

The trip to the hospital passed in a blur. Tank was remembering how he had just been on the same road buying Tess an engagement ring, a ring she might never see. He patted the leather sack on his lap and felt the small square box he had wrapped in his favorite blue bandana to keep from being jostled around.

The sheriff turned his car into the hospital parking lot and told Tank he was parking and coming in. Tank hopped out and ran through the emergency room doors. There were a few other people sitting on plastic chairs and Tank hurried past them to the desk. An elderly lady wearing a pink apron greeted him.

"Tess Green? She came in by helicopter."

"Yes. Are you her husband?"

"Fiancé."

"Okay, well, that's family enough for me," she said, patting Tanks hand. "Ms. Green is in the operating room. If you would please take a seat, I'll let the doctor know you're out here."

Tank mumbled a thank you and sat down in the corner, far away from everyone else. The sheriff came in and spoke with the woman at the desk. Tank saw her nod and smile. The sheriff came over and sat a few chairs away.

"Tank, she made it to the hospital. That's a good sign. She's in good hands."

"Yeah, thanks," Tank acknowledged.

Thirty minutes later, Toby and Breezy ran through the doors. Tank stood up and when they reached him they both wrapped him in a hug that sandwiched him between their two bodies. The word that slammed into his mind was 'family.' He had a great family and he wanted Tess to be a part of that family. The lump in his throat that had been slowly diminishing began to reform.

"Toby." The Sheriff had stood and shook Toby's hand.

"Hey, Norm. Thanks for bringing him over." Breezy, this is an old friend of mine. Sheriff Norman Burger.

Breezy shook his hand. "It's nice to meet you. Any word?" She looked anxiously at Tank and then the sheriff. Both men shook their heads no.

"Breezy, Honey, can you stay here for a minute with Tank so I can talk to the Sheriff?"

Breezy must have said yes. Tank had no idea. His eyes were locked on the door he knew the doctor would emerge from.

"Tank? Tank? Tank!" Breezy was shaking his shoulder.

"What?" he answered quietly.

"Tank, you have to be strong for her. When she pulls..."

"If," he interjected.

"When!" she answered forcibly. "She's going to need you to be there for her."

Tank nodded. He looked over to Breezy and thought back to the previous summer. Breezy had arrived a broken woman with zero self-esteem, and after two months in Happy she was transformed into a courageous, cheerful, kind and happy woman whom everyone loved. It reminded him of Tess. She was broken when he had met her; shy, quiet, but she had remained amazingly resilient. There was an inner strength and toughness to her that he had admired in the first few days of knowing her. The last few months he had watched her blossom into a beautiful, sweet, sensual, fun loving person, and like Breezy, everyone who met her, loved her.

Tank turned to Breezy.

"She said she loved me, Breezy. Right before... "

"Of course, she loves you, Tank."

"Randal was aiming at me and she jumped in front of the gun." Tank's voice shook with emotion.

"She's a brave girl."

"I thought maybe I'd blown it with her. You know?"

"Honey, people make mistakes. She made one and you made one. You don't just stop loving someone because of a mistake. Not if you're really in love."

Tank reached for Breezy's hand. "How'd you get so smart, missy?" he said, with a tender smile.

"I got lucky. Two awesome brothers helped me through the worst time of my life."

"We're the ones that got lucky, Breezy."

Breezy wiped a tear from her eye and leaned against Tank's shoulder.

The emergency room door flew opened again and Tank watched as Sweets Lolly, Grease, Joe, and CC came in. Tank could tell CC had been crying and Joe had a hold of her hand.

They surrounded Tank and Breezy.

"You okay, man?" Sweets asked cautiously. The group had no idea what to expect when they got here.

"Yeah. Tess is in surgery."

"We sent Mindy down to camp to tell your friends. We thought they should know." Breezy explained how his club family had been notified.

"Yeah, thanks," Tank said sincerely.

Grease was standing a little further away from the group. Tank realized that Grease probably thought that he was mad at him because of what his girl had said to Tess that had ultimately sent her running. Tank made his way over to him and draped his arm around his shoulder.

"You okay, brother?" Tank asked.

"I think I'm supposed to be asking you that," Grease said morosely.

"Grease, it's okay. Your girl didn't know."

"Yeah, I know. She's not my girl. You know that."

"Well, I didn't know her name."

"It's getting old, you know?"

"What is?" Tank asked, puzzled.

"Banging different girls all the time. I mean I like sex, but when I see Lolly and Sweets, and Toby and Breezy, and now you and Tess, it just makes me want more."

Tank thumped him on his back. "You'll find her Grease. I think you've banged most of the single women in Montana though, so you may need to move to a different state…"

"Oh, man, that's cruel," Grease interrupted with a little boy's pout on his weathered face.

Tank chuckled. Just then the door that Tank had been eyeing all night opened.

The room hushed as the doctor approached them.

"Mr. O'Brian?" he asked, waiting to see who would step forward.

"That's me. How is she?"

"She came through the operation, but she lost a lot of blood. The bullet penetrated just under her shoulder, grazed her lung and narrowly missed her vertebrae. It passed clear through. She is heading to post op. I'm afraid she can't have any visitors yet."

"Please, doc. Just let me see her. Ten seconds, in and out. Please just let me see her."

The doctor surveyed the group and when he saw the sheriff nodding at him he decided to allow it.

"Okay. Really, Mr. O'Brian, no longer than a minute. You'll have to move your group to the post op waiting room and when she regains consciousness, we'll come get you."

"Thanks, yes. Thank you."

Tank followed the doctor through two sets of doors. When they reached another set, he told Tank to put on a gown.

There were eight beds set up in a large room and a nurse's station in the middle of them. Most of the beds were unoccupied. Tank was looking around the room slightly unnerved.

"This is post-op," the doctor told him. When she's stabilized we will put her in her own room, either in ICU or on another floor depending on how fast she recovers." Tank relaxed a little when he heard the word 'recover'. The doctor noticed and offered him a slight smile.

"She seems like a strong woman, Mr. O'Brian. We lost her once on the table, but it took one zap to her heart to bring her back. I'm thinking positive here and so should you."

The doctor stopped walking and Tank looked at the bed where Tess lay motionless. There was a tube down her throat and a black coil inside a clear chamber was obviously pushing air into her lungs. She was hooked to an IV and noisy monitors beeped loudly. Tank saw the catheter tube running from under the sheets to the side of the bed emptying yellow liquid into a bag.

"God, she so pale," Tank whispered.

A nurse came over to them and the doctor told her that 'Mr. O'Brian' would only be staying a minute. The doctor and the nurse moved back to the nurse's station. Tank moved to the head of the bed and knelt down to be closer to her. He laid one hand on her forehead and the other held her hand.

"Baby, please get better. I'm so sorry I didn't talk to you that night. I was a jerk. I wasn't with anyone, either. I love you so much, Tess. Please wake up so I can make it better. Please, Sweetheart, I know it's selfish, but I need you. I may have two families but without you they'll mean nothing." Tank watched as the woman he loved lay motionless except for the machine induced rise and fall of her chest. A tear slid down his face and he wiped it quickly away as the nurse laid a gentle hand on his back.

"Mr. O'Brian, I promise when there's a change I'll come get you."

The nurse helped him take off his gown outside the post op room.

"What happens now?" Tank asked.

"She was in surgery for a few hours, so she'll probably be out until..." The nurse looked at her watch. "I'm guessing around nine in the morning. The doctor will keep monitoring her and when she wakes up, he'll do a full evaluation. If she needs more time in intensive care, we will take her upstairs to ICU. If she's showing progress they might put her in a step-down unit that will allow you more access."

"Okay, step down. I want step down," he repeated. The nurse smiled at him and told him that someone would talk to him after the doctor saw her again. Tank thanked her and walked to the miniscule post-op waiting room that his friends and family now occupied.

"The Sheriff left, Tank. He said to tell you he hopes everything goes well and he'll be in touch."

"Thanks."

"So, how is she?" Breezy asked.

"She lost a lot of blood. Her heart stopped once on the table." Tank heard a small gasp and watched CC bury her head into Joe's shoulder. "The doc says she's a fighter. She's got a tube down her throat and IV's stick in her arm. She looked so pale," he finished quietly.

Toby put his arm over his brother's shoulder. "Don't Tank. She's a fighter. You know she is. Think about all the shit she's been through. You think a bullet is going to stop that woman? Shit, she'll be running you ragged soon."

Lolly saw where Toby was going with his little lecture. "Tank, she'll have you collecting flowers and vines for her to make new wreaths."

"And you'll be running to the store to get stuff for her to bake. You know that girl can really bake," Sweets laughed.

"I bet you'll have to follow her to the swimming hole, cause that girl loves to lie in those warm pockets of water," Breezy added.

"Okay, guys. I get it. Thanks," Tank said with an actual smile. "Listen, why don't you all go home?" Tank was met with murmurings of, 'no', 'no way', 'and we're staying here,' making him chuckle.

Chapter 33

The group sat down on the chairs and sofas around the pristine room. Tank kept looking over to CC and Joe who were sitting on a small couch whispering to each there. He watched as Joe gently touched CC in small subtle ways. He would run his finger over the back of her hand or slide his thumb over her shoulder. Tank wondered if he even knew he was touching her. He noticed that CC didn't move away from his touches either. Maybe everyone was feeling a bit out of sorts, Tank thought as he looked around the room. Breezy was leaning against Toby, his arm wrapped around her slim shoulders keeping her close. Her eyes were shut, but Tank knew she wasn't asleep. Lolly and Sweets were holding hands talking quietly with Toby. Tank looked to Grease, who he discovered was watching the other couples in the room just like he had been. Their eyes met and Grease nodded, letting Tank know that he saw all the love in the room, too. Tank smiled at him and nodded back.

The room was quiet. Everyone except for Grease and Tank had fallen asleep. Tank saw the door opening and a weary doctor stepped in. When he saw everyone sleeping he motioned for Tank to join him in the hallway.

"Hey, Doc."

"Mr. O'Brian, Miss Green is awake."

"She is? That's great, right?"

"I think it's a very good sign."

"Can I see her?"

"I took the breathing tube out an hour ago and she's doing well breathing on her own. We are going to move her to a different room, but I have to be honest, she's pretty frail."

"Can I see her, doc?" Tank asked again.

"Well, you could, but she doesn't want to see anyone, it's strange. I told her that her fiancé was here, and she started crying and became rather agitated. I can't have her getting upset. I don't think seeing her is in her best interest right now. I'm sorry, Mr. O'Brian."

Tank was crushed and ran his hand over his face.

"I just wanted to tell you she was doing well."

"What should I do, Doc?"

"Well, the first thing you're going to have to do is move your little group to another waiting room," the doctor chuckled good-naturedly.

"Step down?" Tank asked hopefully.

"Yes, to step down."

"Then can I see her? I promise not to upset her."

The doctor was looking skeptical and Tank was worried he was going to be barred from her room.

"Doc, I love her. I was an idiot right before she was shot. I was with her because I was trying to apologize. I need to make it right. Please."

"All right, I'll leave word at the nurse's station that after Ms. Green is settled in her room, they should come get you."

"Thanks, Doc. Really. Thanks." Tank shook his hand appreciatively.

When Tank went back inside the waiting room everyone was standing around anxiously.

"She's moving to step down," he said with a sad smile. His friends smiled and clapped him on the back knowing that Tess had just overcome a huge hurdle towards recovering.

"Why so glum, Tank?" Joe asked perceptively. Tank shrugged his shoulders and told him that he was just tired.

A few minutes later, as the little group made their way to the step-down family waiting room, Joe sidled up to Tank.

"Spill it, Tank. I know you way too well," he said softly so no one else could hear him.

Tank looked at Joe and shook his head. "Yeah, you do know me well."

"So, talk to me, Tank."

"The doctor said that when Tess woke up he told her that her fiancé was waiting to see her, and the doc said she started crying and said she didn't want to see anyone."

"Whoa. What are you going to do?"

Tank looked at him and at the same time they said, "Go see her." Tank chuckled and Joe shook his head.

"Tank, CC said she cried when you didn't talk to her that night. She tried to hide it from her, but CC knew, and then when she thought you... well, she was really hurt."

"Yeah, I'm paying for that stupidity now, aren't I?"

"My point is, maybe you do need to give her some space."

"No chance, man. First she needs to hear me out. Then if she still wants space, I'll give it to her."

"You'd give up on her just like that?"

"I didn't say that, Joe. I said I give her some space, about the size of a hospital room to be exact. I love her. I'll never give up on her."

"Shit! That's good, Tank. I think I need some of your romantic lines."

"You mean to use on CC?"

Joe stopped walking. "What do you mean?"

"Joe, you've been touching her non-stop all night."

"No, I haven't," Joe denied immediately, causing Tank laugh. Just like Tank thought, Joe had no idea that he'd been caressing her.

"Yeah, man. You have."

The little group arrived at the step-down waiting room and were surprised that there were no other families in it. They settled back down and then Toby decided he wanted coffee. Sweets said he wanted a muffin and Lolly needed her tea, so Toby and Sweets took orders and left to find the cafeteria.

It was nearing noon and Tank was beginning to think that the doctor had forgotten to tell the nurses to allow him in to see Tess. Tank exited the room, telling everyone he'd be right back. Joe looked at him and knew where he was headed. Tank stood outside the waiting room door, first doing a little recon. He watched as people, that he assumed were visitors, were simply walking past the nurse's station and going into the rooms of their loved ones. Tank decided to go for it. He put his hands in his pockets and didn't make eye contact with anyone as he pretended to know where he was going. He made it past the nurse's desk but there were still nurses and aides everywhere. Tank continued down one corridor peeking into every room and then he recognized what looked like Tess's hand lying still on a beds white sheet.

Tank tiptoed into the room and saw Tess. Her head was slightly elevated, and her eyes were closed. Monitors beeped her vital signs and he saw that her color was returning to normal. She must have even been allowed out of bed because she was no longer catheterized. Tank sat down next to her and he cautiously reached for her hand.

"Baby," he said softly.

Tess's eyes fluttered open and tears filled her eyes.

"Tess, Sweetheart. Please don't cry. I'll leave. I just needed to talk to you."

"Terry, you're alive," she whispered. The bewildered look on her face worried him.

"What? Of course, I'm alive. Tess, what's going on? You're scaring me a little."

Tears were flowing down Tess's face and she had that deer caught in headlights look.

"Terry, the doctor told me my fiancé was here. I thought... I thought he meant Dan. I thought Dan had killed you and he was waiting here to..."

"Holy crap, Tess, baby. No." Tess was sobbing uncontrollably, and Tank was trying to calm her down when the doctor walked in.

"Mr. O'Brian, I told you she didn't want to see you." The doctor was livid.

"No, Doc. She thought I was dead." Tank was trying to soothe Tess and explain himself to the very displeased doctor. He was staring at Tank like he was nuts.

"Ms. Green, shall I have this man escorted from your room?"

Tess shook her head rapidly. "No, no I thought he was dead."

Tank gripped Tess's one hand lovingly in his own and used the other to wipe the tears from her face. He answered the doctor, but his eyes never left Tess's face.

"Doc, she thought I'd been shot. She thought the fiancé that you told her was waiting for her was the man who shot her and tried to kill me."

The doctor smiled when it finally sank in what the large man and his patient were trying to explain to him. He was relieved to see her smiling so he nodded convinced that his patient was okay and left them alone.

"Tess, Sweetheart. My God. I have so much to tell you. Baby, you saved my life, again. Do you remember that?"

Tess shook her head no.

"Okay, let me start from the beginning. First of all, I am so sorry, so very, very sorry I didn't talk to you that night when you called Toby's." Tess stilled and Tank knew she was remembering how he had refused to talk to her. "Honey, I was an idiot. I know you were only thinking of me. I still don't want there to be any secrets between us, but I get why you did it. You didn't want me to worry, right?" Tess nodded. "And I was in such a good mood about the cabin you didn't want to ruin my good mood, right?" Tess nodded again. "Sweetheart, this is important. You're going to remember this, right?" Tess looked at him with a puzzled expression on her face.

"Tess, I was never, ever, even remotely close to being with another woman that night." Tess opened her mouth to speak but Tank placed his finger on her lips hushing her. "Yes, the little hussy jumped on my lap, and yes, Grease and his girl happened to walk past me at the very moment. But I swear to you, Tess, I never encouraged her or touched her." Tears slipped down Tess's face. Tank placed his hand against her cheek, wiping the drops away.

"Sweetheart, I love you. You have got to get that through that beautiful brain of yours."

"Ter," Tess whispered softly as her tears slowed.

"I'm sorry, too, Ter. I'm sorry I didn't tell you. I knew you'd be upset. I swear I was going to tell you the second I saw you."

"I know, Honey. Tess, you saved my life last night. I drove to Townsend to talk to you and found Randal there. I didn't know he had a gun and when he aimed it at me he had me dead to rights. You stepped in front of the bullet. Tess, what the hell, baby?"

Now Tank had tears in his eyes and Tess couldn't believe that the bigger than life, tougher than nails man sitting next to her had honest to goodness tears in his eyes.

"Ter, I love you. I didn't want you to get hurt." Tank choked back a sob. "Tess, you were almost killed." A lone tear slid down Tank's face and Tess wiped it with her fingers.

"I'd do it again, Ter. You're worth it."

"Shit, Angel, you will never, ever, ever do that again," he said with a sorrowful chuckle.

"What happened, Ter? What happened to Dan?" Tank held her hand tenderly in his. "I shot him, Tess. He's dead."

He waited to see what her reaction would be. Once again her response surprised him.

"Are you okay, Ter? I mean, I'm glad he's gone, but you shot someone."

"I'm okay, baby. I'm not going to lose sleep over it, if that's what you're thinking. The sheriff cleared me too. I'm not headed to jail."

Tess nodded. That was exactly what she had been thinking.

"How long have you been awake?"

"A while actually." Tank noticed she was debating whether to tell him something.

"Tell me, Tess. No secrets remember?"

"Well, I was actually planning my escape when you came in. I was sure you were Dan and I knew I had to get out of here. I was pretending to be asleep hoping he'd leave and then I was going to run."

"To me I hope?"

Tess was quiet. "I thought we were over, Ter."

"Sweetheart, I hate that you thought that. Look at me, Darlin. You and me, we're just getting started. Understand?"

Tess smiled and he leaned down to give her a gentle kiss.

"I guess I better go tell the gang that you're okay. Can they can come in and see you?"

"Of course. Who's here?"

When Tank recited all the names Tess giggled.

"Ter?"

"Yeah, baby?"

"Will you stay with me? At least for a little while?"

"Oh, Darlin, they'll have to drag me out of here."

Tank got to his feet as the doctor came back through the door. "Everything okay in here?"

"It's all good, Doc. Hey, when do you think I can tak
her home?"

"For goodness sakes, Mr. O'Brian, she just got out c
surgery this morning."

"Yeah, I'm just wondering. She looks great doesn't
she?"

The doctor laughed.

"Well, if all goes well, I'd say in a week."

"Hear that, baby? A week. That's the last week of
summer, that's perfect timing."

"Um, Ms. Green, I have to talk to you, privately
please," the doctor said, looking at Tank.

Tank stiffened. "What's the matter?"

"Nothing, it's just something I want to discuss with
Ms. Green privately. Why don't you tell your friend:
how well she is doing and when you come back I'll
be gone?"

Tank didn't like leaving Tess, but he knew his family
and friends would be bouncing off the walls in the
waiting room. When he got back to the room, he
told them how well Tess was doing and that she had
thought he'd been killed. He then had to reveal to
them what the doctor had told him that morning;
that she had not wanted to see him. He explained
that Tess thought he was dead and that it was
Randal waiting for her. Tank saw the relief everyone
was feeling. Tank said they could all see her, but he
needed a minute alone with her first. He told them
her room number and asked for five minutes before
they descended.

Tank quickly walked back to Tess's room and found
Tess clutching the blanket. He couldn't read her
expression.

"Honey, what did the doctor say?"

Tess looked nervous and it frightened him. "Baby,
you're scaring me here."

"Ter, I swear I never planned..."

"Geez, Tess, tell me. I'm worried. Are you all right?
Is it worse than they thought?"

"Ter. I'm pregnant. Six weeks," Tess blurted out
anxiously.

Tank froze, his jaw dropped, and his eyes widened.
It reminded Tess of the first time he saw her after
the shower.

"You're pregnant? For real? With my...."

Tess nodded.

"Ter, I'll raise the baby."

"What the hell are you talking about?" he practically
growled at her.

"It's not something we ever talked about, Ter."

Tank settled into the chair next to her. "Tess, do you
want this baby?" he asked apprehensively.

"More than anything, Ter," she said. "I already love
it." Tank smiled at her.

"I'm not seeing a problem here, Tess."

"It's just, you know...?"

"No, baby, I have no idea what you're talking
about."

"We aren't married. I don't want you to feel like I
trapped you or..."

"Oh, geez, Tess." Tank smiled at her adoringly, stood up and leaned over giving her a long tender kiss on her mouth.

Their friends and family chose that moment to walk into the room. Tess was gently kissed, hugged, and fussed over. Tank had worked his way from her bed and was digging through his motorcycle sack that Toby had brought in. He found what he was looking for and made his way back to the head of the bed.

"Everyone, I have an announcement to make." Tess froze praying he wasn't going to tell their friends now.

Tank sunk down on one knee and looked up at Tess with a huge smile on his face.

"Tess, I think I've loved you from the first moment you saved me."

"You saved me, Ter," she said softly.

Tank shook his head and hushed her with his finger again. "Tess Green, I love you and I know I will always love you. Will you marry me?"

The women in the room gasped and he heard his brother chuckle. Tess was staring at him with her mouth handing open. Tank opened the small white box and Tess saw an exquisite ring nestled inside the cushy pillow box along with two matching wedding bands. Tank took the diamond ring out of the box and looked at Tess, holding the ring by her ring finger, waiting for her answer.

"Yes, Ter. I'll marry you."

The room erupted into cheers and a nurse came in trying to get them to lower their voices. She finally gave up and shut the door.

The doctor stuck his head in the door. "I guess everyone's happy about the baby then," he said cheerfully and ducked back out.

The room became awkwardly quiet.

"A baby?" Breezy said, looking back and forth between Tank and Tess.

"Well, that wasn't how I was going to tell you guys, but yes, she's six weeks pregnant."

Tess looked slightly uncomfortable and Tank realized why.

"And for everyone's information. I planned on asking her to marry me before I even knew about the baby." Tank told them in a hushed voice as he smiled lovingly at Tess. "I love her."

The room became loud again with more congratulations. Tank sat on the bed next to Tess, holding her hand. He wished he could make everyone go away and just crawl into the bed and hold her. He knew she had to be in some discomfort from being shot and he worried she was masking her pain level for the sake of their friends and family. He could see her eyes were closing despite her valiant attempts to keep them open.

"Okay, everyone, listen up. My beautiful fiancé, who is carrying my child, needs her sleep."

"Oh, brother," Toby groaned, making the room ring with laughter.

"Why don't you all go home and tell our family that Tess is going to be fine."

The small party relented to Tank's request. They were all tired and now that they knew Tess was going to be all right they were happy to leave. Everyone kissed Tess goodbye and left the room. Grease was last to go.

"You are staying here?" Grease asked.

Tank sat down in the chair next to Tess's bed. "Not moving until I can bring her home." Grease nodded and left.

"Ter, Honey, you don't have to stay here. Go home and get some sleep."

Tank leaned towards her. "Darlin, I won't be getting any sleep with you here and me there, so I'd prefer to stay, if that's all right with you?"

Tess patted the bed and tried to scoot over but the pain from under her shoulder jabbed at her. Tank saw that she was attempting to move over so he could get on the bed with her, so he simply picked her up and gently moved her. He then climbed on the bed and put his arm carefully around her.

"I love this ring, Terry," Tess said, holding it out in front of her.

"That's where I was when you arrived at camp yesterday. I had to drive into Townsend and then Helena. I wanted to have it ready for the perfect moment."

"I wish I had waited for you, Ter. I just thought, well, you know what I was thinking."

"Yeah and I don't like it."

"It's different, this ring, but I love it."

"It's made out of the sun from my bike."

"Oh my gosh. You made me a ring out of the armor sun on your bike?"

"Yup. Angel, you are as tough as that armor and as beautiful as the sun, so it was a no brainer."

"Oh, Ter, it's the most perfect ring ever. Thank you."

"Sweetheart, thank you for saying yes."

Chapter 34

One week later, Tank pulled into camp with Tess in the front seat. The first very noticeable difference that Tess could see was that the prefab cabin had people running in and out of it and there were light on inside. Tank was grinning as he watched her awed expression when they passed it.

"Ter, it's completely finished?"

"As of yesterday."

"Wow, they work fast."

"Had to. I want us to get married in there as soon as possible."

"What!"

Tank pulled up next to his Harley and ran around the front of the jeep. He purposely did not answer Tess. He wanted what he'd just said to sink in. When he opened her door, she was staring at him and her mouth was slightly opened. Yup, he'd shocked her, he thought to himself with a chuckle.

"Ter?"

"We'll talk in a second, Sweetheart." Tess noticed that none of their friends were running to greet them and she thought that was a bit strange.

When Tess got out of the jeep she looked at Tank's Harley and sure enough, three strips had been cut out of the beautiful sun design. She looked down at her ring and then back up to Tank who had been watching her patiently.

"Thank you, Ter."

"Thank you, Tess," he said with a mischievous smile. When they entered the cabin, Tess saw Breezy, Lolly, and CC were waiting for them. After the hugs, Tess was getting ready to plop down on the couch when Tank steered her to the bedroom.

"Hey!"

Tank shot her a sexy wink. "Darlin, we have a preacher coming in one hour to marry us. No time to sit."

"You have got to be kidding me! Now is your 'soon as possible?'"

"Yup," he gave her bottom a playful swat and left his soon to be bride with her three friends. Tess rubbed her backside and then looked up to see her friends watching her with huge smiles on their faces.

"Can we help you get ready?" Breezy asked wanting to make sure Tess was okay with the surprise wedding.

"Uh, yeah. I guess so."

CC moved and put an arm around her shoulders.

"Tess, if you're not ready you don't have to do this." Tess looked from one woman to the other and then smiled gently.

"I love him. I have ever since I met him. I want to marry him and honestly, this is as good a time as any, right?"

The three women were beaming and Lolly, the toughest of them all, had tears in her eyes as she clapped her hands merrily.

"Well then, let's get you ready!"

Somehow, the women had found a beautiful white lace dress that fit Tess like a glove. It hugged her slim hips and dipped to show her cleavage that was becoming more ample. Every time Tess remarked on how well it fit, Breezy would laugh and remind her that she was an expert on sizes. Before they left the cabin, CC wanted to help Tess put on a pair of white ballet slippers, but Tess ran back into her room and came out with the boots that Tank had bought her.

"Really? You're going to wear those?" Breezy threw her hands up.

"It's symbolic, Breezy. I'm not only marrying, Terry, I'm marrying his club, his motorcycle club."

"Well I'll be damned," Lolly said with an impish grin. "If that ain't the most romantic, unselfish, coolest thing I ever heard."

Tess smiled. Yeah, the boots were perfect.

The women escorted Tess to the new cabin and hurried her inside so Tank wouldn't catch a glimpse of her. Tess realized the gathering was larger than she thought it would be. Car, trucks, and motorcycles filled every area around the new structure. The women ushered her through the large recreation area, which Tess noticed was set up for the reception. Tank, or someone, had obviously hired a catering company because the chairs and tables were all white and the centerpieces gorgeous white roses and green candles.

Lolly went out the sliding doors and asked everyone to take their seats. Tess saw they were also white and arranged so she would be walking down a center aisle.

A lone guitar strummed out the wedding march and Toby came rushing in from a side door wearing a tux. Tess had asked Breezy to find Toby when she was getting ready, to ask him if he would walk her down the aisle.

"Toby, you look wonderful," Tess giggled.

"I ran home to change. Can't have the person giving the bride away looking like a regular attendee can we?" He kissed Breezy who was ogling her handsome husband. CC handed Tess a small bouquet of summer wildflowers, and then Breezy and CC left to find their seats. Toby put Tess's hand on his arm and smiled down at her.

"You are so good for my little brother, Tess. Thank you for saving him."

Tess smiled tenderly back at Toby. "He saved me, Toby."

Toby pushed back the sliding doors and allowed Tess to walk through them first. A gasp went through the crowd upon seeing how resplendent she looked in her gown. Tess looked towards the altar and saw Tank looking sinfully sexy in a black tux. He was staring at her and she could see he was tamping down his emotions because his eyes told her everything. This man truly loved her.

As Toby walked Tess to the altar, she looked around at all the friends and family in attendance. She saw that wildflowers had been placed in mason jars all around the large stone patio that was serving as the altar and small white lights lit the pathway to where the preacher stood with Tank.

Toby gave her a small peck on the cheek before placing her hand in his brother's when they reached Tank.

Tank leaned down and whispered in her ear. "You are so beautiful, Tess, inside and out."

Tess couldn't speak. She was afraid she'd start crying and she didn't want to ruin her make up, so she simply beamed up at her handsome husband to be.

The ceremony wasn't long and before Tess knew it, Tank had her crushed up against his chest, kissing her passionately to the hooting and hollering of everyone around them.

"I love you, Tess," he whispered in her ear after he released her. Tess was still feeling the sensual burn of the kiss and she blushed, which made Tank grin. He loved that he could affect her like that. He couldn't wait for them to be alone tonight. It had been too damn long.

The festivities began with cocktails followed by a delicious dinner. Waiters and waitresses served the large room and a band played a variety of music that had people, young and old, shaking it or swaying on the cleared area being used as the dance floor.

Tess threw the bouquet after she and Tank had cut the cake and as the small bouquet flew through the air, Tess watched as a few of the women dove for it. Unfortunately for them the bouquet practically landed in CC's unsuspecting hands and when she looked up to Tess, the look on her face was priceless, which sent Tess into peals of laughter. Tank then pulled out a chair and prompted Tess to have a seat so he could take off the garter. When he reached under the hem of her gown he felt the boots and his hands stilled. He looked into Tess eyes and then raised the hem up so he could see what he'd been feeling. A huge smile broke across his face, which made Tess giggle.

"Sort of perfect, right?" she said quietly. Tank lifted the hem of her dress so everyone could see what they were laughing about, and the place erupted into cheers.

Tank seductively took off the garter, his large hands skimming her skin sensually and all to the cheering of the people watching, leaving his bride red faced. He sent the little elastic band flying over his shoulder into the crowd behind him. While Tank watched Tess, she watched as men dove on the floor trying to retrieve it. Traditionally who ever catches the garter places it onto the leg of the woman that caught the bride's bouquet.

Tank turned around and helped Tess to stand as they watched the ruckus. The men good-naturedly pushed and shoved one another trying to seize the garter and when the bodies finally separated, a very rumpled, but victorious Joe, stood up holding the garter above his head.

CC sat down in the chair that Tess had vacated and strip tease like melody played from the band as Joe took off CC's high heel shoe and very, very slowly slid the garter up CC's leg. His hands disappeared under her flowery dress and the room was encouraging him to go higher. Tess could see his hands were mid-thigh when CC placed her hand on top of her dress holding his hand in place. She saw Joe give CC a ridiculously sexy wink and then he withdrew his hands and helped her put her heel back on.

Tess gave Tank a little elbow nudge and he nodded, letting her know that he'd seen the obvious sparks flying between their two friends. The chair was quickly taken away and the dancing started back up again. Tess was enjoying being in Tank's arms during the slow songs. She loved to dance but she was tired and so they sat out the faster tempo songs using that time to greet their guests.

The night was drawing to a close and Tank could see his wife was tiring. He gestured to the woman in charge of the wait staff and then took Tess by the arm and led her to the low platform the band was on. The band stopped playing and Tank took the microphone from the stand. He kept his arm firmly around Tess and motioned for a passing waiter. All the waiters and waitresses had trays of champagne. Tank took a glass of champagne for himself and the head waitress handed him a glass of what looked like champagne but was ginger ale and he handed that to Tess.

The room stood, looking at Tank and Tess. Most of them now held glasses of champagne in their hands and the rest had their beers or drinks.

Tank held up his hand and someone started tapping a glass with a spoon to quiet the room.

"My family and friends, thank you for sharing this special day with us. This has been quite the summer." Tank smiled at his wife and then at his friends. The guests agreed with him as they nodded in agreement and murmured with each other.

"Some of it has been good and some not so good." Again, the room hummed with consensus. "I would like to make a toast to my amazing wife and this silver lining summer. You, Tess, have brought me more happiness that I ever hoped to have. We have been through hell, but what we gained is something stronger than any armor made. I love you wife." Tank raised his glass to the room and then looked lovingly at his wife, clinking his glass against hers. "To our silver lining summer."

The End... At least until you read Now It's Perfect. Joe and CC's story.

Zanne Sweeney

Zanne Sweeney a graduate from Kent State University is a teacher, and coach, who loves to write stories that she hopes her readers won't want to put down. "That's the ultimate compliment." When she's not teaching, coaching, or writing, Zanne loves to spend time with her family and fun loving friends. She is a novice photographer, a consummate sports fan, and is never without a book to read.

Thank you for reading my book. I love hearing from you. Please visit my website: https://www.zannesweeney.com and my Facebook Page: https://www.facebook.com/zanne.sweeney.author and I'm on Twitter @zannesweeney

Please don't forget to rate this book. You can also write a review on Amazon or Goodreads.

Happy Reading!

Zanne Sweeney books:
Neighbors
A Chance For More A Readers Favorite Book Contest Award Winner
Someone To Come Home To (This book is published in two editions; Uncut and Abridged) The Uncut Edition is intended for mature readers only.
Finding Happy Book 1 in The Happy Montana Series
Silver Lining Summer Book 2 in The Happy Montana Series

www.ingramcontent.com/pod-product-compliance
Lightning Source LLC
Chambersburg PA
CBHW071153250626
47159CB00001B/71